THE

HUNTED

RETURN

THE

HUNTED

RETURN

JEFF R. SPALSBURY

amazonencore

Text copyright © 2012 Jeff R. Spalsbury
All rights reserved.
Printed in the United States of America.

Published by Encore
P.O. Box 400818
Las Vegas, NV 89140

ISBN-13: 9781612186641
ISBN-10: 1612186645

DEDICATION

Joy Ann Fischer
Editor, hired hand, and dear friend
Who made a difference in my writing

PROLOGUE

Yellow Bird Whitfield crawled deep into the dark cave halfway up the rock cliff, wrapped the wet buffalo robe around her, and prepared to die. Her face, hair, and clothes were soaked with snow and mud from the fall storm. She shivered uncontrollably. Not finding the tribe here had shocked her, but, thinking about it, she realized it had been her mistake. Since Butcher took over her life, he'd never let her see her people. It had been more than three years since she and her two boys, Doc and Red, had last visited the tribe. That was such a happy time. She frowned and wondered if it was the last time she had been happy.

When her horse tripped and went down, she had been thankful that the ground was muddy and soft; otherwise, she may have been injured. Instead, she was thrown safely away from the horse. The horse had struggled up, then bolted down the trail, and was probably back at the ranch by now.

It had taken her another hour to slog wearily through the cold and muddy, slush to the Indian campsite, only to find it deserted. The darkness added to her misery, and the rain had turned to a wet snow. She felt despair gnawing at her soul—with no place to go for help, no way to start a fire, and no food. But she was finally free. Perhaps that was enough, she thought.

Her body trembled involuntarily from her cold, wet clothes. She knew she was exhausted. She wondered if this was how she was going to die. Just fall asleep and never wake. Never see her sons again. Never see Tom again. She felt for the mining claims, which were wrapped securely around her waist inside her buckskin dress. She placed her left hand protectively on them, much as she had when she was pregnant with Doc. If anyone ever found her body, she hoped they would know that she had tried to do what was right.

She heard a noise near the front of the cave—too dark to see what it was. A bear? A puma? Immediately she pulled her knife from its sheath. Her lips tightened as she clutched the knife tightly in her hand. She vowed she would not die easily.

CHAPTER ONE

It was late summer in 1868 and outside the Kansas State Penitentiary, the sun blazed on the burnt earth with hell-like intensity and mixed with the oppressive humidity that made it hard to breathe. Waves of heat shimmered along the horizon and off the walls of the prison. The infrequent breeze only stirred up miniature whirling dust devils that engulfed a person's body in an ugly, choking powder storm. Inside it was worse.

The prisoner stood tall and quiet in front of the warden's desk. Sweat slowly ran down his clean-shaven face and soaked into the shirt buttoned at the neck. The warden looked up at John Warner and wondered what he was all about.

Normally he'd give his "If you're not good, you'll be back" speech, but not this time. In the few months Warner was in his prison, the warden had barely spoken to him. Not that he'd had trouble with Warner; rather, Warner was a loner and spoke very little to anyone.

A tall man, perhaps six foot two, Warner was slim but muscular and strong, with a deeply tanned face that seemed more like leather than flesh. He was in his fifties and still an imposing figure even as he fought the arthritis that now slowed him.

When John Warner first came to the prison, the tough ruffians had tried to intimidate him. John picked the toughest one and knocked him out with one punch. Then he turned to the others and told them, "I want no trouble. Stay out of my way." They did. Even the guards left him alone.

John Warner had come to prison quietly, did what he had to do, and now was going to leave the same way, but much sooner than anyone expected. The warden stood and handed some papers to John. He didn't look Warner in the eyes; nobody did. John Warner's deep-set black eyes seemed to burn right into your soul. The warden thought for a moment about holding out his hand and wishing him luck, but if Warner were to refuse, the guards would soon hear about it and make a big thing of it. He told the guard to take the prisoner out to the front gate.

After Warner left his office, the warden studied his copy of the signed pardon on his desk. Someone had gone to a great deal of effort to get John Warner out. He wondered why.

When John stepped outside the prison, he pulled his hat down to just above his angled gray brows, shielding his eyes from the bright glare. He squinted as he glanced up the road. It was a long five miles to the city of Leavenworth, and it would seem even longer on a sizzling day like this. No matter, he was free. That was all that he cared about. He took a deep breath, and the wind brought the sweet smell of new-cut hay. It smelled like freedom.

A short, dirty man called out to him from an old wagon across the road. "You be John Warner?"

John nodded.

"Man paid me to wait until you were released and bring you into Leavenworth."

John studied the man for a moment before climbing into the wagon and sitting beside him. The driver acted as if he'd taken an instant dislike to John. He mentioned that he'd lost his left leg below the knee in the last year of the Civil War and kept rubbing the stub under his pants. He babbled on about the hot weather and crops, his voice like a rusty gate hinge. John remained silent the entire way into town. When they pulled up in front of the livery stable, the driver gestured with his head that this was John's stop.

"The man who paid me said he'd meet you in the brewery on Fourth Street, across from the courthouse. That way, down Walnut Street," he added with a quick point.

"The man have a name?" John asked.

"He didn't give me one."

John waited, but apparently that was all the man was going to say. It was the first time he had stopped talking. The driver pulled a large red handkerchief from his back pocket and wiped the sweat running down his face and around his neck.

John moved stiffly off the wagon. He stretched and slowly straightened his body, fighting the arthritis pain in his knees and back. Today was his birthday, and he felt his body complaining about the fifty-one years of hard cowboy life.

The sheriff was waiting in the shade of the livery stable office entrance. He was a short, balding man in his forties with the start of a potbelly. The sheriff looked John up and down. He and his deputy were always waiting for the newly released prisoners, whether they rode, walked, or came by wagon into town. The lawmen always carried shotguns, and they always worked in twos.

The deputy poked John in the side with his shotgun, then jumped back as John quickly twisted and glared down at the deputy.

"There're two stages and a train through here in the next twenty-four hours," the sheriff said gruffly. "If you're not out of here by noon tomorrow, I'll lock you up as a vagrant." He took his shotgun and started to jab it at John. "You understand—"

John's right hand shot out quick as a diamondback's strike and engulfed the double-barrels, stopping the jab as if the barrels had hit a wall. The sheriff was thrown off balance and almost fell.

The deputy fumbled with his shotgun's hammer, but John stopped him with a fierce look.

John turned his glare back to the sheriff and, speaking softly but with the threat of danger in his voice, said, "I'll be gone in your twenty-four hours, Sheriff, but if you ever try to touch me with the barrel of this gun again, I'll wrap it around your neck."

The sheriff tried to pull his shotgun back just as John gave it a shove and jammed the stock into the sheriff's soft belly. The move knocked the wind out of the lawman and bent him over.

"Normally, old man, I'd take you down for that," the deputy said to John angrily. "You're just damn lucky the sheriff is here."

"Well, one of us is." John turned and headed down Walnut Street as the sheriff, still bent over, tried to catch his breath.

The deputy held the sheriff's arm until he could breathe normally. "You want me to get that horehound?" the deputy asked.

The sheriff shook his head as he finally straightened. "Forget that, Jim. Just trail after him and let me know what he's up to," he said hoarsely.

The deputy turned and started down the street. The sheriff took a deep breath and grunted. Jim stopped and turned around. "Yeah, Sheriff?"

"Don't mess with him, you hear? Just let me know what he's up to." The sheriff headed back to his office. He didn't like the look of this one at all.

John smelled the brewery a block before he got to it. The sweet aroma of fresh-made beer caused him to pause in the doorway for just a moment and enjoy the richness of the floral, spicy fragrance. After he stepped inside, he let his eyes adjust to the dim light. He glanced around to see if he recognized anyone. He didn't.

Then his eyes narrowed. Across the room, a young man sat watching him. A new Henry rifle leaned against the wall behind him. John glared at the man, and this time there was no backing down. In fact, the stranger seemed to snicker and then grinned at him. It was not the grin of a young fast gun out to start a reputation, but rather the grin of a man who knew something John didn't know.

John dealt with this problem the only way he knew how. He walked over to the stranger. If it surprised the man, he didn't show it. The stranger pushed out a chair with his foot and said, "Afternoon, Big John. Wasn't sure when they'd release you."

John hesitated just a moment. How did this man know him? Only his friends called him Big John. Something was familiar about the man's face, but John just couldn't place it. A moment closed off in his memory, yet his mind kept fluttering around it, seeing and not seeing, without finding an answer. It aggravated him. The stranger continued to grin up at him.

John sat lightly in the offered chair and was about to ask the man who he was and what he wanted when the stranger poured him a glass of beer from a full pitcher.

"They tell me the water is so bad in Leavenworth that the only way not to get sick is to drink beer. I ordered us some steaks."

The stranger filled his own glass, took a long drink, wiped the foam from his lips, and mumbled, "Well, are you going to have a drink? I don't reckon they serve beer in prison."

Normally, Big John would have halted everything and gotten some answers from this brassy man, but it had been a long time since he'd had a beer. He took a long swig, and as he put his glass down, a waiter placed a large steak with onions, mashed potatoes, and gravy in front of him. The smells from the sizzling steak made his stomach growl in anticipation. A hint of a smile crossed his face as he chewed his first piece.

The stranger finished his steak long before Big John, then leaned back in his chair and slowly sipped another glass of beer. Big John continued to eat his food with great pleasure.

Finally Big John leaned back and studied the man sitting across from him.

"You can't quite place me, can you, Big John?" the stranger said. "I don't wonder; it's been fifteen or more years since you last saw me, but I sure remember you." He leaned over and poured more beer into Big John's glass. "I just missed you when you brought Dad back to Fort Madison. What was that, eight years or so ago?"

Big John frowned. "Nat's boy?"

The man smiled. "Paul Hallman, all grown up." He held out his hand and Big John shook it firmly, but not hard. Paul held on to Big John's hand and turned it over. "Your hands and Dad's look alike. Arthritic knuckles and all."

"How's Nat?" Big John asked.

"Hey," Paul exclaimed, "I'm forgetting my manners. Happy birthday." Paul held out his beer glass, and Big John gently tapped his glass to Paul's. "Dad's fine, thanks to you. He said to tell you he's sorry he couldn't make the trip, but he's never completely recovered from the ambush."

"Sorry," Big John said.

"Not me. Oh, I am about his getting shot and all, but he's been home with us for these past years. I've never seen my mother happier, and Dad's gotten to know his three grandsons."

Big John pulled out the papers that the warden had given him. "I've not looked at this, but something tells me you were involved in it."

Paul nodded. "I'm a lawyer. When Dad found out that you'd been sent to prison for robbing a gold shipment, I thought he was going to run right out of the house and break you out by himself. Said you'd never do such a thing. Said you'd starve before you did such a thing."

Paul took a sip of his beer. "I do a bunch of work for the riverboat captains. One of them told me about a captain friend who had witnessed the illegal transferring of gold chests happening on another riverboat. He saw it from his wheelhouse, but he had to pull out before he could tell anyone about it."

"But this?" Big John asked, holding up the pardon letter.

"When I had that lead, I talked to the riverboat captain who saw the switch and figured out how they'd done it. Then it was just paperwork and meeting with judges. That, and politics, Big John. People owed me favors. I'm not into the typical politics, but I have my ways. Once I could prove that you were framed and didn't do it, the rest was easy."

Big John shook his head.

Paul grinned. "And, yes, this gift is one you have to accept. Dad said you'd complain about taking gifts from us. He told me to tell you to remember forty-two days in the wagon."

A hint of a smile crossed Big John's face again.

"And he said that still doesn't make it even in his book." Paul paused and added, "Nor mine. Bringing my dad home after he was shot up in that cattle raid and caring for him all that way is not just any old debt."

"Your dad is a good man."

"You both are." Paul reached back toward the Henry leaning against the wall and handed it to Big John. "Dad said you were the worst shot he'd ever seen with a handgun, but mighty fine with a rifle."

Big John handled the rifle lovingly. "Your dad had to be the second-worst shot."

"Dad said you'd say that." Paul pointed to the Henry. "That's your birthday present from Dad."

Big John placed the Henry in his lap. "When the warden came and told me I was being let out, I could hardly believe it. You and your dad have given me the best birthday I've ever had."

"Well, it gets better. Once I pay the bill here, we are going to the stable and get you outfitted for a horse or whatever you need. Also some new clothes. That prison suit looks ridiculous on you." He handed Big John a small money pouch. "And a little stake is always helpful."

Big John started to refuse.

"A stake to get you started. Dad said you could repay it when you can. I told him I'd be honored to have you come and stay with us, but Dad said you'd have business to take care of."

"Your dad knows me well." Big John sighed softly. "They set me up, and just before I was taken off to prison, the leader, a man named Butcher, comes up and tells me he's killed my wife, Golden Eagle. Said he didn't want any loose ends."

"I'm so sorry." Paul studied his hands and slowly shook his head. "Damn, that's not right." He slapped the top of his legs angrily. "All right, then, let's get you started."

Big John cradled the Henry in his arm, reached out, and gently squeezed Paul's shoulder. "Thanks."

CHAPTER TWO

Once Big John was far out of town, he stopped, removed a small pouch from his vest pocket, and pulled out one of two pairs of wire-rimmed eyeglasses he always carried with him. He put them on and glanced around at the rolling hills ahead of him and a long, narrow sandstone ravine off to his right.

He locked the brake on the wagon and talked softly to the two horses. Then he lifted the Henry, cocked the lever and fired off one shot toward a V-shaped bush at the far end of the ravine. His shot missed, but he was pleased that the horses only twitched and didn't bolt at the unexpected sound. Taking more time, he took another shot and hit his mark. He fired off two more rounds at more-distant objects and hit both of them. He slowly nodded his head in admiration at the rifle he held in his hands. "Thanks, Nat," Big John said softly. He quickly reloaded with four new shells.

Near dark, Big John found a suitable spot and pitched camp for the night under a large cottonwood close to a small stream. The sounds of the stream's rushing water and the dragonflies whooshing about reminded him that he was a free man. After the heat of the afternoon ride, it felt refreshing and cooler by the stream. Like the water, he was free to go where he wanted. And what he wanted more than anything he'd ever wanted in his life was seeing Butcher—dead.

He shook his head. That wasn't true. Wanting Butcher dead was the second-strongest desire he'd ever had. The thing he'd wanted most was Golden Eagle, his Golden Eagle, and when he found her he had made her his wife.

His eyes got misty. Every night in the darkness of that hot prison cell, as he lay sweating on his cot, he'd think of her, and every night his eyes got misty. He wondered if it would be like that for the rest of his life.

After eating, as he rolled out his bedroll beside the wagon, he thought he heard a horse neigh in the distance. He cupped his hand to his ear in the direction of the sound, but he heard only the normal evening noises. He ran his hand over his mouth in thought.

When he finished laying out his bedroll, he placed some long branches under the blanket so it would look like a body. Then he took his old pair of boots and tucked them under the blanket so their bottoms stuck out. Finally he poked a twig in the ground where his head would be and hung his hat on it.

He crawled over the top of the bedroll so it looked like he was wrapping the blanket over himself, but instead he slid under the wagon. In its shadow he slowly got to his feet. Once away from the dim, flickering fire, he silently moved up a small hill until he came to a large rock. He sat with his back against the rock, pulled out his glasses again, and put them on. He cocked the Henry and laid the rifle across his lap, then slowly rubbed his arthritic knuckles.

The small fire by the wagon slowly burned itself out. The moon broke in and out of low-hanging, wispy clouds and turned the landscape into shadowy silhouettes of black and gray. Big John heard a sound almost directly behind him. He quickly sucked in his breath and tried not to move.

Within a few feet of where he sat, two figures moved from around the rock. They stopped just ahead of him. The shorter man waved the revolver that he held in his left hand and sent the other man to the right. They stepped cautiously down the hill. Once they were within six feet of the bedroll, they opened fire, each shooting three times. The shots echoed in the night air, and a flock of nesting mockingbirds squawked and flew noisily into the sky.

The shorter man was laughing when the bullet from Big John's Henry smashed into him and flung him forward, dead. The rifle report echoed through the hills. The second man spun and started firing wildly back up the hill. He got off two shots before the second bullet from the Henry struck him in the chest and lifted him off his feet. He smashed down on his back with his arms outstretched, dead.

Big John slowly rolled over onto his hands and knees and, using the rock for support, painfully stood as his cramped arthritic hips and knees complained. He limped stiffly down the hill, keeping the rifle pointed at the two men.

The shorter man still held his revolver in his hand. Big John kicked the gun from the man's hand toward the wagon. He couldn't see where the other man's revolver had gone.

Big John grabbed some dry sticks and got the fire started again. The fire helped him see, but he still didn't spot the other gun. Certain that both men were dead, he leaned the Henry up against the wagon, painfully knelt beside each man, and went through their pockets. He found a bag of gold dust on each of them. He stood and stared at the men, wondering if he might know them. He didn't.

Unexpectedly, he heard the sound of horses approaching. He glanced at the Henry but realized the rifle was too far away for him to get to it before the riders entered his camp.

Five horses came to a hard halt, and all the riders had their guns out. Big John grimaced as he slowly raised his hands into the air, thinking that he was a dead man. As the kicked-up dust settled, he realized that the leader was the sheriff from town. The lawmen quickly studied the scene in front of them. The sheriff told one of his deputies to check the man in the bedroll, then turned to Big John. "Sorry about your friend."

The deputy held up the blanket and said with a grin, "They plumb killed his blanket." He kicked at the branches and old boots stretched out on the ground.

The sheriff got down stiffly from his horse and told Big John to put his hands down. He pointed to the blanket.

"Thought I heard a horse," Big John said. "Figured if it were someone friendly, he would ride in and we could share some coffee. When nobody came in, made me nervous."

"Did you know them?" the sheriff asked.

Big John shook his head.

The sheriff kicked the boot of the short man. "They beat up a shop owner in town and got away with a bundle of stuff and a couple of horses." He turned to another deputy and said, "Malcolm, see if you can find their horses."

"Gents, can I fix you some coffee?" Big John asked.

"Be obliged," the sheriff said.

As Big John poured the coffee, Malcolm rode up with four horses. "Got them all, Sheriff."

Big John went to the first horse and ran his finger over the brand, a Rocking B.

"Know the horse?" the sheriff asked.

"Yup. From Montana Territory." Big John dug into his pocket, pulled out the two bags of gold, and showed them to the sheriff. "Do you know whether the shop owner had any gold that these two took?"

The sheriff took a bag, opened it, and studied the gold. "He gave us a complete list of what was taken. He would have mentioned any bags of gold. He didn't." He handed the bag back to Big John. "Was that blood money?"

Big John nodded his head slowly. "I reckon." He paused, then added, "For my blood."

"There's a reward for these two. You want to come back with us to collect it?"

Big John shook his head. "I'd like to keep the gold bags, but the rest is yours to share with your men."

"Going to use the gold to help pay your way back home?" the sheriff asked, pointing to the gold.

Big John looked at the two bags in his hand. "Nope. I plan to give them back to the fellow who paid these men. One bag in each eye."

The sheriff took off his glasses and slowly cleaned them with a green bandanna. He grinned up at Big John. "It's hell getting old, isn't it?"

Big John hadn't even realized the sheriff was wearing glasses.

"If it's not the eyes, it's the knees, the hands, or the back," the sheriff added. "Something is always aching. Even riding a horse has gotten mighty painful. The stable owner said you really wanted to get a horse but went with the wagon. If you're heading to Montana Territory, I'd say that was one smart move. Not that riding in a wagon isn't painful—it's just less painful than a horse. How come you didn't take the train?"

"Rode on one once. Scared me worse than the worst stampede I've ever been in. That train was shaking this way and that, making horrible squealing and groaning sounds and going faster than any man was meant to go. Ugly black smoke kept pouring into the cabin and made all of us cough and wheeze. Told the good Lord that if I got off that thing alive, I'd never ride on one again."

For the first time that evening, the sheriff smiled. "My boys are tired, but I've a feeling they'd much rather head back home than spend the night here. I know I would. We'll take the bodies back with us. I figure you'd have only planted them shallow and without a reading if we hadn't showed up."

"Probably not even that," Big John said.

The sheriff grinned. "For a man one day out of prison, you've had yourself quite a day. The warden told me you got out on a pardon." He held out his hand. "We didn't do well at our introduction in town, but I'd like to wish you luck."

Big John took the sheriff's hand. "Thanks, Sheriff. Appreciate that."

The sheriff had his deputies load the bodies onto two of the extra horses.

As they headed out of the camp, the sheriff, the last to leave, bent from his saddle toward Big John and said, "A man who would pay that much money to kill you and send killers all the way from Montana Territory is a mighty dangerous enemy. I'd suggest wearing your glasses all the time."

"That sounds like good advice, Sheriff. Thanks."

"In case you didn't know, the Army closed the Bozeman Trail. Bunches of scalping Indian tribes are unhappy with all the miners and settlers pouring into their land. Too much trouble for the Army to handle. I suspect you won't run into any wagon trains on the Oregon Trail this late in the season, but you might. If you do, tag along with them before cutting north on the Montana Trail."

"Thanks for the information."

"Oh, and one last thing." The sheriff pointed back toward the wagon. "I had my boys throw the blankets, foodstuffs, and tarpaulin our two killers were carrying into your wagon. I figure they won't need them, and after they shot up your blanket, it's the least they should do for you." The sheriff chuckled at his joke, turned his horse, and followed his men.

Big John watched them go. Butcher knew he was out of prison. These two wouldn't be the only ones after him. He cursed softly.

Butcher had too many men for Big John to just ride into his ranch and shoot him. He wanted Butcher dead but wasn't about to back-shoot him. Big John wanted Butcher to see the man who killed him. He wanted his face to be the last thing Butcher saw before he died. He had to do that for his Golden Eagle.

CHAPTER THREE

Late in the afternoon, the train, puffing clouds of black smoke and soot, slowly moved around the bend of the prairie hillside when the engineer saw a large tree trunk lying across the tracks. He immediately pulled the brake lever, causing the train to come to a screeching, sparks-flying, sliding halt.

People in the passenger cars were tossed about like loose potatoes. Boxes and cases slid onto the floor. Two women screamed, and three men stretched out the windows to see what was wrong.

As soon as the train stopped, two outlaws with masks covering their faces entered through the back door of the last passenger car. They fired in the air and demanded that everyone put their hands up, remain quiet, and turn over all their valuables.

A pregnant woman at the front of the car stood and screamed in fear. The first robber quickly fired at her. The bullet hit her in the left arm and slammed her back against the seat. She slumped to the floor, semiconscious.

Doc Whitfield jumped from his seat across the aisle and knelt by the woman's husband, who was trying to stop the bleeding.

The robber who shot the woman said loudly to Doc, "You. Get back to your seat and put your hands up. If you want to die, that's a good way to do it."

Ignoring the robber, Doc took the husband's hand and whispered, "I'm a doctor. I want you to press where I show you." Doc pressed the man's finger down against the wound in his wife's arm. "Good. Don't let up."

Doc wiped the blood from his right hand with a bandanna he'd pulled from his pocket. Satisfied that his hand was no longer slippery, he stood and faced the two outlaws. Doc had dark piercing eyes and long straight black hair. He wore black wool pants and a black vest over a white shirt, unbuttoned at the top, which was unusual. His long, delicate fingers waited confidently beside the black-handled .45 Colt strapped low on his right hip.

"You," the robber said, "get your hands in the air."

"I'm a doctor. A man who shoots a pregnant woman can't be much of a man."

The robber frowned at Doc. "I don't care who—"

Doc drew and fired so quickly the outlaw didn't realize what had happened until the bullet struck him. He stared down at his chest in amazement and then fell backward to the floor. The second outlaw glanced at his dead partner, then at Doc with his smoking Colt in his hand. The outlaw immediately threw his revolver to the floor and raised his hands over his head.

Five seats ahead of Doc, a tall, slender, dark-haired man stood holding his Wells Fargo badge toward Doc in one hand and his revolver pointing at the outlaw with his other. "I'll take care of this one," he said, "while you take care of the woman."

"Obliged." Doc quickly reholstered his Colt. He grabbed his bag from his seat and pulled his medical instruments out.

Half an hour later, the woman was sitting back up in her seat and holding her arm. "I'm so sorry," she said to Doc. "I just panicked. All I could think of was my unborn baby."

"Understandable. Fortunately, the wound is minor. The bullet went right through the flesh of your arm. You've just got to be sure to keep the wound clean." He patted her gently on the hand. "The medicine I gave you will keep it from hurting too much. You didn't lose that much blood, and the baby's just fine."

She leaned her head on her husband's shoulder. "It's our first."

The husband asked, "Can we name the baby after you, if it's a boy?"

"Well, I'd be honored," Doc said, grinning. "But strange as it sounds, I'm a doctor and my first name is Doc. So, unless you expect your baby to be a doctor, I think you should just give it the name you'd planned."

They smiled their thanks as the husband shook Doc's hand.

Doc had just returned to his seat when the Wells Fargo agent came up and asked, "Might I speak with you for a moment?"

Doc nodded for the agent to join him.

The man sat beside Doc and pulled out his identification papers. "I'm with Wells Fargo. Special Agent Robert Mock. I was debating going after the outlaws when they first came in, but I was concerned about the other passengers if it turned into a shoot-out."

"What happened out there?"

"They pulled an old dead cottonwood log over the rails. Luckily, it didn't cause any damage to the train."

"Good."

"When I saw you draw, I immediately recognized you." Robert laughed gently. "I'm sure you don't remember me, but I was with Bob Bates in St. Joseph three years ago. You shot the two men who tried to rob the gold you were returning for Dave Kramer."

"That seems a long time ago," Doc said.

"Are you a real doctor now?"

"Yup. It's been a rough three years in New York at the medical school."

"Rough because you were in medical school, or rough living in New York?"

Doc laughed. "Both. You must be from there."

"Was. I never liked being a big-city boy, but it wasn't until I joined with Mr. Bates at Wells Fargo that I realized how much I love being out West. I notice you're carrying a new Colt. Seems I remember you were using an old Dragoon back then."

"Your boss is responsible for that. About a year ago, he took me to visit an old friend of his, Richard Jarvis, the president of the Colt Armory in Hartford. Mr. Bates wanted me to show him my Dragoon. The company hadn't been doing well since Mr. Colt died, back in '62, and Root, the chief technician, died in '65. The company is working hard to design a new gun to compete with Smith & Wesson.

"Well, as we were walking up to the factory entrance, a little girl I'd helped heal in New York saw me and came running up to me to say hello. She turned out to be Mr. Jarvis's niece, and suddenly I was being treated like some really important person.

"When we went to the target range, I drew and fired my Dragoon. Mr. Jarvis got so excited he immediately wanted to buy my gun. Said he wanted to add it to his collection. When I said no, he offered to trade my gun for one of his new ones. They were switching to metallic cartridges, but the weapon he had me try, well..."

Doc paused, trying to find the right words to explain. "Well, I felt bad about it, but I just didn't like how it felt. I didn't want to hurt his feelings, but Mr. Jarvis was not to be denied. So then he brought me an experimental single-action revolver with black ebony grips.

"The first time I held and fired it, I was hooked. Then I felt guilty about trading my old gun for this one, but Mr. Jarvis was so delighted at how much I loved his new gun, he made me feel as if I were doing him a favor. It's an amazing weapon." Doc pulled his Colt and showed it to Robert.

Robert asked if he could hold it. "This gun is wonderful," he said as he shifted it back and forth in his hands. "When do they expect to have it for sale?"

"I got the impression that it could be another two to four years. They only had three prototypes." Doc grinned, slightly embarrassed. "Of course, now they only have two. I don't think they even have patents on it yet."

Robert handed the weapon back to Doc. "What about ammo?"

"Mr. Jarvis made sure I had plenty. He said he'd ship me more if I needed it, but I hope that won't be necessary."

"You heading home? Montana Territory, wasn't it?"

"Yup. My mother, Yellow Bird, is in trouble because of a man named Butcher. He was the reason my brother Red and I had to leave."

"I'm sorry about your mother. Anything I can do to help?"

Doc shook his head no. "But thanks for the offer."

Robert glanced out the window. "Hey, we're going to be stopping in the next town so I can turn that outlaw over to the local sheriff. I've got him hog-tied in the baggage car with his dead buddy. That should give him something to think about, huh? We're going to be there for a few hours. How about I buy you dinner?"

"I'd appreciate that."

* * *

After dinner in the hotel dining room, Robert and Doc walked leisurely back to the train. As they passed the saloon, a drunken cowboy called out to Doc, "You know how to use that Colt, or do you just wear it for show?"

Robert leaned toward Doc and whispered, "Ignore him. He's drunk."

"You guys think you're so tough. I'll take you both on. And if you don't turn around and face me, I'll shoot you both in the back."

Doc and Robert turned around slowly. There were three drunken cowboys now. Robert said, "Come on, fellas, we sure don't want any trouble with you three."

"Well, that's too bad, 'cause you've got it."

"So the three of you are going to take the two of us on?"

"Nah, I'll take you both on by myself."

Robert smiled, friendly-like, and said, "Well, how about we do a little test down by the corral before you shoot us?"

"Why?"

Robert shrugged and flipped his hands up. "Well, for one thing, you don't want to shoot an innocent woman or child, do you? And secondly, as my pappy always said, it's always good to know what you're up against in a gunfight."

The cowboys drunkenly agreed with Robert and told them to lead the way.

Robert turned and walked with Doc.

The three drunks staggered behind them to the corral.

"What are you up to?" Doc whispered.

"Obviously, common sense and words won't work with these three. I figure I'll just let them see you draw."

Doc frowned, then grinned. "Hum, interesting. Yes, a most interesting approach."

When they were at the corral, Robert pointed to an empty cornfield where the tattered remains of an old scarecrow flapped in the wind. "Here's what I suggest. I'll throw a coin out in front of you. When it hits the ground, you draw and shoot at the scarecrow."

"And what will that prove?" the drunken gunfighter asked.

"Well," Robert said with a shrug, "if you hit the scarecrow at the same time, then it should be an interesting showdown. If, on the other hand, one of you is a great deal faster than the other one, then it's going to be a bloody mess."

"Okay, throw your coin," the cowboy said.

Robert took a gold coin from his vest pocket. "Gentlemen, take your positions." He flipped the coin up in the air.

The moment the gold coin touched the ground, Doc drew. He fired his black-handled Colt so quickly that one moment his hand was empty and the next the Colt had already fired. His shot cut the center pole of the scarecrow in half.

The cowboy-gunfighter had his revolver half out of his holster. His two friends stared at the dangling scarecrow, broken in two, now held together only by the tattered shirt that had scared the birds away.

The gunfighter looked down at his gun, still only halfway out of his holster. He grimaced as if in pain. He scowled at the scarecrow's shirt swinging gently in the breeze and back down at his hand, which still held his half-drawn gun. "My God," he mumbled, suddenly sober. Frowning, he turned to Robert and asked, "Am I drunk?"

"What do you think?" Robert asked as he bent and picked up his gold coin.

The cowboy-gunfighter ran his left hand over his face. "Not that drunk." He turned to his two friends, still shaking his head. "Why didn't you stop me?"

"You get a burr under your saddle and nobody can stop you," one of them answered.

The third said softly, "Ain't never seen no one draw a gun like that in my whole life."

The cowboy-gunfighter finally released his grip on his gun and let it drop silently back into his holster. He gulped nervously. "You just saved my life, huh?" he asked Robert.

"I 'spect so," Robert said.

The cowboy turned to Doc. "Sorry. If it weren't for your friend, I'd be lying in the street—dead."

"That's probably correct. Apology accepted."

The cowboy started to say something else, thought better of it with a shake of his head and frowned. Finally, he added softly, "That was mighty dumb."

"Well, you might want to think about no more heavy drinking," Robert said. "It could be bad for your health if I'm not around."

The cowboy managed a weak smile. "Thanks. You're right." The three cowboys turned and headed back into town. He said to his friends, "If I ever do anything as stupid as that again, you just take out your gun and hit me on my head."

Doc and Robert grinned at each other. Doc said, "Thanks. That was pretty smart thinking."

"Well, I'm okay with a gun, but not nearly as fast as you." Robert grinned. "Besides, I try to use my brain rather than my gun."

"I'll remember that."

"I'll walk you to the train." Robert smirked and added, "But just to keep you out of trouble. Sorry I can't go on with you, but the sheriff needs me to stay here until the judge arrives tomorrow. I would have enjoyed traveling with you."

"Me too."

"What's your route?"

"This train to Cheyenne and then a stage to Denver and on to Quiet Valley in the Rockies. I need to pick up some help before I head to Elk Forks."

Robert shook Doc's hand. "Luck to you. I'll tell Mr. Bates I saw you in action again on the train."

"And I'll tell him how you prevented me from being in action again. I think that will please him more."

"Fair enough," Robert said with a laugh.

CHAPTER FOUR

Dave Kramer turned the street corner in Quiet Valley and stopped abruptly. The two Owens brothers had been waiting for him. He grimaced as he realized he'd left his gun and holster on his desk in the newspaper office. Dave spread his hands and said, "Men, I'm not carrying."

"Foolish mistake on your part, Kramer."

Dave grimaced, realizing that they were about to shoot him and there was nothing he could do about it. He watched the eyes of the two gunmen, expecting them to draw instantly, but they were no longer focused on him. The two men were looking over his shoulder. Dave glanced around and watched as a tall, handsome young man in a long, black cape walked determinedly and rapidly up to them. The man had flipped the right side of his cape over his shoulder, exposing a deadly looking black-handled Colt revolver slung low on his right hip. "I'll be damned," Dave said. "Doc!"

When the man was close enough so the Owens brothers could hear him without difficulty, he said, "Easy to be brave against an unarmed man."

Before the brothers could draw, the Colt seemed to leap into the man's hand. Both men jerked back at the speed of the draw. Their hands froze on the handles of their weapons.

"Casey, Marcus," Dave said seriously to the Owens brothers, "you remember when my friend Bob Bates from Wells Fargo was in the Queen Bee and told about when I was working for Wells Fargo. This man beside me was taking gold I recovered for Wells Fargo back to St. Joseph. Two men tried to take it from him. They even had their guns drawn. My friend here drew and killed them both. You remember that?"

Casey, the younger of the Owens brothers, slowly licked his lips and nervously let his hand slide off his revolver's handle.

"Yup," Dave continued. "I bet my friend here would even be willing to reholster his Colt and let you have another go at it. What do you say, Doc?"

"Sure. However, this time when I draw, I'll have to kill them," Doc said. He slid his Colt back into his holster almost as quickly as he'd drawn it.

"Well, that certainly seems reasonable," Dave said agreeably. Dave faced the two men. "It shouldn't be a problem, right? Two of you and only one of him."

Casey shook his head violently. "Hey, no." He turned to his brother, "I didn't even see him draw."

"Faster than a blink." Marcus pushed his revolver out of his holster; the gun fell to the dusty street with a thump.

Casey didn't want to even touch his gun. He untied the leg strap, unbuckled the gun belt and let it drop around his boots. The brothers slowly raised their hands.

Sheriff Mac McMakin hurried to them, shotgun in hand, panting. He frowned at Dave and said harshly between gulps of air, "How many times have I told you not to be walking on the street without your gun?"

Dave grimaced. "You're right, Mac. That was stupid of me."

"Stupid is too kindly a word for what I'm thinking about you right at this moment."

"And this must be Sheriff McMakin," Doc said with a grin, "who you persuaded to come up to Quiet Valley and have an easy life till retirement."

Mac's bushy eyebrows squeezed together, his eyes narrowed, his nose flared, and he asked, "And just who might you be that you know so much about me?"

Dave grinned. "It's all right, Mac. Say hi to Doc Whitfield."

Mac leaned back in surprise. "The same Doc who saved your bony hide after you got shot up in Abilene and the one Bob Bates told us about?"

"The same," Dave said.

"So, what happened here?" Mac asked Dave as he kept an eye on the Owens brothers, whose hands were still in the air.

"They decided not to have a gunfight with Doc." Dave paused a moment in thought. "In fact, I reckon the Owens boys have decided it's time to leave the Territory of Colorado and never return. Right, boys?"

The brothers' heads bounced up and down rapidly.

Ted Jones, tall with sandy hair, ran up the street still wearing his shopkeeper apron and carrying his Henry rifle. In a gravelly voice he asked, "Were they going to shoot you unarmed?"

"I think that was their original plan."

Sheriff McMakin growled, "I think we should just hang them."

"Hey, Mac, that's not very friendly. Why, I'm sure if we let them get on their horses and leave, they will. Since they tried to kill an unarmed man, it shouldn't take long for you to get the word out that these two aren't welcome in Colorado Territory any longer."

"I'd still prefer to hang them." Mac's bushy eyebrows drew together in a frown and he pushed out his lips in thought. He glanced at Dave and shook his head in annoyance. Finally, after a deep sigh, he said to the two men, "You snakes, get to your horses and get out fast before I change my mind. And when I say out of the territory, that means all the way out."

Marcus Owens started to reach down to pick up his gun from the ground, but Doc made a small guttural sound. Marcus glanced up and saw that Doc had his hand on his Colt.

Mac pointed his shotgun at Marcus. "You touch that gun, and Casey will be an only child," he said firmly. "I'd suggest you just mount up and consider yourself damn lucky that you aren't gurgling at the end of a hemp rope. And when you get to your horses, you can leave your rifles as well. Just throw them on the ground. And don't stop at your place either. I can see it from here. Just be glad you're leaving with your lives."

Marcus started to argue, but Casey grabbed his arm and said nervously, "Let's go."

The brothers ran to their horses, pulled their rifles and dropped them to the street, then quickly mounted and galloped out of town.

Ted said to Doc, "I don't know who you are, but I owe you a big thanks. You just saved my best friend's life."

"As it happens, Ted," Doc said, "Dave is also one of my best friends."

Ted looked askance at Doc and asked Dave, "Do we know him?"

"Sort of, Ted. This fine-looking man is Doc Whitfield—all grown up and a real doctor."

"Really!" Ted said. He immediately went over and hugged Doc warmly, much to Doc's surprise. "Bless you," he whispered to Doc.

Doc laughed as he patted Ted on the back. "Dave wrote me that the doctor fixed your voice after that big gunfight you two were in. Sounds like he did a great job."

"It's a bit husky and gravelly, but it works for me." Ted glanced around the street and asked, "Where'd you come from, anyway?"

"I came in on the stage and was heading for the newspaper office when I saw those two acting suspicious at the corner. They'd glance around the building, look down the street, then dance back. They were far too rough looking to be on a social call. So I dropped my bag and hid behind the wagon over there and waited to see what they were up to. When Dave came out of the newspaper office, it was apparent they were after him."

"Well, your timing couldn't have been better," Dave said. He started toward the wagon and said over his shoulder, "Since you just saved my life, I guess the least I can do is carry your bag to my office."

* * *

Back in the office of *The Quiet Weekly*, Dave had just told Doc, Ted, and Mac to sit when Dave's wife, Elizabeth, rushed through the door. "Are you all right? I just heard that two men tried to kill you and some stranger saved your life."

"The same stranger who saved my life once before," Dave said as he held her tightly.

Elizabeth pulled back, a puzzled look on her face. "You told me that only four men had ever saved your life—Ted and Jamie Blackfoot, too many times to count, Slim at the cave, and Doc..."

Doc had stood when Elizabeth came through the door; now she quickly went and hugged him. "You look just like Dave described you, Doc, only taller. Thank you for saving him so long ago, and thank you for saving him today."

"I'm getting more hugs than I've had in a long time." Doc grinned down at her. "This is very nice."

Elizabeth laughed, then reached up and kissed him on his cheek.

"And that's even better," Doc said with a smile.

Elizabeth turned to Dave. "He'll be staying with us," she said in a voice that made it clear there would be no argument. "I've got to get back to the baby."

Dave reached down to give her a quick kiss good-bye, but she'd have none of that and kissed him passionately. She turned and hurried out the door.

Dave turned back to the group, his face slightly crimson. He shrugged. "She does worry some about me."

"I'm glad you explained that," Doc said. "I never would have figured that out by myself."

They laughed as everyone sat back down.

"All right," Doc asked, "explain to me why two men would want to shoot an unarmed man in midday?"

Dave leaned back in his chair. "Sloth, avarice, and an evil wish for power."

"Oh, right, just the usual stuff," Doc said. "And how did you manage to get yourself right in the middle of it?"

Ted smirked. "He wrote several editorials about the Owens brothers and their activities in rather precise detail. I believe they took offense."

Mac nodded emphatically. "Point was, we were certain they were responsible for some of the robberies and extortion going on, but we could never prove it. People were too afraid to tell me, but we knew."

"So," Doc said to Dave, "you decided to try to force their hand by writing about them."

Dave shrugged.

"And after that you decided to set yourself up as a target by walking around without your gun on. That seems a bit suicidal," Doc added with a disarming smile.

Mac started laughing. "Nah, just stupid. Just plain stupid."

Doc and Ted joined Mac in the laughter, while Dave squirmed in his chair, embarrassed.

"Don't you have some telegrams to send or criminals to go catch?" Dave said to Mac.

When Mac gave no response, Dave asked Doc, "What brings you to Quiet Valley? I'm delighted to see you, but you're sporting a new Colt. And the last letter I got from you telling me that you had your doctor's degree also mentioned that you were worried about your mom."

Doc sighed and turned serious. "She hasn't been seen for some time. Butcher won't let her go to church anymore. I got a telegram from our friend Tom Frost saying that he's worried about her. I sent a telegram to Red. He's on his way to Elk Forks to meet me. It's time for a showdown."

Dave frowned. "You need help, don't you?"

"I hate to ask. You've a wife, a child. I don't have the right to ask, yet I don't know who else to turn to. Maybe you could just give me some advice."

Dave drummed his fingers on his desk. "The odds are against you—you know that. That man you're up against, what was his name?"

"Butcher."

"Right. You told me he has a bunch of outlaws and gunslingers on his side."

"He does, or did. I suspect that hasn't changed."

Dave slowly leaned back in his chair and glanced over at Ted.

Ted patted his Henry rifle. "We're going hunting again, aren't we?"

Doc turned quickly to Ted. "I don't want—"

Ted interrupted. "He needs a bunch of babysitting to keep him out of trouble."

"But Dave wrote me that you and Henrietta are expecting your first baby. You two can't just ride up to Montana Territory and leave your families."

"He's right about that," Dave said. "Our womenfolk are not going to be pleased."

Mac looked at them. "I'd go, but these old bones couldn't keep up with you. But there is something I can do."

"What's that?" Dave asked.

"I've friends in Denver. How about you go as deputy US marshals?

"You can do that?" Dave asked.

"I think so. Let me send some telegrams. Fortunately, your name is well known in Denver."

"Thanks to you, no doubt," Dave harrumphed.

Mac grinned sheepishly. "Just a few stories among friends." He pondered a moment, then added, "I think it might be best if I get home and tell Donna. Once your women hear about this, they're gonna want to talk to her."

"Good idea," Ted said. "I can tell you that I don't relish telling Henrietta. But we owe Doc. We can't let him ride off to face that killer and his gunmen alone."

"But, Ted," Doc said, "you don't owe me."

Ted grinned. "You see that dummy sitting over there who can't remember to wear his gun? Well, without him, my life would be about the saddest thing I can think of. Yup, I owe you, Doc."

Dave frowned. "Doc, I have to be honest with you. There's no way our womenfolk are going to let us go off on this fight unless we give them some assurance about when we're coming back."

"I understand. A week, Dave. Just give me a week. Red and I have already decided to give the ranch to Butcher. I'll get word to Butcher to send us our mom when we get to Elk Forks and we'll sign over the ranch to him. If he doesn't, then we give him a show of force. He's not interested in our mom, just the ranch. I believe the three…" Doc glanced at Ted, "the four of us can convince him it wouldn't be worth a showdown."

"Interesting plan," Dave said. He stood. "One week, Doc. Well, Ted, let's get home and deal with the toughest part of this— trying to convince our wives that we have to go."

Doc stood and flipped his cape around his shoulders.

"Son, where did you get that thing?" Mac asked.

"A gift from a patient who couldn't afford to pay me, an English tailor," Doc said. "He custom sewed it for me. I figure if it can handle a New York City winter, it might be great for Montana. It's warm and sheds the rain." Doc gave it a sweep with his right arm, and it flowed across his shoulder. "I was worried about being able to draw, but the way he cut it, it works just great." He drew so fast, Mac and Ted both jerked in surprise. "I can even draw when it's not flipped back, and no one even sees it happen."

"Ha! I couldn't even see it while I watched you," Ted exclaimed.

Doc grinned as he flipped his cape back.

Dave laughed. "Still hate wearing a hat, huh?"

"I've got a hood that goes with this when the weather is bad, but you're right, hats aren't for me. Must be my Indian blood."

"As fair as you are, I'd say your dad's French blood overruled your Indian blood except for your straight, black hair," Dave said.

"And beard. According to Mom, I wasn't supposed to have any facial hair." He took his hand and rubbed his four-day growth of beard. "Yet here it is. Mom always called me her white baby." Doc's face turned sad. "It seems like forever since I've seen her."

"That's about to change," Ted said.

Dave didn't smile as he said, "I agree."

CHAPTER FIVE

Thunder rumbled ominously as black clouds billowed across the sky toward the town of Elk Forks, Montana Territory. An occasional flash of lightning silhouetted a small buggy pulled by one horse moving slowly down the long, pine-tree-lined trail to the lush, grassy valley below and the town of Elk Forks.

In town, the front lamps of the saloon-hotel had been burned out for more than an hour, but inside the lights were still turned up high. Joe Simms, the bartender and owner, flicked his damp towel across the already spotless bar and glanced nervously over at the poker table against the back wall. He was a short, stocky man with a round head that at first glance looked bald, but it was only that he kept his light-colored hair cut almost flush with his scalp. Joe bit on an unlit cigar, moving it from one side of his mouth to the other. He never bothered to light it. Normally he chewed up two in an evening; he was grinding out his sixth one tonight.

The door to the saloon opened, letting in a fierce gust from the impending storm. With some effort, Reverend Percy Ansley closed the door behind him and hurried to the bar as he shook the raindrops from his heavy black frock coat.

Reverend Ansley, the town preacher, undertaker, and drugstore owner, had bags under his eyes and a tiredness that seemed never to leave him. He was already old when he came to Montana Territory. He'd followed the eager gold miners first to the Gregory Gold Diggings in Colorado Territory, then on to Bannack and Virginia City and finally to Elk Forks. Now he was past seventy and weary. All his adult life he had tried to help those he could with his ministry or his patent medicines. Those he couldn't help, he buried.

Joe tilted his head toward the poker table. "They've been playing since late this afternoon. I didn't think Tex would come back today. They played until late last night, and Jesse told me they were supposed to be watching the ranch. The others went to Helena on Friday."

"When is Butcher due back?"

"He should already be back. Tex lost big last night, but Jesse got him to go home. Considering how drunk Tex was, I was surprised he went. Then this afternoon, here they show up again."

"So what's going on?" the reverend asked.

"Tex won some games for a while. Then about an hour ago, he started losing. He blames it all on Layton. Won't let Layton stop. He even kicked his cowboys out of the game so it would just be between them." Joe pointed with the cigar in his mouth to another poker table, where three cowboys sat silently watching Tex and the gambler. "Jesse won't let them start anything themselves, but in a showdown, they sure ain't going to help Layton."

"Have you sent for Ben?"

"Oh, yeah, Reverend. First thing I did when I figured there was going to be trouble. But Sammy told me the sheriff was out at Femora's mine. I sent Sammy out to fetch him, but I don't think he's going to be able to make it back in time. I'm not sure he'd even want to."

The reverend gave an understanding flick of his head. "Yes… yes, not against Tex. I don't expect he'll show." The reverend sighed softly and looked at the poker table where the two players faced each other.

Tex, a big man, sat with his back to the reverend and Joe. Every motion of Tex's arms strained the sweat-stained, close-fitting gray flannel shirt against his muscular back. Layton, the young gambler facing him, was thin with sharp, handsome cheekbones and wavy brown hair. His face was untanned, inscrutable. Except for an occasional glance at Tex and the quick movement of his hands with the cards, Layton's upper body was still. His fancy coat, ruffled white shirt, and tie seemed out of place in this rough, harsh setting.

Tex glanced at the cards just dealt him and glared across the table at the young gambler. "Damn you!"

Layton made no reply.

Tex took a large gulp of whiskey, draining his glass, then grabbed a bottle and tried to pour himself more. Realizing that the bottle was empty, he threw it against the wall behind the gambler and yelled drunkenly, "Simms, you stupid jackass, bring me another bottle."

"Give me the bottle, Joe," the reverend said. "I'll go see if I can talk some sense into his drunken head."

Outside, the storm had reached the outskirts of town, although it hadn't started to rain yet. The sky was filled with long flashes of lightning, streaking across black curtains of darkness. The driver of the buggy looked up at a sign that read Hotel D'Horse and smiled. A hotel for horses—he liked that. He drove the buggy to an open area outside the barn and stopped in front of a broken wagon. The man unhitched his horse, led it into an empty stall, and quickly took care of its needs. He glanced into a small room attached to the livery stable and saw a man asleep but decided not to wake him.

The driver walked out onto the main street and glanced up at the sky. A drop of cold rain bounced off his cheek. He'd ridden in and out of cold wet snow and wind all the way from Helena. He knew that before morning the street would be a river of mud or slushy, icy snow. He wore a black cape with a hood pulled over his head. As he hurried across the deserted street to the hotel-saloon, he glanced up at the sign over the building—Simms's Bar, Saloon & Restaurant.

The stranger stopped and silently inspected the four horses hitched in front, warily noting they all had the same brand. He ran his finger over the brand, a Rocking B, and shook his head. "Bad box," he whispered dejectedly. "Too soon. Ox pie!"

The reverend was back at the bar sipping a cup of hot coffee. He'd gotten nowhere with Tex.

The sound of the wind rushing in as the stranger opened the door caused everyone except Tex and Layton to look away from the gambling table. Joe bit into the leafy remains of his sixth cigar and mumbled to the reverend, "I surely do wish that had been Ben."

"Joe, you don't really expect him, do you?"

"A man can wish for a small miracle, Reverend. Isn't that what you told us in your sermon this morning?"

The three cowboys sitting together let their attention go back to the poker players after glancing briefly at the stranger.

The stranger, after some effort against the wind, closed the door, turned, and quickly studied the saloon. It was a large, long room, divided into a bar and an eating area. Kerosene lamps hanging from the rafters provided a yellowish light. The stained and worn wood plank floor was still wet from people coming in from the earlier storm. Faded chintz wallpaper covered the side and back walls. Off on the right of the room were three long tables with benches for serving meals.

A rough oak bar sat in the middle of the room and was plain but functional. The stuffed heads of an elk and a deer hung on the wall and watched over the room from each end of the bar. An old, discolored, long-forgotten hat was perched on one of the elk's antlers. Behind the bar a long shelf held liquor bottles and glasses. Two faded posters advertising rye whiskey and a picture of a steamboat were tacked to the wall above the shelf. A faded square on the back wall outlined the space where once a large mirror had hung.

The old potbellied stove at the end of the bar faintly leaked smoke from the stovepipe poking through the ceiling. A spittoon rested beside the wood used to feed the stove. Eight feet in front of the bar were six tables with spindle chairs used for card playing and drinking. Only two tables were occupied.

The stranger recognized Tex immediately, and also one of the three cowboys sitting at the adjacent table.

The stranger felt the tension in the room. He moved to the bar, pushed the hood off his head, and placed his gear on the floor. He looked over at the bartender and the reverend and asked softly, "Trouble?"

Joe leaned over the bar and in a half whisper said, "I'm afraid there's going to be, if the sheriff doesn't show up pretty damn soon."

"Oh, how's that?"

The reverend moved closer to the stranger, introduced himself, and told him about Tex and Layton in a whisper. When the reverend was finished, the stranger looked over at the three cowboys and asked, "What about them?"

"Three ranch hands from the Rocking B Ranch. Jesse is the foreman. Tex works for the owner, a man named Butcher."

"Tex Huffman," the man said softly.

"Yes. How'd you know that?"

The stranger didn't answer. Instead, he asked, "And he's got an older brother?"

The reverend nodded.

"You can't escape destiny," the man mumbled softly.

The reverend and Joe exchanged puzzled looks.

Before the reverend could ask him what he meant, the stranger asked, "Why doesn't the gambler just lose?"

Joe looked at the stranger and shook his head. "Not him. The first honest gambler I've had in this place in months. He'll play it straight, right down the fence line."

"And probably die for it," the reverend added.

The stranger stared at the gambler for a long, silent moment and with a grim smile mumbled softly, "Against Tex he doesn't have much of a chance."

The reverend frowned worriedly and said, "I'm afraid you're right."

"I'd like a room," the stranger said to Joe. "And I'd give a whole lot for a cup of hot coffee."

"Sure thing," Joe said, almost glad for the diversion. He brought a ledger book up from under the bar with a quill and ink bottle. "Just sign your name or make your mark. I'll get you some coffee. Reverend, how about you? Another cup?"

"Don't mind if I do, just as long as I know that Ann made it and not you."

Joe gave a snort, took what was left of his cigar out of his mouth, and spit into the spittoon on his side of the bar. He bit back down on the shredded remains of the cigar and hurried into the kitchen.

The stranger signed his name and closed the book. He unclipped his full-length cape until only the brass clasp at his neck remained attached. When Joe returned with the coffee, he took his cup with his left hand.

Joe was handing the other cup to the reverend when Tex gave a roar, kicking his chair over as he jumped to his feet. He waved his gun at the gambler. "You two-timing bastard. You worthless, cheating son of a bitch."

Layton got slowly to his feet and let his arms hang by his sides. His face showed no fear.

Tex took two steps back. His face glowed with anger. He returned his gun to his holster and yelled, "Okay, you rotten cheat. I'll give you a chance. You draw when you're ready."

Layton sighed. "I don't have a gun, Tex." His voice was as calm as his face.

"Hell you don't. Never yet knew a cheating gambler who didn't carry at least a derringer on him. You'd better draw when I count three, else I'm going to blow the hell out of you.

"One."

Layton stood calmly facing Tex, and except for his lips tightening, he didn't move.

"Two."

The three ranch hands had moved off to the side and were now frozen in suspense.

Suddenly the stranger yelled out. "Hey, clodhopper."

Tex had been ready to draw. He glanced over his shoulder.

"Yeah, clown. That's right, Tex. You worthless, back-shooting coward. I'm talking to you," the stranger said.

Tex turned around slowly, his face scrunched up in puzzlement, trying to figure out who this person was.

The stranger had stepped a few feet away from the bar. He flung his cape back with his right arm and the cape flowed smoothly over his shoulder, exposing a deadly looking, black-handled, shiny Colt on his hip. His right arm hung easily by his side, and the Colt seemed to be trying to reach out for his hand. In his left hand, he held his cup of coffee about waist high.

"You know, Tex, you're so dumb you wouldn't know whether anyone cheated you or not. The only time you're real tough is when you face down a man without a gun or you shoot someone in the back."

"Do I know you?" Tex managed to stammer.

"You know me." The stranger made a partial smile. "But it doesn't really matter if you can't come up with my name, because tonight you're three-seven-seventy-seven."

"I'm what?"

"That's the width, depth, and length of an outlaw grave," the reverend blurted.

"Ain't no one going to..." Tex went for his gun. He had it partway out of the holster before the stranger even started to draw. The stranger's arm flowed in an effortless motion that stripped the Colt from its holster in a blink. Two times the Colt roared, almost faster than the mind could comprehend, and Tex was lifted off his feet as his arms flailed in all directions. His body crashed on top of the poker table, then slowly slid off, upsetting the table with a crash and sending chips, cards, bottles, and money cascading across the floor.

The eyes of all the men slowly turned to the stranger. He still held the coffee cup in his left hand. He stared at it in amazement, not realizing that he still held it. Then, with a frightening calmness, he slowly brought the cup up to his lips and took a sip. The Colt was still in his hand, and a slight wisp of smoke languidly drifted out of the barrel. The three ranch hands were nervously aware that he was watching them closely over the edge of the cup.

The reverend hurried to Tex. He glanced up at the gambler, who hadn't taken his eyes off the stranger since the shooting. Layton held a derringer in his right hand. He quickly reattached it to the release mechanism inside his ruffled sleeve, then walked stiffly to the bar. "I think I need a serious drink, Joe."

Joe was still staring at the Colt in the stranger's hand. He looked up, startled, and with shaky hands poured Layton a drink from the nearest bottle.

Layton turned to the stranger and said, "Thanks."

The stranger had watched Layton replace his derringer. "Not sure you needed my help."

"Oh, I needed it, all right. I've never used it before. Never had to. Not sure it would have been enough against Tex."

The stranger moved back to the bar, set his cup down, and reloaded his Colt, keeping his eyes on the three cowboys.

The cowboys stood around Tex's body as the reverend examined him. Two holes formed a small, irregular line on his bloodied white chest.

"Take him home, boys," the reverend said as he stood. "He never knew what hit him."

Two of the cowboys dragged Tex's body out of the saloon, feet first. The third man, old and weather-beaten, came up to the stranger. "I won't say Tex didn't deserve to die, but if I were you, son, I'd get the hell out of Elk Forks—" The cowboy stopped in midsentence and stared hard at the stranger.

"What's the matter, Jesse?" the stranger asked in almost a whisper. "It hasn't been that long since you lied to protect Tex, his brother, and the others. Do you ever wake in the middle of the night and regret what you did?"

"You can't be you. You're dead." Jesse shook his head in disbelief.

"That's right, Jesse. You of all people should know that, huh? Give Butcher a message for me, will you? Tell him the lark buntings have returned, just a little later than he expected. You tell him to bring my mother into town by Friday, along with any belongings she wants with her, and we'll be out of his life forever. You tell Butcher I'll even sign over the ranch to him in exchange for my mother.

"If he doesn't bring her in, Red and I will be coming out to get her. He won't find that a pleasant experience if that's how he wants to play it, and I don't care how many gunfighters he has working for him.

"But when you see Richie, Cole, and Tex's brother, Rocky, back at the ranch...you tell them that's a different matter. Shooting my uncle in the back makes it real personal. You understand that, don't you, Jesse?"

Jesse tried to speak, but nothing came out. He kept shaking his head as he backed away from the stranger. Finally he turned and ran from the saloon as though he'd just escaped from the clutches of a hideous nightmare.

The reverend watched Jesse rush out of the saloon. He hadn't been close enough to hear the conversation, but he figured that Jesse was probably telling the stranger to get out of town, and fast.

However, the look on Jesse's face was one of fear. No, that wasn't it; the look was of terror—pure, unadulterated terror. The reverend rubbed his eyes tiredly. He'd seen too much of this type of trouble.

He went to the stranger.

"If Jesse was telling you to get out of town, then I'd follow that advice, son. There's going to be a pack of trouble coming into Elk Forks, and soon. And it's going to be looking for you."

"Why would that be, Reverend? He drew first. It was a fair fight."

The reverend heard a tone in the stranger's voice that bordered on disdain, but he wasn't sure. Something was strangely familiar about this man, but what was it?

"When Butcher hears about Tex, he's going to come charging in here with his whole crew," the reverend said. "And leading the charge will be Tex's older brother, Rocky."

The reverend studied the stranger's face closely to see if his words had made an impression. That haunting feeling returned. Something about this man he knew, but what was it? "Rocky is a professional gunfighter," the reverend continued. "He's as mean a man as I've ever met."

"I know about Rocky, but thanks for the warning." The stranger smiled grimly at the reverend. "Rocky won't shoot me in the back like he did my uncle. Not this time, Reverend."

The reverend stepped back, his mind racing, trying to come up with a name. "Herb Whitfield. They shot him in the back." He rubbed his forehead with his fingers as he frowned at the man in front of him. "My God, you're Doc Whitfield, aren't you? My eyes are getting old. I should have recognized you right off. You've grown at least three inches, and with that week's beard…" He shook his head in confusion.

"It's me, Reverend. Back from the grave."

The reverend reached out and shook Doc's hand.

"They told us you and your brother were dead."

"You mean Butcher told the town that."

"Of course. I always wondered, but when you and Red never returned…" The reverend shrugged. "Did Tom know?"

"He knew," Doc said.

"So your mother knew all this time."

"Yes. Tom became our voice to her."

"I'm glad. I wondered how she could hold up so well after word of your death. Of course, she came to church twice a week. That's where she'd meet with Tom, once on Thursday to practice Sunday's songs on the organ, and then again on Sunday.

"Then one of her guards saw her talking to Tom. All these years, we've been able to pull off the meeting without the guards knowing. They'd drop her off at the church and then come here to drink until she got out. Then this July, one of them decided to stroll into the church and saw them talking. That was it. She hasn't been seen by anyone since then." He shook his head. "I'm worried about her."

"So are we, Reverend."

"And if anything has happened to her?" he asked.

"That better not be the case." Doc's face turned grim.

"But if it is?"

"Butcher's not stupid. He never married my mother, so he has no rights to the ranch, the land, the stock, or the water."

"He could force her to sign the deed. He thinks you and Red are dead."

"When Tom wrote me that they'd been seen together, I sent a letter to Mom at the ranch. I knew Butcher would never let her read it, but after that letter, he knows we are alive. Alive and dangerous. Tom said a neighbor saw my mom just before I left New York, so we know she was still alive a few weeks ago."

"New York?"

"I just graduated from medical school. I'm a real doctor, so I finally caught up with my name."

"Butcher's going to want you dead."

"I 'spect so, but all I want to do is get her out of here forever."

"Butcher's not going to let that happen after what went on last winter. A bad winter, between the weather and the Indians. He lost a bunch of money. I hear he and his men have robbed gold miners at Bannack, forcing them to give up their claims to him and then making them keep working their own mines."

Joe had been listening. "He keeps the gold and gives them next to nothing to live on," Joe said bitterly. "We think he's been responsible for robberies all over, but so far the vigilantes haven't come looking for him. Not yet."

"I'm not here about all that," Doc said. "I'm here to get my mother. That's all. Is the new sheriff going to help us, or is that position still owned by Butcher?"

"Ben's not a bad man, but he's weak," the reverend said. "He's not about to go up against Butcher and his gunmen."

"We're hoping Butcher will trade my mom for the ranch. For some reason he's always wanted our ranch. I could never figure out why. He's not a cattleman. It's a good spread, but no more than others around here. It just doesn't make sense. He's a greedy soul but not a fool. I'm hoping my offer will work."

"And if it doesn't work?"

"Then we'll just have to do whatever it takes to rescue our mom. I've often…"

The salon door flew open and a group of armed men rushed in before Doc could finish his thought.

CHAPTER SIX

Five people stood in line for a seat at the restaurant when Dave and Ted got there. Dave looked ahead of him and put a smirk on his face. He turned to Ted and said in a loud voice, "The thing I really can't stand is when a big, redheaded man pushes his way to the front of the line."

Ted glanced at Dave in astonishment. "Dave!" he exclaimed in his guttural voice.

"I think we should just pick up that big ox ahead of us and shove him out in the street. Small buffalo need to be put in their place."

"Hush, Dave," Ted said. The others in the line stared at Dave nervously. The large man, three people in front of Dave, had already turned and walked back to them. He frowned down at Dave. "Seems like you're looking for trouble," he said in a hard voice.

"See that muscle?" Dave said as he flexed his arm. "Let's see what you've got."

The big man flexed his arm and a huge bulge formed under his shirtsleeve.

"That's not a muscle; that's a tree trunk," Ted said. "Dave, apologize to this man before he kills us both."

"Nah," he said with a laugh. He patted the man on the chest. "You aren't going to let a little muscle scare you, are you, Ted? I'm going to show you how we do it in Quiet Valley. I'm going to put my arms around this little buffalo and throw him right out the door."

Dave wrapped his arms around the man and with much grunting tried to lift him once, then twice. Before he could try a third time, he started laughing as the large man wrapped his arms around Dave and started hugging him warmly. "Hiya, Dave."

Ted stared at them for a moment, trying to fathom what was going on. Then, abruptly, he smiled. "Aha! It's Doc's brother, Red, isn't it?"

"Yup." Dave managed to gasp between his laughter. "Red, say hello to Ted Jones."

Red reached out a huge paw and shook Ted's hand warmly.

"And here I was figuring Dave had chewed some loco weed, and we were both going to need a doctor to patch us up after you got through stomping us," Ted said with relief.

Dave grabbed Red's shoulders with both hands and stepped back. "Let me look at you. Tiny as ever, and you still have the biggest smile of any man I've ever met."

"Thanks to you," Red said.

"Don't be giving me that. Back in Kansas, you were the one who saved my life. I sure didn't expect to run into you here. Figured you'd already be in Elk Forks."

"Train went as far as Carlin, Nevada. That's as far as the Central Pacific has gotten on the way to here but that's still astonishing. You should see them laying track. It's incredible. It's the biggest engineering project I've ever seen, and I've seen some big ones around the gold mines. They hope to join with the Union Pacific sometime next year.

"From Carlin, thanks to a letter Mr. Bates gave me, I was able to hitch a ride with some railroad people on a freight wagon to Salt Lake City. Missed the Montana Trail stage to Helena by a few hours. I had to wait an extra day for the next one."

"What do you hear from Doc?"

"Nothing. I'm worried that instead of waiting, he'll try to go up against Butcher without us."

Dave nodded seriously. "But Doc's smart."

"Yes, but he's plenty worried about Mom. Butcher might try to force his hand before we get there." Red placed his arm around Dave and said in a choked voice, "I sure am glad to see you. I wasn't sure you'd come, what with the odds against us so."

"Well, Red, you know I'd do anything for a piece of your apple pie."

Red glanced at Ted.

Ted shrugged. "Someone has to keep him out of trouble. Besides, I want to see if your apple pie is really as good as he keeps telling me."

"I'm much obliged to you both." Red stared at the badge on Dave's vest. "Something new?"

"Our friend, Mac, is the sheriff in Quiet Valley, and he used some of his influence to get these. He thought it might make things easier for us."

"Or harder," Red said. "Not everyone takes kindly to authority in Montana Territory."

"Nevertheless, this time we want to make sure the law is on your side," Ted said.

"After dinner we'd best get some rest," Dave said. "Four and a half days on a rocking coach to Helena will make us appreciate our bed tonight."

"I heard the food is terrible, so I packed some good stuff to fortify us," Red said with a grin.

"Apple pie?" Dave asked.

"Maybe," Red said with a mischievous smirk. "But only if you promise not to throw me out of the food line again."

"Considering that I couldn't even lift you an inch, that's an easy promise to make."

"Any chance we could get an early sample tonight?" Ted asked.

"I certainly can tell you're a friend of Dave's. After dinner, dessert's on me."

* * *

After dinner, Ted finished his large helping of apple pie on the hotel front porch, sighed, and said, "Well, I thought Dave might have been exaggerating about your pie, but he wasn't. That was the best I've ever had, but if you tell my wife I said that, I'll deny it."

"I promise not to tell her." Red laughed.

"So," Ted asked, "how'd a delicate little boy like you get into baking?"

Red leaned back in his chair and explained, "My mom and dad died during a diphtheria epidemic. It was just my *grand-mère* and me. I was too young to understand it, but we were in big trouble. No money, no food, and no hope. Doc's mother and dad came and took us into their home the day of the funeral. That was up in Fort Benton."

"What's a grand-mère?" Ted asked.

"Oh, right. Well, Doc's dad started calling my grandmother grand-mère, the French word for 'grandmother,' and soon we were all calling her that. She told me once that she liked it because it made her feel like a special part of the family.

"It seems like Doc was interested in medicine from the moment I met him. I was two years older than he was, and he was such a cute little kid, you couldn't help caring for him. Anyway, while he was healing things, I'd hang out with Grand-mère in the kitchen and watch her cook. Doc's mom and dad loved her cooking, so soon I was cooking too. But the part I loved the best was baking."

"What did you do after you got Doc to New York?" Dave asked.

"I took a boat to California." Red grimaced. "Don't want to ever do that again. When I wasn't leaning over the railing, heaving up things too horrible to describe, I was holding on for dear life. My stomach and my body were unquestionably not made for sea travel. That's why I'm so excited about the rail making it all the way to here."

"So what happened once you got to California?" Ted asked.

"A surprising adventure. I bought an old, used chuck wagon and loaded it up. I took it to the most active gold mining area I could find and started cooking." Red stopped and grinned at them. "The gold poured in. I couldn't cook enough or fast enough. I hired two wagons to do nothing but travel back and forth from my place to the valley and buy me supplies. Soon I had a huge tent and tables everywhere, and the gold just kept pouring in."

"What about security?" Dave asked.

Red roughly scratched his flowing red hair. "Well, as you pointed out, I'm not what you'd call a tiny young man."

"Ah," Ted said with a quick grin. "The master of understatement."

"One evening two men started to go at it, and I could see it was going to explode quickly into a big fight. The tent was full of my customers, and I didn't want that type of trouble, so I grabbed a large cast-iron skillet and went up to their table. They were sassing each other so loud, they didn't even see me come. I took that skillet and slammed it down on the table between them. The sound was like an explosion. The plates on the table must have bounced a foot and everyone in the place along with them."

Red stopped and suppressed a laugh at the memory. "Once that skillet hit the table, there wasn't a sound in the whole tent. The two men almost jumped out of their boots, I scared them that much. I told them if they ever wanted to eat at my place again, they'd either have to make up or take their fight onto the street, 'cause I wasn't going to put up with no fighting in my place.

"The one man, Jake, said I wouldn't stop serving them. And I told him I would, so either make up or no pie or apple dumplings at my place forever." Red paused.

Dave grinned. "And?"

"Jake said to Roy, 'No way I'm risking that.' And Roy's head was bobbing up and down in agreement. 'Me neither,' he said. They shook hands and everyone in the place applauded. Word got out quickly after that not to mess in Big Red's place."

"Right!" Ted said. "That's what I tried to tell Dave this evening when he started that fracas in the restaurant, and I hadn't even met you yet."

"So how could you manage to just up and leave?" Dave asked.

Red looked down shyly. "I have more than twenty people working for me now. I put my lead man in charge. He's an old Swede and about the most honest man I've ever met. I helped him pay to bring his wife to California when he didn't make it panning for gold. He became most beholden to me and started working at my place.

"I'm embarrassed to say it, but I have more money than I know what to do with. I fronted some gold mines and they hit some big strikes too."

Red shook his head, then shrugged. "The problem is that I didn't want that to happen. I just wanted to bake in my kitchen, be happy, and have people enjoy my cooking. Make enough money to be able to pay my bills and live well. That's not so bad, is it?" Red asked, as he looked at Dave.

Dave started laughing as he shook his head. "That's not bad at all, Red. Not a bad dream at all."

Red leaned back in his chair, laced his fingers together, and said, "Good. I didn't think so either." He scratched his beard. "So what happens? All this money just kept pouring in and confused everything. Money can sure be a nuisance. Rather than baking, I had to do all this other money stuff."

"Yup, that certainly does sound tough," Ted said, trying hard to look serious. "All that money and no time to have fun."

"Precisely!" Red said. "That's my point." He frowned. "Oh, all right, I know you're fooling with me, but it's like you said. I'm a really good baker."

"I can't argue with you on that point," Ted said with a quick wave of his fork. "Have you told Doc about your good fortune?"

"I think I'll spring it on him sort of gentle-like after we find Mom." He scratched his beard. "Never figured having money would be such an annoyance. Always thought it would be the other way around."

"In the meantime," Dave said, "you can keep baking for us." He held up his empty plate. "Seconds?"

"These pies are supposed to last us until we get to Helena," Red protested.

Ted stretched his plate toward Red. "But we need our strength for that tough ride on that nasty, dusty stagecoach. You can't have two deputy US marshals get off the stage in Helena in a weakened condition."

"And remember, Red, we're only eating this pie to keep your dream of being a happy baker alive," Dave added with a grin.

Red served them another slice of pie as he grumbled, "I'm starting to think I should have pretended I didn't know you and let you throw me into the street."

CHAPTER SEVEN

Jesse was surprised to see the lights still on in the ranch house when he, Ray, and Shorty rode up the trail toward the ranch with Tex's body. A soggy snow had fallen the whole way back from Elk Forks, and their slickers hadn't kept them dry. They were tired, cold, wet, and worried.

"Shorty, you and Ray take Tex's body to the shed beside the bunkhouse," Jesse ordered. "I'll see if I can find Rocky and Butcher and tell them what happened." He slowly bit his lip as he rode up to the house. This was news he didn't want to be bringing to Butcher, who would already be angry at them for going into town and not staying at the ranch. That was Tex's fault. Tex had made them come with him. Jesse had seen Butcher go crazy after hearing bad news before, and this news was certainly bad. And Rocky would explode when he heard about his brother. Both these men were dangerous when angry.

Jesse knocked hesitantly on the door and jumped when Cole opened it. "What are you doing here at this hour, Jesse?" Cole demanded with a scowl.

"I've bad news for Mr. Butcher." Jesse noticed that Cole's pants and shirt were wet and covered with mud.

"Yeah, well, he's not in the mood for more bad news, and I'm not either, so you'd better tread softly."

Cole followed Jesse into the study. Butcher was sitting behind a large oak desk, holding a drink. He looked as if he'd had many drinks, and his eyes were bloodshot. His large, bulbous nose was a bright red. "Did you find her?" he demanded.

"Find who?" Jesse asked.

"That Blackfoot woman, Mrs. Whitfield, you worthless sod. Have you found her yet?"

"Sorry, Mr. Butcher. I don't know what you're talking about."

Rocky came from the next room holding a new bottle of whiskey and handed it to Butcher.

"The Kid told me that he, Tex, and a couple of the boys snuck off to town yesterday and then again today when they were supposed to be here keeping a watch on things," Rocky said, his speech slightly slurred from the whiskey. "She wouldn't have gotten away if they'd done what they were told to do. I'm going to pound on Tex when I see him." He turned toward Butcher. "Jesse don't know nothing about your woman," he said.

"Well, what are you doing here, then?" Butcher demanded.

Jesse glanced worriedly at Rocky. "Bad news, I'm afraid, Mr. Butcher. Tex was killed at the saloon this evening."

Rocky took three quick steps, grabbed Jesse by the front of his wet slicker, and slammed him against the wall. "How? Who did it?"

Jesse shook in fear. "I think it was Doc Whitfield."

"You drunken old crow bait! Whitfield and his brother have been dead for years," Rocky screamed at Jesse.

Jesse shook his head. "He told me to tell Mr. Butcher that the lark buntings have decided to return this year."

Butcher jumped from his chair, his face ashen, and quickly took a big gulp of whiskey from his glass. "You sure he said 'lark buntings'?"

"Yes, sir. He also told me to tell Rocky and Cole that he's looking for them and Richie too."

"Damn!" Cole said. He quickly sat and asked Butcher, "Do you suppose that's why Mrs. Whitfield took off?"

Butcher shook his head. "I knew they were alive, but I never thought he'd come back here and challenge my hand." Butcher pounded his fist on the table. "Did he have a vigilante group with him?"

Jesse's voice squeaked nervously. "Just him. I didn't see his brother either. He got a room at Simms's place. Doc told me to tell you to bring his mother into Elk Forks by Friday, and you can have the ranch."

Butcher tried to pace by the desk, but he weaved unsteadily on his feet. Finally, he placed his hands flat on his desk and just leaned against it and glared at Jesse. "He said I could have the ranch. In exchange for their mother."

"That's what he said. Said he'd sign it over to you."

"Damn." Butcher pounded the desk with his fist. "And she's gone." He took a deep breath and asked, "And if I don't?"

"Then he's going to come out here for you, and he said he didn't care how many guns you had."

Rocky slammed Jesse roughly to the floor. "Why the hell are you still here, then? Why didn't you and the boys kill him?"

"I've never seen a man draw so fast." Jesse stayed on the floor and was too frightened to look up at Rocky. "Tex had his gun half out before Doc even started to draw, and he shot Tex two times in the chest. Tex never got off a shot."

"Well, he's not faster than me," Rocky said as he clumsily pulled his gun and pointed it at Jesse.

"Rocky!" Butcher yelled. "Put your gun away. You're half drunk, and if the Kid is fast, I don't want you to be going after him full of whiskey."

Rocky glared at Butcher and reluctantly shoved his gun back into his holster.

"Go and fire off three quick rifle shots, Cole," Butcher said. "That will bring in the men who are still out searching for the Indian. Tell them to bed down for the night. We ride to town tomorrow morning before sunup." Butcher glared into his empty glass. "We'll take all the men and hit Doc while he's still asleep. Let's see how many guns he has against mine."

"What about Roy, Shorty, and the Kid?" Cole asked.

"Leave them. They're lucky if they can hit the ground. I want guns with us, not three stupid cowboys that only know about herding cattle. They can keep looking for the Indian woman." He slapped the top of the table. "No, get them to round up all the cattle they can find. We need money."

CHAPTER EIGHT

Doc had his Colt halfway out of his holster before he realized that the five men weren't after him. Doc recognized the older one immediately. Conrad Spear was short and stocky, with leathery skin as tough as a buffalo hide and a thick, shaggy gray mustache hanging over his upper lip. He had a spread on the opposite side of the valley from Doc's ranch. Conrad rushed to the bar. "We need Ann, Joe. Esther's gone into labor."

Doc looked questioningly at the reverend.

"Ann's a midwife," he said quietly.

"I thought she wasn't due for another month or so," Joe said.

"She's early. Something's wrong. She's hurting awful bad," the younger man said anxiously.

Doc recognized Martin Graham. His thin, pointed, untanned face always looked serious. He had wild brown hair that peeked out around his floppy hat, and his dark overalls were always covered with gray mine dust. He was thin but muscular from taking over and working his father's mine when he was fourteen, after the fever killed his mom and dad.

"I'll get Ann up," Joe said. "You get Esther into the side room over there." He pointed at a door off to the right. "A bed's already set up there."

"This wouldn't have happened if she'd been at home," Conrad yelled at Martin.

"She was at home, our home where she belongs. She's not your little baby anymore," Martin yelled back. "She's my wife."

"She'll always be my daughter, and you sneaking off and marrying her won't change that."

"Well, that was your doing. We didn't sneak off. We wanted you there, but you would have none of it."

"Hey! Hey!" Doc shouted. "Enough, already. Both of you, shut up!"

Conrad turned angrily to Doc. "Who the hell are you, telling me—"

"I'm Doc Whitfield," Doc interrupted.

"You're dead," Conrad sputtered, not believing his eyes.

"Not yet. What I am is a real doctor, and it sounds like Esther needs my help. So let me tell you something. The last thing your daughter and your wife needs right this minute is to have the two men she loves raisin' Cain. Do you hear me? You two sound like a couple of baby coyotes yapping over your territory."

The men dropped their heads, embarrassed.

"Martin, I want you to run across the street to the stable and fetch me two large carpetbags from the buggy parked in front of a broken wagon by the barn. They have my medical instruments."

Martin stared at Doc, not believing who he saw.

"Martin!" Doc said. "Now!"

"Right." Martin snapped from his trance and hurried out the door.

Conrad frowned at Doc.

"Save that look for later, Conrad. It's your daughter we need to worry about. Sounds like your bullheadedness has already cost you your daughter and a chance to have that son you always wanted."

"You're out of line, boy."

"You two have been yelling at each other since long before I left. You've been more a dad to him than his dad. Seems like you lost not only him but your daughter as well. That's what I'd call really out of line."

Conrad scowled at him but didn't say anything.

"Come on," Doc said. "We've got to get her out of the elements."

Doc, Conrad, and Conrad's three cowboys hurried out to the wagon. The wet snow was falling hard, coating everything with a slick, icy layer.

Doc slipped and a cowboy grabbed his arm before he fell. "Oops. Not good to have the doctor break his rump before delivering a baby," Doc said.

"You look too young to be a doctor," the tall, thin cowboy drawled. He was a young, good-looking kid with the whitest teeth and the bluest eyes Doc had ever seen.

"You look younger than me. How many times have you heard that since you became a cowboy?"

"A bunch. I guess we've all got to start young." The cowboy grinned.

"Got that right. Even doctors." Doc crawled into the covered wagon. Mrs. Bale, Conrad's housekeeper, held Esther's head in her lap. She glared at Doc and demanded, "Who are you?"

"Hi, Mrs. Bale. Remember me? Doc Whitfield?"

She frowned in thought, as Doc felt the blankets on top of Esther and noticed that they were wet. "I'm a real doctor now, Mrs. Bale." He touched her arm and realized that Mrs. Bale was also wet, and shivering. He didn't like that. Esther's faced contorted in pain as she looked up at him.

"Yup, Esther, it's me, Doc. Guess what? I'm a real doctor. Went to school in New York City, got a degree and everything. I'm going to help you have a grand new baby. All right?"

"Doc?"

"Honest, it's really me."

"They told us you were dead."

"Sometimes it's best not to believe everything you hear."

She reached up her hand and Doc took it gently in his. "Like Betsy," she whispered.

Doc grinned as he remembered Esther's dog. "Yeah, but I'd just as soon you didn't have eight little ones, like what happened when I helped Betsy deliver hers."

He reached under the blanket, ran his hand over her tummy to feel the location of the baby, and frowned. "We're going to bring you inside and get you snug and warm."

"I'm powerful scared, Doc. I don't think I can walk."

"Nope, and I don't want you to. You just hold on to Mrs. Bale until we get something to carry you in on." He gently patted her hand. "Don't be scared, Esther. I'm here and Mrs. Bale is here, and everything is going to be fine. I'm a really good doctor." He smiled reassuringly at her.

"Thanks, Doc," Esther whispered.

He glanced up at Mrs. Bale. "When we get Esther inside, I want you to get into some dry clothes. I'm going to need your help tonight, and I can't have you freezing in wet clothes."

"Ann and I are about the same size. I'll borrow some of hers."

"Good." Doc crawled back out of the wagon and said to Conrad, "You get some dry blankets from inside and replace those wet ones covering her, but don't move her. Not till I tell you. You understand?"

"Is she going to be all right?" Conrad asked.

"The baby's not in the right position. It's going to be a long night."

Conrad grabbed his arm. "I lost my wife when she was giving birth to Esther. Don't let that happen to Esther."

"Not if I can help it, Conrad."

"But it's bad, isn't it?"

Doc nodded quickly. "Not as good as I'd like, but I didn't come back to Elk Forks to lose a friend. Get those blankets." Doc hurried into the hotel.

"Reverend, I need a stretcher."

"I don't know of one hereabouts."

Doc thought a moment. "Do you have a loose coffin lid?"

"Right. We could wrap a blanket or two around one and use that." The reverend waved to the cowboy that had kept Doc from falling and said, "Sinful, come with me. I'm not as strong as I used to be."

"Hey, Sinful," Doc yelled.

Sinful turned around.

"I didn't have time to say thanks for saving me from falling on my behind. How'd you get a name like Sinful?"

"My momma gave me that name to keep me from being sinful. Raised me on prunes and proverbs."

"Did it work?"

Sinful looked seriously at Doc and sadly shook his head. "Nah. I became a cowboy."

Doc frowned for just a moment, then in unison they grinned at each other.

Martin returned with Doc's bags as Sinful and the reverend hurried off. Doc quickly opened one bag, pulled out a smaller bag and went around behind the bar. He pulled out a porcelain mortar and pestle from the bag, opened two small vials, and soon was crushing the contents. "Joe, I need a bottle of the best whiskey you've got, and one that's not been opened."

Joe quickly got it, along with a glass.

Doc smiled at Joe. "No, Joe, it's not for me. Open it and give me the bottle."

Joe did as Doc asked and watched Doc precisely pour a measured shot into the contents of the mortar. Joe wrinkled his nose. "You going to make poor Esther drink that?"

"Smells pretty bad, doesn't it?" He opened another vial and, with an eyedropper, splashed four drops into the mixture. "Okay, that hides the smell some. Find me a big spoon."

Doc hurried out to the wagon. Conrad had replaced the wet blankets around his daughter and draped a dry blanket over Mrs. Bale's shoulders. Conrad stood outside the wagon as the wet snow fell on him. Doc gestured his approval at the dry blankets. Martin was on his knees beside his wife. "All right, Esther," Doc said to her. "I want you to swallow this. It tastes terrible, but it will help your pain."

"I thought the doctor was supposed to be kind to his patients," Esther said with a pained smile.

"If it's any consolation, I put a shot of whiskey in it, just to spice it up for you. Martin, you and Mrs. Bale gently lift her head while I spoon this good stuff down her."

As soon as he'd gotten the medicine into Esther, the reverend and Sinful showed up with the makeshift stretcher. Following Doc's instructions, the men carried Esther into the bedroom. Doc quickly introduced himself to Ann and told her to get some warm clothes on Mrs. Bale. He ran out to where his medical bags were.

Doc quickly grabbed the two smaller bags, glared at Conrad and Martin, and said, "It's going to be a long night, gents. If you care for this woman, I'd suggest that you mend some fences. And let me warn you, if I hear any yelling or angry words coming from out here, I'll come out and shoot you both in the foot to give you something to really yell about. Is that clear?"

Doc hurried into the bedroom and quietly closed the door.

CHAPTER NINE

Conrad pointed to the table on its side, the blood, chips, and cards on the floor.

Joe frowned. "Doc took out Tex Huffman tonight, just a bit before you showed up. I haven't had time to clean it up yet."

"What happened?"

"Tex accused me of cheating," Layton explained. "Doc stepped in and saved my hide."

The reverend waved his hand dramatically. "Doc had the fastest draw I've ever seen. Tex didn't have a chance. Doc believes Tex was one of the men who shot his uncle in the back. You remember Herb Whitfield."

"Nasty business." Conrad paused in thought. "Butcher claimed Doc and his brother, Red, had shot their uncle, and that's when the boys disappeared. Next we heard they were both dead. You say Doc was fast?"

"The fastest draw I've ever seen, and I've seen some fast ones," Layton said. "And I had the best view."

"You and your boys had anything to eat?" Joe asked Conrad.

"Not since lunch."

"How about I rustle you up some steak and eggs? Just remember, I'm not Ann, but I do a fair job at the stove."

"That would be much appreciated, Joe. It's been a tough afternoon for us."

Joe looked over at the upended bloody poker table and said, "You have no idea."

"Joe," Layton said. "Least I can do is clean up this mess."

* * *

Two hours later, Granville, Conrad's foreman, came to the table where Conrad sat, aimlessly playing a hand of solitaire.

Conrad didn't look up. Granville fumbled with his suspenders and fidgeted for a bit before he said, "All the boys have been fed and are sacked out on the floor in the restaurant area." He paused, waiting for a response. When there was none, he cleared his throat and said, "Boss, you know I'm not one to pry, particularly where you're concerned, but Martin looks like he's hurting real bad."

Martin sat alone at another table with his hands clasped together. His face was contoured in pain and sadness.

Conrad scrambled his cards angrily and frowned at Granville. "How many years have you and I been together?"

Granville gave a toothless grin and said, "More years than I can remember, boss."

"In all those years, you've never lied to me, Granville. Tonight I want you to be totally honest with me. I didn't do right by them two, did I?"

Granville ran his tongue over his lips and tried to decide how to respond. Finally he said, "Martin's a good man, boss. He loves your daughter a powerful lot. I think he loves you too, but you won't let him in." Granville pulled his suspenders in and out nervously. "I know it hurt you a bunch when Esther married Martin and he took her to his place. But it hurt her a lot too. This last year has been tough on all of you."

"Have I been a stupid old fool, Granville?"

"Well," Granville said, nervously crisscrossing his suspenders. "I'd never call you stupid."

Conrad smiled wryly. "But the old fool is true, huh?" He stood. "Damn." He patted Granville on the shoulder. "Thanks for being as honest as always, Granville. Between you and Doc, I've taken some soul-searching hits tonight."

Conrad picked up his coffee, fortified it with a shot of whiskey, and carried it to the table where Martin was sitting.

Martin glanced up and said, "I don't want to fight with you, Conrad. I'm tired of always fighting with you. I just want to pray for Esther."

"No fighting, Martin, but I need to talk to you. May I sit down?"

Martin turned his head away from Conrad, but after a moment he sighed softly and said, "Yes, sir."

Conrad sat across from him. "I have some things to say to you, Martin, and they will be hard for me to say, but I want you to let me finish without interrupting me. Will you do that?"

"Yes, sir." Martin didn't look at him, only stared at his clutched hands.

"I know how hard this night is for you, Martin. I lost my wife, Esther's mother, Ruth, during childbirth on a night like this, and all the pain of that night—all that I lost—is flooding my memories." Conrad stopped and rubbed his rough, knurly hands together. "This cold makes my hands ache something fierce." Then he shook his head, knowing he was stalling. He took a deep breath and continued.

"After my wife was gone, all I had was this tiny little baby girl to love and care for. And I believe I did a good job raising her, with a lot of help from Mrs. Bale. The problem was, I never thought about the day when she'd leave and go off on her own. I chased all her other suitors away, but you wouldn't go. You were always polite, but you never backed down from me. Not once. Tonight, thinking back about those days, I realize I was secretly impressed with you."

Martin glanced quickly over at Conrad, his dark brown eyes showing his surprise.

"Still, things went the way they went, and I ended up losing my daughter. Doc Whitfield was correct. I should have been gaining a son, but instead I lost my only daughter." He took a sip of his coffee.

Martin wasn't sure if Conrad was through. He wasn't.

"Martin, my little girl is in that room fighting for her life, and I can't tell her how sorry I am, but I can tell you. You know I'm a strong, bullheaded man, but I love my daughter, and what I did to you hurt her. That's not acceptable." He took another sip of coffee. "I'd be honored if you and Esther would move into my house."

Martin shook his head.

Conrad held up his hand. "Hear me out, Martin. I'm not telling you, I'm asking." He looked away for a moment, then added, "No, I'm not even asking. I'm begging you. I want to see my grandchild grow up, and I don't want to ride five miles to your mine every time I start missing the baby. I'm getting old, and when I'm gone that means you and Esther will be getting my ranch. I need to start teaching you how to handle a spread. I'll build an extension to the west wing so you can have your own wing to live in. Mrs. Bale has missed Esther as much as I have. And you will need help with the baby..." Conrad's voice faltered, and he didn't finish.

Martin's forehead creased in thought. Finally he let out a long, slow breath and said, "I'll do it for Esther." He held out his hand.

Conrad shook Martin's hand firmly. "Thank you, son. I know I don't deserve it, but thank you."

Martin's face remained serious.

Conrad, his eyes unexpectedly teary, took a large bandanna from his pocket and blew his nose. Then he took a deep breath and composed himself.

"All right, son, there's one final bit of business that needs to be settled." Conrad sighed quietly. "I want to welcome you to the family. I realize I'm a year late, but Esther won't be happy until we've knocked down the fences between us. Even Doc saw it right off when he told us to settle things." Conrad shook his head. "And I don't want him spanking our rumps again."

For the first time, Martin smiled. "I surely agree with you on that."

"Good. Then, Martin, I'm here to tell you I'm sorry. I'm saying I made a mistake." Conrad paused and took a deep breath. "A bunch of them. I want us to be friends."

Martin leaned back in his chair. "Conrad, you don't know how long I've dreamed that you and I could be friends. Not just because of Esther but because of my respect for you."

"Damn!" Conrad tried to hide the pain he felt at Martin's words. "I've got some making up to do to you, Martin." He shook his head, took a big gulp of the fortified coffee, and said, "You know, when Esther was little she always told me that when she married, I'd have a son, and he would call me Dad."

Puzzled, Martin studied Conrad, not certain that he understood what Conrad was suggesting. He tilted his head to the side.

Conrad smiled gently at Martin and shrugged.

A smile slowly formed on Martin's face. "Esther's never going to believe this—Dad."

Conrad held out his hand. "Welcome home, son! Sorry it took so long to get that front door open for you."

CHAPTER TEN

At 3:23 in the morning, Conrad and Martin heard a baby cry. Then there was silence. They paced in the bar area of the hotel. Joe had intended to go to bed but decided to stay in case he was needed. He was fast asleep in a chair tilted up against the wall.

"Why don't they come out and tell us what's going on?" Martin asked Conrad in frustration.

"I wish I knew. I'd like to just go in and ask them, but that damn Doc has made me feel like a naughty little kid tonight," Conrad said, "and I'm old enough to be his grandfather."

Just then Ann hurried out and raced to the kitchen. "Can't talk. Need stuff."

As Ann hurried back, Martin asked, "Is she all right?"

Ann stopped. "You have no idea how lucky you are. They'd both be dead if Doc Whitfield hadn't been here. There's no way I could've handled her birth." She closed the door.

Martin turned to Conrad. "She said they'd both be dead. That means they are still both alive."

"And she said there was no way she could have handled her birth," Conrad added.

"Yes, but was she talking about Esther or the baby?"

"Son, as you know, I'm not one for getting drunk or even heavy drinking, but how about you and I have a small shot? We need it."

"I agree. I feel as if I've been in the worst mine explosion I've ever been in and had a mountain of rocks stomp me flat. Every time Esther moaned or screamed tonight, I felt her pain through my whole body. I'm exhausted, and I can't imagine how's she's handling it."

Layton walked up to their table with a bottle and three glasses. Conrad glanced up in surprise.

"Doc saved my life tonight. In case he needs anything, I want to be here for him." He quickly poured three drinks and raised his glass. "To Esther and the new baby. If Doc is half as good a doctor as he is a quick draw, she's in the best of hands, and I've got a feeling he's the best."

They clicked their glasses and drank. After their drink, Conrad and Martin sat facing the bedroom door, each too tired to even pace. Layton went back to a corner table and quietly played with a deck of cards.

At 4:11 a.m. Doc walked out of the bedroom with Ann. "Ann, you get to bed, and when you wake, you can spell Mrs. Bale." He reached out and patted her on the arm. "You were magnificent tonight." She smiled her thanks and went over and gently woke her husband.

Doc turned to the men. "Well, gents, you have a little girl."

"How's Esther?" Martin asked as he jumped to his feet.

"She's been through the roughest night of her life. She's shown more courage than any man I've ever seen and is about as exhausted as one person has a right to be, but she still insisted on seeing you two."

Doc eyed each of them seriously. "She's not out of danger by any means, and that means anything you say or do in there could make the difference as to whether she lives or dies."

"We understand," Conrad said.

"I hope to hell you do, because if either of you upsets Esther, I'll bring you back out here and thrash the both of you. And believe me, gents, those are not idle words."

"It's okay, Doc," Martin said. "Dad and I have settled it all."

Doc raised a questioning eyebrow at Martin. "Show me. You go in there and say a few words, then get out and let her sleep. I'm going to be in there with you, so make no mistakes."

Esther lay in the bed, her face ashen, but no longer in pain, with the tiny baby tucked beside her in her right arm. Mrs. Bale stood by her with a large smile.

Martin hurried into the room. He quickly knelt beside Esther's bed and gently took her right hand. Conrad moved to the left side and took a bit longer to get down on his knees.

Esther studied the baby. "Isn't she beautiful?" She paused as a wave of pain crossed her face. "I don't want you two to fight anymore. It just hurts me more than I can tell you."

"It's all right, Esther. Dad and I are through with all that."

Esther stared at Martin. "Martin, you called him Dad."

Conrad smiled and said, "Yes, he did, Esther." She turned her head toward her father, puzzled. "He has other news for you as well."

She looked back at Martin.

"Your dad wants us to move back to the ranch so Mrs. Bale can help us with the baby and he can start teaching me how to run the place."

Doc glanced up at Mrs. Bale. Her mouth was open in surprise, and tears were running down her cheeks.

"Really?" Esther said as she too started crying softly. "Dad, you aren't just saying that because of the baby?"

"Honey," Conrad said, "it took this little darling"—he pointed to the sleeping baby in Esther's arm—"and Doc over there to knock some sense into this old rock head of mine, but Martin and I are here to tell you that there will be no more fighting."

"Well," Martin added, "at least none that we can't handle as friends."

Conrad laughed gently. "Right. Welcome home, honey."

"Oh, Daddy, you have given me the best gift I could ever ask for." She squeezed Martin's hand. "Thank you, dear. I know that had to be hard for you to do too."

"Not as hard as having Doc scold us like schoolkids," Martin said.

"That's the first thing we agreed on," Conrad said, with a quick grin up at Doc.

Doc walked to the end of the bed and said, "And now I'm here to give Esther her second-best gift, which is for you to leave and let this new mother get some well-deserved rest."

After they were gone, Doc knelt and whispered to Esther, "Mrs. Bale is going to place the baby in the crib and sleep in the rocking chair beside her. I tried to convince her to let me stay, but she'll have none of it."

"You don't argue with Mrs. Bale," Esther said in a thin, weak voice.

"I remember." He grinned at Mrs. Bale. "I guess that's why we all love her so."

Mrs. Bale shook a warning finger at Doc. She took the baby from Esther's arm and gently placed her in the crib. "I'll come and get you if there's a problem."

She held out her hand to Doc as he stood, but he shook his head and held out his arms. He gave her a long hug and whispered to her, "It's all right, Mrs. Bale; I won't tell anyone that I gave you a hug. I wouldn't want to tarnish your image."

They looked down at Esther. She was asleep with a faint smile on her face.

"Thank you for taking care of my little girl tonight. Both of them."

"You made a difference tonight, Mrs. Bale."

Her smile was weary as she said, "No, Doc. You did. You were magical tonight. We were just your extra hands." As he turned to go, Mrs. Bale whispered after him, "Thanks for bringing her back home to me, Doc. You've given me three presents tonight, and I won't ever forget it or you."

Doc grinned, nodded his head, and winked.

Once outside, Doc quietly closed the door and smiled at Conrad and Martin. "If I hadn't heard that with my own ears, I'd never have believed it. I'm so proud of both of you."

Conrad took Doc's arm. "Is she going to make it?"

"After what you two did and said in there, I'd say she has a good chance. The next three days will be iffy, but you keep giving her the love you just showed and by the end of the week, you should be able to take her and the baby home."

Conrad grasped Doc's hand and shook it wildly. "I don't know how to thank you, Doc. Whatever you want, whatever I have is yours."

"Well, Conrad, how about giving me back my hand in one piece."

"How about I buy us all a drink?" Conrad said with a smile that refused to end. He glanced over at the corner table and saw that Layton was already heading for the bar to get a new bottle. Layton had a big smile on his face.

Doc stifled a yawn. "Yes, a small drink, and then I'm off to bed. This has been a much longer day than I expected, and I need a bit of sleep before trouble comes looking for me."

Conrad's face hardened. "Butcher. Joe told me about what happened. Don't you worry about that, Doc."

"Conrad, I don't want you getting involved. You are a new granddaddy. You just worry about Esther and her baby. Say, Martin, what are you going to call her?"

Martin smiled at Conrad. "Esther said if it was a girl, she wanted to name it after her mother."

"Ruth," Conrad said, his eyes blinking rapidly. "I'd like that. What were you going to call it if it was a boy?"

"She wanted to name him after you."

"And how did you feel about that?" Conrad asked.

"I agreed, sir...Dad."

CHAPTER ELEVEN

The details in the shadows along the trail slowly came into focus as dawn started sending beams of colored light over the long valley. The storm had passed and the sky was clear, but the temperature was only a little above freezing. A group of nine riders moved silently toward Elk Forks. At the edge of town, Butcher paused to pull his bandanna over his face and the others did the same. He pointed with his finger for Cole to take two men and circle to the rear of Simms's Bar. Butcher wanted Rocky with him. Rocky wanted to kill Doc in an ugly, thirsty way. Butcher smiled behind his mask. That was fine with him; he never did his own killing.

Butcher sat in his saddle giving Cole enough time to circle behind the saloon. He studied each building to see if there was movement, if there might be a trap. The town was silent. Not even a barking dog. Satisfied that it was safe, he moved forward cautiously.

The road into town was lightly frozen mud. The frosty sheen from the street sparkled in the pale dawn light. White puffs of the men's breath through their bandannas matched the steam coming from the horses' nostrils. It had been a cold ride. For the last half mile Butcher had the men place their shooting hand inside a pocket to be sure it was warm when needed. They formed a solid line across the street and headed methodically toward the saloon.

Butcher was angry that Richie hadn't returned to the ranch last night, but he'd deal with him later. He'd discussed his plan with Cole and Rocky before they left. They'd charge into Simms's Bar, find the rooms Doc and Layton were in, blast them full of bullets, and shoot anyone else who got in their way or saw them.

They were all riding stolen horses, so there was no chance the horses could be traced to him. The sheriff was no problem; he would stay hidden until the shooting stopped. Butcher was certain the plan was foolproof.

Jesse had said that Doc rode in alone, so that meant Red was coming later, perhaps today or tomorrow. Butcher had sent two men last night to wait at the summit. Red never had been a gunman, so a couple of rifle shots and that would be the end of the Whitfield boys. Then all he had to do was find that damn Indian mother of theirs, get his money and mining deeds back, kill her, and the ranch was his.

Butcher's mealymouthed old bay slid on the soft mud and started crow-hopping around the slippery street. It almost threw him off, and he had to grab the saddle horn as he was twisted over sideways. He heard the shot and felt the bullet whiz over his head before it struck the chest of the man behind him. The shot lifted the man out of his saddle and dropped him into the muddy street. At once, everyone was firing at the source of the shot.

Butcher snarled when he realized that the old gray-haired man in the wagon firing at him was Big John Warner.

"Damn!" Butcher hollered. "One man." He yelled frantically, "We can take him. Kill him. Kill him." The horses were out of control, twisting and bucking in the street.

Suddenly, dozens of shots came from the saloon door and windows. Another of his men screamed as he was shot in the side and fell from his horse. The horse went galloping wildly down the street.

A horse was shot and collapsed in the muddy street. The rider fell to the ground, then stood and fired off two shots. He immediately went down in a stream of bullets from the saloon. The man lay in the mud on his back, screaming in pain. Smoke filled the street.

Butcher fired wildly at the saloon, then realized that only he, Rocky, and Jesse were still on their horses. He yelled from behind his mask, wheeled his horse, and, bending low, raced out of town with Rocky and Jesse close behind him.

When Butcher glanced back, he saw John Warner crash over the seat of his wagon. It looked as though Cole had managed to kill him as he raced around from behind the saloon. Shots from the saloon missed Cole, but the two outlaws with him ran into a volley of bullets. One man was shot off his horse and went skidding across the street, facedown. He didn't move after he stopped sliding. The gunman's horse tripped on the dead horse and went down too, sliding against the wooden walkway across the street. The other gunman fired wildly until his weapon was empty. He tried to flee and was near the end of the street when two bullets struck him in the back. He crashed headfirst onto the mushy ground.

Cole crouched low on his horse as he urged it faster and faster. Men hurried out of the saloon and were firing wildly at him. Cole heard the high-pitched sound of bullets whizzing past, but none hit.

Soon the four gunmen were out of range. "That was an ambush! Jesse said Doc was alone," Rocky yelled at Butcher as they urged their horses on.

"Kill him," Butcher mumbled to Rocky.

Rocky turned, drew his weapon, and shot Jesse from his saddle. Jesse slammed hard against the road and didn't move.

Cole caught up with them after a few minutes. "They don't seem to be following us. What're we going to do?"

Butcher did a quick count. They'd come in with nine men, and now they were down to three, Rocky, Cole and himself. "Get back to the ranch. I need to think."

"I need a drink. A bunch of drinks," Rocky growled.

"So do I," Butcher mumbled.

CHAPTER TWELVE

At the sound of the first shot, Doc reached for his Colt and jumped from his bed. He ran out of his room in his waist-high underdrawers and almost bumped into Layton standing in front of his door, pointing his shotgun down the hall. "What's going on?"

"Don't know, but there's plenty of shooting."

Doc noticed the chair against the wall. "You been outside my door all night?"

"Well, night was pert near over when you went down. You looked plenty tired, and I didn't want anyone sneaking in on you."

Doc nodded. "Appreciate that. Come on." They ran down the narrow hallway to the saloon. Mrs. Bale stood outside Esther's door holding a huge old revolver that looked like a cannon in her hand.

No one else was inside the saloon. Doc and Layton ran out on the wooden walkway, where Martin, Conrad, Conrad's three cowboys, and Joe Simms all stood with smoking weapons in their hands. A gray horse lay on its side across the muddy street, pinned against the walkway, whinnying pitifully. Another horse lay dead by the corner of the building. One man was facedown in the mud in front of them, dead. Two other outlaws were sprawled down the street, also dead. Two more riders were wounded and lay helpless, moaning in pain.

"Put that poor old flea-bitten gray across the street out of its misery, and get one of the boys to gather up the loose horses," Conrad said to Granville. "Martin, why don't you and Charlie get the guns away from those two wounded boys and drag them out of the mud."

"A bunch of them rode in, I suspect to get you," Conrad said to Doc. "If that man in the wagon across the street hadn't opened fire, they would have gotten us all asleep."

"What happened to him?" Doc asked.

"Shot dead, I guess."

"Where's the sheriff?"

"Nowhere to be seen. Not only crooked but dumb," Conrad snorted. "If his brains were dynamite, there wouldn't be enough to blow his nose."

"I'm going to check him out," Doc said, pointing to the wagon across the street.

Conrad started to tell him to wait and put on some boots and clothes, but Doc jumped off the wooden sidewalk in his bare feet. He tried to run across the muddy, half-frozen street to the wagon, but four steps into the street, he slipped and went down, sliding three feet across the slick surface. He remembered to hold his Colt up so it wouldn't get muddy, but he also felt his underdrawers moving south.

Sinful hurried out to him. "Doc, you all right?"

Doc lifted his head from the muck and spit mud out of his mouth. "Sinful, did I do what I think I just did?" he sputtered.

"Well, if you're asking me if your underdrawers are down around your knees, I'm afraid so."

"Bad box!"

"But that's not all."

"What could be worse?"

"You landed in a big pile of fresh horse droppings." Sinful tried to keep from grinning at Doc. "But you did manage to keep your Colt clean."

"Here," Doc said as he stretched his arm up and gave his Colt to Sinful. "Since that's the only thing I did right, take care of it for me." He jerked around in the muck until he could pull his underdrawers back up. Finally he stood and looked down at himself. The cold, wet mud and horse dung dripped off his body. "Any suggestions?"

Conrad yelled over at him. "Doc, I'll get some blankets. You come back over here and step in the horse trough and try to clean yourself up. Sinful, you go over and check on the man in the wagon."

Doc trudged disgustingly to the trough as Conrad returned with two blankets. "Doc, you surely have a powerful odor about you. You smell worse than the inside of my boots after a week on the trail."

"Hey, boss," Charlie called out. "We've got one man shot bad and the other is a bit better."

"Any place I can work on them?" Doc asked Joe.

"The butchering room. I've a long table for butchering game."

"That'll do."

"Charlie," Joe yelled. "Drag their worthless hides around to the back door. Someone will need to go inside and pull the back-door bar."

"I was wondering why they didn't try to come in the back way," Conrad said to Joe.

"They probably tried, but that door bar is one strong lock," Joe said with a grin. He took a blanket and stepped gingerly into the mud in front of the trough, while Conrad held up another blanket behind the watering trough for privacy from the wooden walkway. "This should wake you up fast," Conrad said.

Doc pulled off his underdrawers, set one foot cautiously into the lightly iced watering trough, and gave out a horrible yell as he put his other foot in. "Oh, mercy heavens, that water's cold enough to freeze a man into a fence post."

As he leaped up and down in the icy water, he remembered his mom telling him that Blackfoot Indians never felt the cold. They took a daily bath in the river during the winter. Where was his Blackfoot Indian blood when he needed it?

"I think this feller is still alive," Sinful yelled to them from the wagon.

"Get him around to Joe's butchering room," Conrad said.

"I'm coming to help you, Sinful," Layton said. "He's the one who saved us all, so he deserves same special care."

Doc quickly washed the mud and horse manure off his body, continuing to yell and hopping from one foot to the other. When he splashed water on his face and chest, he yelled even louder.

Conrad looked over at Joe and winked. They were trying unsuccessfully not to laugh at Doc.

"I'm sure glad you two are enjoying this so much," Doc growled at Conrad and Joe.

"Ain't never seen a man dance and wash with such speed in all my days," Joe said with a broad grin.

Finally Doc stepped out of the trough onto the wooden walk and, grabbing the blanket from Conrad, hurried into the hotel to his room.

Conrad studied the watering trough. "I'll get one of my men to empty this, clean and refill it," he told Joe. "It's too dirty to drink and too thin to plow. I surely don't want one of my animals using it."

Joe nodded solemnly. "Tell him to use a stick and throw away Doc's underdrawers."

"Maybe I'll just have him bury them," Conrad said.

"Yup, good idea."

As Doc ran past Mrs. Bale, she called out to him. "Esther and the baby are having trouble. Hurry back when you're dressed."

Doc raced down the hall, thinking, I've got three men shot and a problem with Esther and the baby. I need more of me.

He hurried into his room and quickly dressed. Baby first, he said to himself. He ran back to Esther's room.

"Is there a problem?" Conrad asked as Doc sped by.

"Not sure," Doc called back as he rushed into the room and closed the door behind him.

After a few minutes he ran back out and asked Joe, "Where's Ann? Is she up yet?"

"In the kitchen."

Martin burst in. "Is Esther all right? The baby?"

Doc was already running to the kitchen and just waved his hand. "No time."

Mrs. Simms had just pulled out a batch of biscuits when Doc hurried in.

"Mrs. Simms."

Ann smiled at him. "Doc, you called me Ann last night."

"Sorry. Ann, you know I'm a good doctor—"

"The best I've ever seen," Ann interrupted.

"Thanks, but what I'm trying to say is that I'm a good doctor, but there's still a bunch I don't know. When I delivered babies in New York, afterward there were always nurses who helped the mothers."

"Is there a problem?" Ann asked with concern.

"I thought when a baby was born that mothers just knew how to feed them, and Esther isn't having any luck. Mrs. Bale hasn't been around a new mother in years, and I..." Doc shrugged.

"Oh, Doc, come on. I'll teach you. If you're going to be a frontier doctor, this is something you'll need to know. Many young mothers have trouble starting to breast-feed their first baby. They aren't like animals, where it comes naturally. Some need a little help and instruction. It will be just fine."

They hurried back to Esther's room. After about five minutes, Doc came out and grinned at Conrad and Martin. "Everything's fine. Esther just needed some instruction getting started feeding the baby." He turned to Joe. "You've one great wife there, Joe."

Joe grinned. "I try to tell her that at least once a day."

"Good man. All right, show me to the wounded."

CHAPTER THIRTEEN

Doc walked wearily into his room and sat on the edge of the bed. John Warner lay in the bed with a white bandage around his head. Big John squinted at Doc, trying to focus.

"How's the head?" Doc asked.

Big John frowned at Doc. "Who are you?"

"I'm Doc Whitfield. I'm the one who patched you up. A bullet creased the side of your head and knocked you out, but it didn't do any serious damage that I can see."

"Where am I?"

"I had you moved to my room. I figure a man who saves my life deserves that at least."

Big John gently turned his head to better face Doc. "Saved your life? I don't understand."

"Butcher and his men were here to kill me."

"Butcher hurt you too? I'm sorry I missed him. What'd he do to you?"

Doc told Big John about his mother, and about how Butcher had his uncle back-shot and tried to frame him and his brother.

"Sorry," Big John said, weariness and sorrow apparent in his one-word reply.

"And your story?" Doc asked.

"Name's John Warner. My friends call me Big John. Butcher framed me for gold that he stole, then had my wife killed." Big John's eyes had a sad, faraway look. "You want to hear the details?"

"Only if you want to and feel up to it. I don't want to pry."

"Don't normally talk about it, but I'd like you to know. I guess if I saddle a cloud and ride to the great beyond before I kill him, I want someone to know—someone who hates him as much as me."

It took Big John ten minutes to tell his story. "You going after him?" he asked when he had finished.

"Yup, but not today. I'm waiting for more help."

"I've got to go with you," Big John said. He started to sit up.

Doc placed his hand gently on Big John's chest. "Easy there. After what you've just told me, there's no way I'd leave you behind. But to just make sure you're up for the trip, I want you to try to sleep. That bullet shook up your brain. Give it time to get back to its old self."

"You won't sneak off without me?"

"I promise, Big John," Doc said. He saw the skeptical look on Big John's face. "I'm a man of my word. I won't go without you. You hungry?"

Big John shook his head almost imperceptibly. "I want to be the one to kill him, Doc. I want him to know who killed him. I don't care if he kills me, just so I kill him too."

"I understand. Get some rest. The more guns we have, the better for all of us." Doc stopped and added, "But I don't want him killing you, all right? Killing him is fine, but not you."

Big John gave him a weak smile and nodded.

"Sleep. You have my promise. I won't go without you. We go together when we go."

Doc left his room and was almost to the saloon when Conrad's hand Charlie rushed down the hallway to him. "We've got another one. One of Butcher's men. His name's Jesse, and we carried him back to the butchering table."

Doc's face hardened. "I'm on my way."

Jesse was laid out flat on the table, covered with blood. He avoided looking at Doc. Between painful breaths, he explained, "Rocky turned and shot me on the way out of town. Not sure why. I'd understand if you just let me bleed to death, Doc.

"I was scared when I lied about those men not back-shooting your uncle." He sighed in pain. "I don't reckon I've had a peaceful night's sleep since I did that."

Doc took Jesse's hand away from the wounded shoulder and inspected it.

"I've got no right to ask, but before I die, I'd be ever thankful if you'd forgive me," Jesse continued, his face knotted as he fought the pain. He finally looked Doc in the eye. "I just don't want to go to my maker with that lie on my soul."

"Why'd you stay with them?" Doc asked.

"Scared. Too scared to leave. Who'd have me? I'm an old man, Doc. Not worth much, can't do much. Who'd take me in? No family, no friends. Who'd want me?"

"I've got bad news for you, Jesse."

"You're not going to forgive me, Doc?"

"No, worse than that. You're going to live."

"Without your forgiveness, I'd rather die."

Doc leaned on the table and frowned at Jesse. "I can't think of one good reason to forgive you." He paused and lowered his head, refusing to look at Jesse. Finally he said, "But no man should carry that much torture in his soul."

Jesse looked at him, hopeful.

"So, Jesse, I forgive you. I don't know why I should, except it's the Christian thing to do. I also know what it's like to be scared and alone."

"Thanks, Doc," Jesse said. "Now you can just let me die. I'm not afraid of dying anymore."

"I can't do that, Jesse. I'm a doctor, and my job is to patch you up and not let you die."

"Why? I'm a no-good, hobbled-up, old, dishonest cowboy. There's nothing ahead for me but swabbing some saloon floor and dumping out spittoons. If I can even get someone to hire me to do that." Tears flooded Jesse's eyes and ran down his face.

"If you die, I'm going to take back my forgiveness."

"Doc, you wouldn't do that. Please don't do that."

Doc shrugged.

Jesse stared at the ceiling, his face squeezed in pain. After a bit, he said, "If I promise to live, will you forgive me?"

"Jesse, I'll make a deal with you. If you tell me all you know about Butcher and his operation, I'll forgive you and promise you a job for the rest of your life on our ranch."

Jesse's voice choked. "That's more than I deserve."

"I agree, and I'm not even sure why I'm making it, but that's my offer. Before you went turncoat, you were kindly to Red and me. Maybe it's for the old times that I'm doing it. Not sure. Just don't make me regret it."

"I promise, Doc. I swear to God, I won't make you regret it."

"All right, then it's done. But you've got to want to live. You've given me your word."

"I'm not lying this time, Doc. You've got my word." Jesse turned his head away. "I've only lied once in my life, and it's been the most terrible thing I've ever done. Thanks for giving me another chance."

"All right. I'm going to put you to sleep for a bit and get that shell out of your shoulder. Okay, close your eyes…"

* * *

Doc trudged tiredly into the saloon in the early part of the afternoon. He sank into a chair, joining Conrad, Joe, and Martin at a table near the front door.

"You're a bloody mess, Doc," Joe said.

Doc glanced down and realized he was covered with dried blood from the wounded he'd worked on. "I'm out of clothes."

"Ann said you'd need a hot bath after all you've been through. You go back to the kitchen. She's got food and hot water waiting for you. While you're eating, she'll fill the tub. I'll slip over to Anderson's Mercantile and get you some new clothes."

"Tell Todd to put it on my bill, Joe," Conrad said.

"I can pay—" Doc started, but Conrad interrupted him. "Not a matter whether you can pay, it's what I want to do. You go and grab some grub and have your bath. We'll chat after you look"— Conrad sniffed, —"and smell better."

"Thanks. That mud bath this morning woke me up but didn't clean me as good as a real one," Doc said. He rose and walked slowly back to the kitchen.

* * *

Conrad grinned as Doc strolled to the table with his new clothes on. "Doc, you not only look cleaner, but your smell has definitely improved."

"I sure feel better." He glanced around at the table with everyone there. He sat next to Conrad and handed him a piece of paper. "This note was attached to my new clothes. Tell me about this Todd Anderson."

Conrad quickly read the note and smiled. "That was good of him to thank you for taking care of everyone. That's Todd. He owns the store across the street. You'd like him. He's honest, gentle, and funny. Almost as big as Red was—" Conrad stopped and frowned.

Doc understood. "It's all right, Conrad. Red's alive too. You can make that 'as Red *is*.'"

"Oh, that's good news. I was afraid I'd stepped on the wrong side of the fence. Anyway, Todd's a fine man, married to a lovely woman, April, and has two of the sweetest little wild girls a man could ever want."

"Speaking of which, how's our new baby, Ruth, doing?"

"She's surely the cutest little nipper I've ever seen." Conrad grinned at Doc. "And I'm not even a little bit prejudiced."

"I can see that. Is she sleeping?"

"They all are," Martin said. "My Esther, baby Ruth, and Mrs. Bale."

"So's Ann," Joe said. "The last twenty-four hours have been wild for all the women."

"And us," Doc said.

"Joe and I brought in a small bed so Mrs. Bale could be right there with them," Martin said. "Mrs. Bale is so excited about us moving back to the ranch." Martin shook a little baby rattle and grinned at Doc. "I made this for the baby. I can't get used to how tiny she is. So perfect and so tiny."

Martin turned to Conrad. "I've prayed that there was some way we could work out our differences for Esther's sake, but I never imagined it would be baby Ruth that would do it."

Conrad pulled on his walrus mustache. "Baby Ruth and Doc over here."

"I guess I never realized what a big responsibility it would be to have a baby until I held her this morning." Martin sighed. "Mrs. Bale is so great."

"Mrs. Bale runs my house as if it were hers," Conrad said. "Thank goodness." He turned to Doc and said seriously, "Mrs. Bale did mention that she thought you looked real pretty in your drawers this morning."

"What! She didn't say—" Doc stopped when he realized Conrad was joking with him. Everyone at the table started laughing.

"What was that cannon Mrs. Bale was holding this morning?" Doc asked.

Conrad laughed. "You don't want to get on the bad side of Mrs. Bale. That was her late husband's gun, but as huge as it is, don't be fooled. She knows how to shoot it."

"What is it?"

"It's an old Walker Colt. You get hit with a bullet from that monster and you won't get back up. I challenged her once to a contest to see which of our handguns had the most firing power. She fired one shot from that thing and blew one of my fence posts apart. I didn't even bother firing my gun. Like I said, you don't want to get her mad at you."

"Well," Doc said, with an admiring shake of his head, "it was apparent to me that nobody was going to get past her to Esther or the baby without a fight."

Conrad turned serious. "We were lucky this morning."

"I know," Doc said. "I feel responsible for what happened. I don't like having you and your family here with me. But I don't want to move Esther for at least another three or four days."

"But she's doing fine, isn't she?" Conrad asked.

"Thanks to you two, once you stopped butting heads. She's coming along great, but remember, it hasn't even been twenty-four hours yet. She had a tough delivery. Plus a major gun battle outside her room this morning. That isn't the setting that I'd prescribe for a peaceful and quiet recovery."

"She started crying this morning when I was with her," Conrad said. "When I asked what the matter was, she said she's just so happy that Martin and I are friends. It made me feel so guilty for all the pain I've given her this last year."

"It takes a mighty big man to admit that," Doc said.

"I tell you, Doc, there aren't words I can use to thank you for forcing me to ride that line last night."

"Just keep loving them, Conrad. That will be all the thanks I ask."

"Doc, you look exhausted. Why don't you go down for a while?" Martin said.

"After a bit. Whatever happened to the sheriff?"

"Gone," Conrad said.

"Gone! Where'd he go?" Doc asked.

"He looked at the carnage this morning, got on his horse, and rode off. I suspect he didn't want anything to do with this mess. When I checked the jail, I found his badge and the jail keys thrown on the desk."

"You think he'll join up with Butcher?" Doc asked.

"Not him," Conrad said. "He's out of here."

"Probably lookin' over his shoulder the whole way," Martin added.

Conrad grinned at Martin. "That's a good one, Martin. He's not sure who's going to be shooting at him, Butcher or us."

"I've got other news for you, Doc," Conrad said. "About your mother."

"Me too. Jesse filled me in," Doc said.

"Jesse?" Martin asked, confused.

"Yeah. The same Jesse who lied about Red and me to protect Butcher's killers and force us to leave the territory. Yes, we had an interesting conversation."

Sinful was leaning back against the wall, delicately cleaning his fingernails with a huge dagger. He stopped and leaned forward. "Well? Don't just leave us hanging. What'd he say?"

"What is that thing?" Doc asked.

"This is my toothpick." He grinned at Doc's skeptical look. "It's called an Arkansas toothpick." He twirled the huge knife expertly, balancing it on its handle in his palm. The razor-sharp blade sparkled in the light like a jewel.

"You be careful with that thing. I don't want any more blood on me today."

Sinful laughed. "You afraid I might cut off my finger? I might if you don't get on with your story."

"You sure get a whole lot of joy out of jawing me, Sinful."

"You bring out the best in me, Doc." Sinful's bright blue eyes twinkled in the reflection from the late-afternoon sun that came through the window and made his golden hair glow.

"What I bring out in you, I wouldn't call your best," Doc said with a quick grin. "Jesse told me that Rocky just turned around and shot him out of his saddle as they were riding out of town after the raid. Jesse doesn't know why. Anyway, he staggered back to town where your boys found him."

"Butcher rode in here this morning with his boys as nonchalant as if they were going to a church meeting," Joe said thoughtfully. "The only ones they expected to find were Doc and Layton."

Layton agreed. "Right. When Jesse and the boys took Tex's body back to the ranch, Conrad and his cowboys hadn't shown up yet."

"Nor the man in the wagon," Martin added.

"Right," Layton said. "So Butcher might have thought Jesse had ridden them into an ambush."

"An interesting theory," Doc said. "Jesse was all set to die, but he wanted me to forgive him before he did."

"Did Jesse die?" Sinful asked.

"Hush, Sinful," Granville said sternly. "Let Doc talk."

"Jesse said his soul would never be at peace if I didn't forgive him." Doc shook his head. "Tough call. I blame him for not telling the truth, but he told me that Rocky and Tex threatened to kill him if he didn't lie. Poor old Jesse was in a deep coulee."

Doc sighed and shrugged. "So I told him that I forgave him, and then he said he was ready to die. Well, that's not the result I wanted. I explained that I was a doctor, and I don't take kindly to my patients dying, but he said he didn't have anything to live for. He was an old cowboy, and he didn't want to live out the rest of his life cleaning out spittoons, so he was just going to die."

Everyone at the table was silent, listening intently.

"You know," Doc said, "if a man wants to die, sometimes all he has to do is will it, and it will happen. He had a bad shoulder wound, and I figured he just might pull it off."

"So what did you do?" Sinful asked.

"I just told him I took back my forgiveness. If he was going to die, then I wasn't going to forgive him." Doc stopped and glanced around at the serious faces watching him. "Well, that upset him something fierce." Doc explained how he'd worked out a deal with Jesse.

Sinful gasped. "Dang! Let me see if I got that straight. If he told you about Butcher, you'd give him a job and forgive him, but if he died, then his soul was doomed."

"As I said, Sinful, a man's got to want to live."

"Dang it, Doc." Sinful shook his head. "You're one hell of a doctor. How is he?"

"He's doing fine. He told me a bunch." Doc turned to Conrad and said, "Why don't you tell me what you heard, and I'll see if it squares up with what Jesse told me."

"One of the outlaws you patched up wanted to talk real badly," Conrad said. "He's afraid we're going to hang him, and I have to admit that thought did occur to me. He's hoping if he talks it might help his chances. Apparently, your mother escaped from the ranch either Saturday or yesterday.

"Everyone was over at Helena having a good time except Tex, Jesse, and three of the hands. They were supposed to be watching the ranch and I guess your mom, but Tex made the boys come into town with him. The youngest cowboy was sick in bed, so they just left him in the bunkhouse. Tex was angry that Butcher had left him behind. He wanted his own good time.

"This talkative one also told us something else. He overheard Rocky and Cole talking. Your mother took all of Butcher's mining deeds and all his gold and silver."

"You think he's telling the truth?"

"He's plenty scared, so I don't think he was stretching his blanket."

Doc thought for a moment. "Jesse said Butcher was unnaturally upset about her being gone, but he wasn't sure why. Normally, he said, my mother was seldom seen by any of the ranch hands."

"The Kid told me Butcher had everyone out looking for her until Jesse showed up," Conrad added. "Offered a hundred dollars in gold as a reward to the man who found her, but they had to bring her back alive."

Doc sat back in his chair. "Gold and silver. How much do you think Butcher had?"

Conrad shrugged. "The Kid said he'd seen one large chest."

Doc shook his head. "The man who saved our hides—his name's Big John Warner—said that Butcher stole two large chests full of gold from a bunch of miners down in Virginia City and Bannack and blamed Big John for it. Butcher told the miners Big John was transferring their gold to a bank down in Leavenworth, Kansas, where it would be safer."

"Some of those miners can be so stupid," Conrad said. "I thought I recognized Big John when Sinful and Layton carried him in here. He came to me looking for work early this spring. Appears he built a cabin back up on the ridge for his Blackfoot wife. I didn't have a job, so I couldn't help him."

"How'd Butcher steal the gold?" Martin asked.

"Switched the chests at the river stop in Fort Madison, Iowa. Big John brought the chests down by riverboat from Fort Benton. From there, he was to use a wagon to get them to the bank in Leavenworth. A riverboat captain saw them do the switch from his wheelhouse, but he had to pull out before he could tell anyone about it. A son of Big John's friend, a lawyer, heard about it from another riverboat captain, found the captain who saw the switch, and figured the whole swindle out. He got John a pardon and out of prison."

"No wonder he wanted Butcher," Conrad said.

"Worse. Butcher had someone kill his wife, and he told John about it as they were hauling him off to prison."

"Damn," Conrad and Martin said in unison.

Doc shook his head. "I reckon Butcher hauled the chests back here and hid them at the ranch. I can't see Mom hauling chests of gold from the ranch. She must have had help."

"Tom would have helped her, but I saw him taking three big freight loads of lumber south a few weeks ago to the mining camps," Conrad said. "No way he could have been there for her." Conrad pulled on his walrus mustache. "The boy said there weren't any horses missing. They figured she must have run away on foot."

"Have there been any Blackfoot through here in the past week?"

"Not that I've seen, but they keep to themselves, so it's hard to know," Joe said.

Doc laced his fingers together and stared silently down at them.

"The merchants all came over while you were working on the wounded." Conrad paused, choosing his words deliberately. "The merchants feel threatened every time Butcher and his boys come to town. They may not help us, but they won't help him."

"Too many innocent people are becoming involved because of my troubles." Doc's voice was a whisper.

"The boys and I have already set up guards. Just like watching a high-strung herd. There'll be no more sneaking up on us like this morning."

"Thanks, Conrad," Doc said, still looking at his hands. "I'll take my turn."

"No, Doc. You don't get a turn, and I don't want you fretting none about this. You saved my daughter and my grandbaby last night. Way I figure it, I still owe you one. You're just stuck with us."

Doc smiled. "I couldn't imagine better folks to be stuck with." He stood. "I know I'm tired and my mind's not working straight, so before we do anything and make any decisions, I need to get some sleep." He waved to a pile of blankets over in the restaurant section of the saloon against the wall. "I'll be over there if anyone needs me, but wake me gentle. My Colt will be under my blanket-pillow."

As he walked to the blankets, Sinful suggested, "How about I tickle your nose with a turkey feather if we need to get you up?"

"Interesting approach, Sinful, but no." Doc wrapped a blanket around his shoulders before lying down on top of another two blankets.

Sinful smiled broadly at Doc. "All right, how about I just yell at you like a Sioux is getting ready to scalp you and then hide before you can get a good aim."

Doc yawned and slipped his Colt under the blanket by his head.

"On second thought, let's go with the feather. 'Night, Sinful." Doc smiled and closed his eyes.

"Sleep easy, Doc. I'll be watching over you."

CHAPTER FOURTEEN

The gunman stood patiently waiting in the narrow space between Reverend Ansley's drugstore and funeral home and McCoy's Feed & Grocery Store, right across the street from the log jail in Elk Forks. Periodically, he bent forward and looked cautiously around the building to see if Doc Whitfield was coming down to check on the two prisoners. This late in the afternoon, the sun was behind the mountains, and it was already starting to get dark. The temperature was dropping fast.

The bounty hunter was glad he had taken the flannel-lined, heavy brown canvas coat from the miner he'd killed and robbed last week. He had his hands inside the pockets to keep them warm, although he hadn't buttoned the coat. He wanted quick access to his gun. He'd considered using his rifle, but Doc Whitfield would be only ten or twelve feet away when he shot him. An easy kill.

What had Butcher said? Don't let him draw on you. Just shoot him in the back and get out. If you get fancy, he'll kill you.

The outlaw took a nervous breath and grimaced. He was missing his two front teeth, and sometimes he sucked in air when he was nervous and it made a whistling, hissing noise. He heard the sound and forced himself to breathe more slowly. Too much money to lose by giving away his position. Two hundred dollars in gold. Easy money, easy shot. Even if there were more than one, he'd catch them by surprise and they'd all be dead. He silently moved his feet up and down, trying to keep them warm.

* * *

Doc came out of Esther's room and said to Conrad, "Go on in. She's ready to share baby Ruth with her granddaddy."

"Everything all right?"

"She's fine. Amazing daughter you've got there, Conrad." Doc laughed. "Amazing granddaughter too. But watch out for Mrs. Bale. She's real protective of that little girl."

Conrad hurried into the room.

Sinful walked over to Doc and said, "Mrs. Simms made dinner for the prisoners." He held a wicker basket in one hand.

"You eaten yet?" Doc asked.

"Nope."

"Here, let me take it. I've already eaten. I need to go down and check their bandages anyway."

"Okay." Sinful grinned. "Do you think they've escaped yet?"

"Well, we've surely given them enough opportunities. Nobody guarding them, two horses tied up out in front. Conrad thinks they're so dumb they don't have enough sense to spit downwind."

Sinful scratched his two-day growth of beard and grunted. "Not sure I understand why you want them to escape. Don't you think they'll just head back to Butcher?"

"Conrad and I believe they've seen all they want of this part of the territory. They both have some bad wounds, but they can ride if they go slow. My guess is that they know if they go back to Butcher, he'll be just as likely to shoot them for meanness since they wouldn't be any use to him. And the young one is mighty frightened of gargling on the end of a rope."

"Well, that would be enough reason for me." Sinful slowly rubbed his throat and frowned at the thought.

"I just might forget to lock the cells when I leave," Doc said.

"For a man who handles a Colt as fast as I've heard, you sure are a strange case."

"That's 'cause I'm a doctor first. The Colt is just to keep me being a doctor as long as I can."

"You want me to tag along?"

"Nah, you go eat. Granville's out in front keeping a watch on things." Doc pulled his cape on and took the basket in one hand and his medical bag in the other.

"If your cape were red, you'd look just like Little Red Riding Hood off to see Grandma," Sinful said with a laugh.

"Well, then, I'm certainly glad it's black," Doc replied with a quick smirk.

Granville sat in an old chair covered with buffalo hides. He jerked around when Doc came out the door.

"You all right?" Doc asked.

"My old body gets a little cramped when sitting for a long time, but boss brought me out a bottle to ease the pain." He gave Doc a toothless grin.

"How about staying warm?" Doc asked.

"These old buffalo hides are like sitting next to a pretty woman. Keeps a man cozy and warm."

Doc walked down the dark street. Few lights were on. The events of the morning had frightened the town. It had started freezing again, and the street was slippery. He went slowly down the wooden walkway until he came to McCoy's Feed & Grocery

Store, where he had to cross the semifrozen muddy street to the jail.

He made sure he had good footing as his boots sank into the still soft mud. He didn't want a repeat of the morning's performance. He frowned at the horses still tied up to the hitching post, their nostrils steaming with each breath. Need to get someone down here and take care of those, he thought.

When Doc reached the middle of the street, suddenly there was a loud KA-BLANG behind him. He immediately dropped his medical bag and food basket, slid his hand inside his cape, drew and turned toward the sound.

As he turned, a man in a long brown canvas coat fell forward, facedown, onto the wooden walkway. The man's gun skittered silently over the half-frozen mud toward Doc. Behind the fallen man, a tall redhead with a full, bright-red beard frowned at him. He held a large, cast-iron skillet in his hand.

"Red!" Doc exclaimed.

"I hated to hit him so hard, but he was getting ready to shoot you in the back." He sighed painfully. "Hi, Doc."

Granville was on his feet and yelling, "Doc, you all right?"

"I'm okay." Doc yelled back. "Someone just tried to bush-whack me."

Doc caught a movement out of the corner of his eye and spun toward the side of the jail. Dave walked out and grinned at Doc. He whistled softly and Ted came out from behind an old shed. They were carrying their Henry rifles.

"We were ready just in case Red's skillet didn't do the job or if there were others," Dave said.

Martin and Sinful rushed out the saloon door with rifles in their hand. They ran down to Doc.

Doc waved that everything was all right. "Someone tried to back-shoot me," he yelled. "These are friends."

Doc quickly reholstered his Colt, hurried to Red, and grabbed him in a long bear hug. "It's been far too long, big brother." He had a hard time keeping himself from choking up.

"Who are they?" Sinful asked. He squinted in the dim light. "Dang, they be US marshals."

Ted picked up the basket from the street and grinned at Dave. "With this basket, Doc looked like Little Red Riding Hood coming down the street."

"That's just what I told Doc when he left Simms's," Sinful exclaimed.

Doc turned and said, "Don't be encouraging Sinful, Ted. He's been jawing on me since I arrived in town. How long have you been here?"

"For a while. When two men tried to ambush us over the pass, we decided we'd better sneak into town cautious and quiet-like and find out how the wind was blowing."

Conrad and John Warner hurried out of the saloon and ran down the walk. Conrad had his gun out, and John carried his Henry. "You all right, Doc?"

"You surely do have a bunch of people worried about you," Red said to Doc.

"Red, is that you?" Conrad asked. "You get any bigger you could hide a freight wagon behind you."

"Gentlemen, it's far too cold for us to jabber out here," Dave said. "Doc, why don't you finish your business in the jail? Perhaps this man," he said to Sinful, "will stand guard."

"Pleasure, Marshal."

"Me too," Red said. "It's been too long since I've seen this little brother of mine. I'll keep my skillet close in case there's more trouble."

"Okay," Dave said. "When you're done, we can fill each other in back at the saloon. I don't know about you, but my feet feel like two icicles."

"What about him?" Sinful asked, pointing to the back-shooter lying on the walk.

Doc hurried to him and quickly checked him. He shook his head. "He's in hell, chatting with the devil. Tell the reverend we have another one for him."

Red shook his head sadly. "First man I ever killed. That makes me feel real bad."

"Red," Dave said softly, "there's nothing righteous about killing a man, but this one was about to shoot your brother in the back. If it was necessary to kill someone, at least you killed a very bad man who has probably killed more innocent people than we will ever know. A man who would shoot another man in the back is the dregs of the earth. God understands."

Red nodded, but his face still showed remorse.

Doc stood and gently gripped his brother's arm. "I know it's hard, but thank you for saving my life."

Doc said to Sinful, "Why don't you pull that coat off that back-shooter? He probably stole it from someone, and he doesn't deserve to be buried in it."

"Why, that's mighty kind of you, Doc." Sinful grinned. "How about I give his gun to Granville? It appears a bunch better than his, once I clean the mud off it."

"Don't you want it?" Doc asked.

Granville shook his head at Doc. "He don't want it and he don't own one, and it's a good thing. He's still trying to make it up to me for when I tried to teach him how to shoot. He darn near killed me. If you put a gun in Sinful's hand and tell him to shoot that jail building over there, maybe—and I'm saying only maybe—he'd hit it once after six tries."

"Granville," Sinful said indignantly, "just think of all the other things I'd hit while I was trying to shoot the jail."

"Exactly," Granville said with a wave of his arms. "When the boss told me to teach Sinful how to shoot, none of us realized how dangerous that would be!"

Sinful shrugged. "Granville told me to shoot the barn, but it kept moving."

Doc started laughing. "What do you mean, it started moving?"

"Honest, Doc, that barn just up and moved every time I pointed the gun at it."

Granville explained. "Doc, at first I thought he was squinting to see better, but after the second shot I realized he was closing his eyes."

"The noise really spooked me. It's like when a firecracker goes off. You close your eyes in anticipation of the noise."

"Horrible," Granville said.

"Hey!" Sinful said. "I shot our dinner that night."

Doc looked puzzled, and Granville explained. "He plumb killed a poor old chicken running across the road. They were all running for their lives. I tried to stay behind him, 'cause I never knew where his next bullet would go."

Conrad laughed. "That was it. When he killed the chicken, I told Granville to take that gun away from him and never let him touch another one."

"Those were the best words I heard that day," Granville said with a toothless grin.

"What about the rifle he's holding?" Doc asked.

"After that experience with a handgun, I took Sinful far from the ranch to see how he'd do with a rifle. Happily, he's a bit better with it."

"Nah, I'm not. Granville is just being kind. At least I don't close my eyes when I shoot a rifle. I'm still not sure how I killed that man this morning." Sinful shook his head. "But no gun for me. I really don't like 'em. The boss and Granville decided the folks of Montana would be much better off if I just stuck with my toothpick."

"And interestingly enough," Conrad said, "he's extremely good with that." Conrad patted Sinful on his shoulder. "Well, Sinful, if you're going to get the back-shooter's coat and gun, you can just drag his body to the reverend's place. Come on, boys, the marshal's correct. It's too cold out here for any more jabbering."

CHAPTER FIFTEEN

Sinful hurried into the saloon wearing his new coat and grinned at the men sitting around two tables they'd shoved together. "Our jailbirds took Doc's hint and just flew away."

"Toward Butcher?" Doc asked.

"Nope. Just as you figured. Off toward Helena and points south, I 'spect. They were moving real slow 'cause they're hurting, but I imagine they were thinking that riding slow and free beats the alternative."

"Good. Two less to worry about," Conrad said.

"How'd you do it, Doc?" Sinful asked.

"Why, I just told them that since the sheriff had run off, the only law in town was that grizzly old rancher with the walrus mustache. And that he was back at the saloon soaping up a new rope for a cottonwood party. Then I threw the jail key on a table where they could reach it as I walked out."

"What'd you mean, a grizzly old rancher?" Conrad huffed. "You should have said that handsome, slightly mature rancher with the good-looking mustache."

"Next time I describe you, that's exactly what I'll say."

Conrad turned to Dave. "Doc's filled us in about you and your friend Ted."

"Good. Then you realize that although we carry the badges of United States marshals, our assignment is for one week and specifically to help Doc and Red get their mom away from Butcher."

"How'd you know to sneak into town?" Big John asked.

Red pointed at Ted. "His hawk eyes saved us."

Ted looked embarrassed and said to Dave, "You tell them."

Dave leaned back in his chair and lit his pipe. "What Red said was true. The three of us met up in Utah and rode the stage to Helena together. Talk about a nasty, exhausting, dusty ride." He shook his head at the memory. "The only thing that saved us was that Red had packed enough victuals to feed a cavalry troop."

"As hard as that trip was, for Red's meals I'd do it again," Ted said.

"The only thing we questioned," Dave added, "was that Red didn't know we'd be meeting up with him, so all that food he carried had to be intended for him."

"No," Red said. "I'm at an age where I might have met a fair damsel, and my baked goods always win their hearts. Instead, I had to share it with these two ungrateful urchins." Red shook his head dramatically.

"All I can tell you, gents," Dave said, "is we ate like starving wolves for four days, and he still had food left in his baskets."

"Well, she might have been a really hungry damsel," Red insisted with a grin.

"Like they say, only a fool argues with a skunk, a mule, or a cook." Dave grinned back at Red. "Once we got to Helena, we leased two horses from Travis on Main Street for Ted and me and we got Red a wagon with two horses."

"Sign of the Iron Horse," Granville said. "The Travis brothers are good boys."

"I agree. They treated us well. I was surprised at the size of Helena. They told me there were already ten thousand people living there," Dave added.

"Red had to bring some trunks full of his pots and pans from California, so we needed a wagon, plus we didn't want to have some poor horse suffer by carrying the big moose."

"Hey, watch it," Red said with a grin. "Doc has his Colt and I have my favorite pots and pans."

"Red and I were riding together in the wagon with my horse tied on behind when we took off from Helena. We were chatting like a couple of crows socializing at a migration. Things were going so smoothly that I'm afraid we got a bit careless.

"As we neared the top of the pass, Ted told us to shut up. I realize that none of you know Ted well yet, but he's the politest man I know. I don't think I've ever heard him say 'Shut up' once in all the years I've known him, so for him to say that meant mighty big trouble ahead.

"He told us he just saw a reflection off something. Like perhaps a rifle barrel? I asked, and he told me yup. He suggested that he'd go ahead on foot and scout out where he saw the flash.

"I wasn't keen on the idea, but since I couldn't offer a better suggestion, it was agreed that he would slip on ahead by foot and we would follow in forty-five minutes. Red and I talked about it for a while, and Red decided we needed to wear a couple of his cast-iron skillets for protection. One in front and one in back."

"That must have been a sight," Sinful said. "Weren't they heavy?"

"Not for Red, but I felt as if I had two frozen gold sacks attached to my body. Red likes his skillets big like him. When we left, he had to boost me into the wagon. I held my Henry in my lap, cocked and ready. We were moving slowly, and Red and

I were constantly scanning the rocks before us, but we didn't see anything. We reached the crest of the pass and halted the horses to give them a chance to blow.

"Red turned to me and said that maybe it was a false alarm, and just then there were four quick rifle shots. Red dove off the wagon on one side, and I went off on the other. Those damn pots almost killed me when I hit the ground. I still have circle bruises on my chest from them. After I staggered to my feet, I tore off my shirt and pulled those skillets off so I could move around. I was afraid if I left them on and fell on my back, I wouldn't be able to get back up. Red had crawled under the wagon, which wasn't easy for a man of Red's size."

Dave leaned forward for emphasis.

"I was running around the wagon with my shirt off, trying to see where the shots came from, when way down the trail I saw a man riding a horse faster than a hungry cougar chasing a meal.

"While I was watching the rider, there was another shot. The man fell sideways but hung on and kept riding. Then he went out of sight. A few moments later, Ted rode up with this big grin on his face and asked me why I was running around naked. I ignored his smart remark and asked where he got the horse, and he told me it was a gift."

"Well, it was," Ted said seriously. "Its owner was getting ready to shoot you, so I shot him instead, thus I get his horse."

Dave relit his pipe and leaned back again in his chair. "And that's the logic that makes him the merchant and me the newspaperman."

Everyone laughed.

"So," Martin asked, "what happened then? Who was it?"

"We went up and buried the body. Don't know his name, but he was riding a Rocking B horse," Dave said.

"Butcher's," Doc said.

"Yup. When Ted first snuck up the mountain he wasn't sure if it was one man or more. Then when he saw the two men, he wasn't sure if they were really waiting for us or just resting, so he settled down where he could watch them. Once we got to the top of the pass, they took out their rifles and started aiming them at us."

"You said there were four shots," Conrad said.

"I killed the first man and the second killer turned and fired once at me," Ted explained. "It was a wild shot 'cause he couldn't even see me. I got off two more shots, but he was already on his way to his horse. By the time I could get a clear shot, he was down the road a bit."

Dave laughed. "A bit! Don't let him kid you. That man was a long way off, and Ted still managed to put a slug into him. Ted's a good man to have backing you up."

"How far do you think it was?" Sinful asked.

"Oh, I reckon three hundred yards or more. Keep in mind that the Henry's better at short range and not that accurate over a hundred fifty yards."

"Dang!" Sinful exclaimed. "Remember, Ted, I'm on your side."

Ted lifted his coffee cup toward Sinful and said, "I've got you covered, Sinful."

Dave continued. "After that happened, we realized that our casual journey was over. If Butcher had gunmen waiting for Red, that meant trouble of the worst kind.

"Not knowing what was happening here, we rode close to town and hid the wagon, then walked in real quiet-like. Once again, Ted was the one who saw the back-shooter. Since we weren't sure how many there were, Ted and I took up positions on the jail side of the street, and Red said he'd take care of the back-shooter."

Ted shook his head. "Red darn near caused me to panic. I could see the killer, and I had him in my sights. As I'm watching, here comes Red, this giant of a man as quiet as a leaf drifting from a limb, sneaking up behind him. I thought sure the killer would hear him, spin, and blast poor Red, but nope, the killer doesn't have any idea there's a giant standing right behind him. I'm worried that if he turns around, I'm not sure I can hit the killer without hitting Red. I was never so glad to see Doc start down the street when he did."

"Ted's right," Dave added. "I didn't have a great angle on the killer either, but I was plenty worried about Red. Then Doc steps into the street, gets to the middle and bang, Red pounds the back-shooter with his skillet. One mighty loud clunk, and the man drops on the walkway to meet his maker."

"I still feel bad about killing him." Red sadly shook his head.

"I'd have felt worse if you hadn't," Doc said.

"Yeah," Sinful said, "but I beefed my first man this morning, and I know how Red's feeling. Those aren't good feelings. I know that man would have killed me, but it still don't make me feel good."

"Bad times," Conrad said. "There's never any good comes from killing another man. But sometimes it comes down to a choice, and you have to make a tough call. These men you killed came looking to kill us. We were just defending the ones we love."

He paused. "You both did good. I'm glad you don't feel right about it. If you kill a man and feel good about it, that's the devil talking to you. When you feel bad, that's means you're on God's side and He understands."

Conrad turned to Dave and asked, "So, Marshal, what's the plan?"

"That's a good question." Dave said. He looked at Doc. "From what you've told us, you gents put a hole in Butcher's gang this morning. Riding in with nine men and back out with three will force Butcher to do some serious regrouping. I 'spect he'll shortly find out he's lost three more, what with the two at the pass and the back-shooter not showing up." Dave shrugged. "Doc, what do you want to do?"

Doc frowned. "What I—we—wanted was to get our mom back. After today, that's all changed. On the train ride out here, in my mind I figured with your help, if Butcher wouldn't trade the ranch for Mom, then we could ride there and confront him. Then Ted offered to join us, so that made another Henry." Doc nodded at Ted. "So on the ride from Quiet Valley to here, I'm thinking with your two Henrys and my Colt we'd succeed. But instead, this is what happened: Mom's missing and Butcher is still loose." He flung his hands up in bewilderment. "I don't know what to do."

"I do," Big John said quietly.

Everyone turned to him.

"You've all heard my story, so you understand that I want Butcher dead as much as Doc and Red do. Even so, the only important thing is finding their mother." He paused a moment and frowned in thought.

"The way I see it, we can't go off looking for her until we take care of Butcher. If he has time to regroup and hire more guns, we'll all be looking over our shoulders the whole time we're searching for her."

"I agree with you, Big John," Dave said. "We've all seen that Butcher has no problem shooting people in the back." Dave tapped his pipe empty into a small clay pot on the table. "So the only difference in your plan, Doc, is that we've got three Henrys instead of just mine and Ted's, with Big John joining us."

Conrad pulled on his mustache. "Yup, I'd say that's the best way of dealing with Butcher. Doc, what about the baby and Esther?"

"They're both doing good. What they need is rest. They're coming along fine. I don't perceive any problems."

"We've got enough guns here to protect our women, if Butcher circles around and comes back through town," Martin said. "With Big John, you should have enough firepower to hit the ranch. Go and kill that bastard."

"When?" Doc asked.

"Not early," Big John said. "That would put the sun in our eyes. If we leave here by midmorning tomorrow, that would put the sun in their eyes by the time we reach the ranch."

They agreed.

Sinful grinned at Big John. "Are you saying not early because of the sun, or just because you want to sleep late?"

Big John gently patted the bandage around his head. "Maybe a bit of both."

"Well, since I've got the next watch, I'm looking forward to sleeping late tomorrow," Sinful said. He glanced at Conrad. "If that's all right with my boss."

Conrad leaned back in his chair. "Ah, Sinful, for a boy who works as hard as you do, you sure know how to work lazy too."

"Why, thanks, boss."

Everyone laughed.

CHAPTER SIXTEEN

The five men were silently alert as they rode to the ranch. It was clear and not as cold as it had been; the weekend storm had blown past the valley, and white clouds stood out against a bright blue sky. Water dripped from the ice on the plants and trees beside the trail, but the trail itself was dry.

"They must be expecting us," Dave said to Doc. "I think your idea of circling the ranch and going in by Red's hidden path is the best bet."

"Do you think Butcher's men may know about it?" Ted asked.

"Nah, I doubt it," Red replied. "You follow a little stream up a ways until you get to a ten-foot-high cliff with a waterfall pouring over it that looks impassable. The only reason I found it, I was chasing a steer up that stream and suddenly that little maverick disappeared. I'm thinking to myself there's no way a steer is going to leap over a ten-foot waterfall. I went closer and behind a huge old mountain larch was a path that led around the cliff."

Big John pulled his hat down gently on his head and winced slightly.

"Big John?" Doc asked.

"It's fine, Doc. Still a little tender, but I'd feel lost without my hat."

"Hmm. I'd still rather you not be placing any pressure on that wound for a few more days."

"Really, Doc, it's fine." He immediately changed the subject. "I like going in from the side of the ranch a bunch better than just riding straight in. Dave's right. They must know we're coming after them, so any surprise we can give them will work to our advantage."

Two miles from the ranch entrance, Red rode in front and led them south of the ranch and then up a wide, shallow stream, around the waterfall to the top of a tree-covered ridge. After another forty-five minutes, they came to a large Douglas fir grove overlooking the valley. They tied their horses and moved surreptitiously from tree to tree until they had a clear view of the ranch below.

Dave handed his binoculars to Doc and whispered, "Take your time, Doc. This is not the time to be impatient. You boys know the layout better than we do, so look for likely spots for shooters. You too, Red."

Red used Ted's binoculars.

Big John put his distance glasses on and studied the ranch intently. The last time he'd been there was when Butcher hired him to take the gold down the river. There was a large, one-story ranch house. Five corrals, a large barn, and two smaller barns sat off to the left of the house. On the right was a long bunkhouse with benches flanking the door. A corral beside the bunkhouse held twelve horses. Farther on were three large sheds and a dilapidated barn. Another corral, a large one, held thirty or more steers.

Doc glanced over at Red. "There's been a bunch of changes since we left."

"Like what?" Dave asked.

"When we left there was only the ranch house, one barn, a pigpen and chicken coop, a corral, and a small bunkhouse. The bunkhouse has been expanded. It's at least three times as big as when we left, and everything else is new."

"See anything suspicious?" Dave asked.

Red and Doc shook their heads.

"Let me take a look," Dave said, taking back his binoculars. He studied each building slowly. Finally he turned to Ted and asked, "What do you think?"

"It's mighty quiet down there." Ted rubbed his hand over his face. "Yet I've searched around the outside perimeter of the buildings, and I don't see a thing. Either they are hiding so well we don't see them, or..."

"Or what?"

"Or they've left."

Dave leaned against a tree. "I hadn't considered that. Doc, do you think that's possible?"

"There's more ways to leave this valley than past town. I know we hurt them yesterday, but I figured he had more men working for him than what rode into town yesterday."

Big John pointed to the corral. "Twelve horses down there. I don't see them just taking off and leaving that many."

The men stood silently, pondering their choices.

"So," Dave said, thinking aloud, "there might be twelve gun hands down there, or there might not be any."

"Or any number between," Ted said.

Big John shook his head. "And there's no easy way to sneak up on those buildings. We come from any direction, they're going to see us. I surely don't like the idea of just riding in and not knowing what we're going to find."

"Look at that." Ted pointed toward the bunkhouse.

"Let me see your binoculars," Big John said, tapping Dave's arm. "Three men are carrying a body out of the bunkhouse," he reported. "Interesting."

"What?" Dave asked.

Big John handed the binoculars back to Dave. "You take a look."

"Two of the men aren't packing," Dave said. "Only one has a gun on, and he's wearing it high on his waist." He glanced at Big John.

"Yup," Big John said. "Those men look just like me. Ordinary cowboys." He shook his head, puzzled. "I'm going down. If they get me, you make sure you get Butcher."

"Whoa, Big John," Dave said. "We'll all go. But let's swing around to the right and come in near that run-down barn. We've got the firepower with our Henrys. If we run into trouble, we spread out, use the barn as cover, and go after them."

Red's eyes widened. "That's mighty brazen."

"Yeah, I don't like it much either, but sometimes you just have to charge in. We'll go in slow, and at the first shot, hug the ground and find shelter. Don't stay on your horses."

They remounted and circled the valley above the ranch in single file, trying to stay in the trees as much as they could. Finally Dave rode down the hill and out into the open. The others followed, nervously glancing around. All was still.

"This not knowing is worse than if they just opened fire," Ted whispered in his hoarse, gravelly voice.

The riders soon came up behind the old barn. Much of the siding was gone, so it was easy to see the barn was empty inside.

Dave whispered for them to dismount. "We'll go on foot the rest of the way. Big John, you take the nearest shed. Doc, you and

Red take the next one, and I'll go after the one closest to the bunk-house. Ted, you cover us. If they're empty, join up with me."

Quick glances told Big John, Doc, and Red that the first two sheds were empty. Dave ducked inside the third, then waved urgently for them to join him. When they got there, Dave pointed to the body lying on the floor. "What do you think, Ted?"

"Could be the man I shot. Looks to be the same clothes."

Doc checked the man out. "If they'd patched up his wound, he probably wouldn't have died. It appears he just bled to death."

"All mighty strange," Dave mumbled as he shook his head. "If it's a trap, I surely haven't figured it out yet."

Ted glanced out the open window. "There's no one about that I can see." He turned to Dave and shrugged his puzzlement, then abruptly waved for them to be still. They all heard the same thing. An intense argument was going on in the bunkhouse.

"If they were planning to ambush us, they certainly wouldn't be arguing about it," Big John said. "I'm going to step in and see what this is all about."

Before anyone could stop him, Big John walked out of the shed to the bunkhouse door. He flung the door open and stepped in, holding his Henry rifle in front of him.

Dave followed, about five steps behind Big John. He'd already pulled out his Adams revolver and carried his Henry in his left hand.

Three men sat at a table with their hands up. One man was saying repeatedly, "Please don't shoot. Please don't shoot."

Ted, Doc, and Red rushed into the bunkhouse. Big John told the shorter cowboy, who had the revolver, "Unbuckle your gun belt and let it go to the floor."

"Yes, sir, mister. We don't want no trouble. Whatever you want. Please don't shoot us." He saw the badge on Dave's vest. "Please don't let him shoot us, Marshal. We ain't done nothing."

"Put your hands down but keep them on top of the table," Dave told them. "Red, Ted, check out this place."

After a quick check, Ted called back, "Empty, except for these three."

"What were you arguing about?" Big John asked.

"We don't know what to do," one of the cowboys answered.

"What do you mean?" Doc asked.

"Mr. Butcher, Rocky, and Cole rode in here yesterday with their horses about dead. We'd just brought in a few head of cattle and were getting ready to go out after more. Cole told us to saddle three new horses and take them up to the house. When I asked what was going on, he just shook his head at me and told us to stick around. I know better than to question Cole.

"About two hours later, Luther rode in. He was all shot up, and there was blood all over his horse. He talked to Mr. Butcher and Rocky. Then Cole told me to take Luther to the bunkhouse and patch him up. Before we can get to him, he falls off his horse. Me and the boys carry him here. We try to patch him up as best we can, but he's looking all white and sickly.

"About ten or fifteen minutes later, a stranger rode in."

"Yeah," the short cowboy agrees. "Another gunfighter type wearing a long brown canvas coat. He spoke to Mr. Butcher for a few minutes, then rode off toward town. A bit later, Mr. Butcher, Rocky, and Cole all rode off again, but not toward town. I went up to the main house, and the doors were wide open. I didn't know what to think.

"When I got back here, Luther's all still, but he's still breathing, except he's not talking or anything. He feels clammy and has cold sweat all over him. We take turns watching him through the night, but just a few minutes ago he makes a really ugly sound and stops breathing." The cowboy shrugged. "So we took him out to the shed, and we were trying to figure what to do when you came in. We didn't shoot Luther—honest, Marshal."

"I know, boys. We did," Ted said. "Your friend Luther was trying to shoot us in the back."

"See, Shorty? I told you he was no good," the youngest cowboy said.

Shorty looked up at Dave. "My brother's correct, Marshal. He did tell us that, but we needed work. It's hard to get work for the likes of us. Everyone is crazy with gold fever, and there aren't that many cattle ranches around."

"What were you doing with the cattle?" Ted asked.

"Jesse woke us before sunup on Monday and told us to round up as many head as we could. He said Mr. Butcher wanted us to take them down to the closest gold mining camp right away and sell them for whatever we could get for them."

"Why?" Doc asked.

"Not sure. Strange time to be doing it." He scratched his head. "A peculiar weekend. Tex forces us to go to town Saturday and Sunday, and he gets killed. We get back Sunday evening, and everyone is out looking for Mrs. Whitfield. On Monday after Jesse got us up, we find the bunkhouse is empty except for us. When we go out to saddle our horses, all the gun hands were heading for town in the dark."

"They never returned. Did you meet up with them?" the youngest cowboy asked.

"Yup," Big John said. "They's all dead or wounded. What you saw come back is all that's left."

"All dead," Shorty said in a hushed voice.

"Where's Richie?" Doc asked.

"He went out looking for Mrs. Whitfield on Sunday, and he ain't never returned."

"Which way did your boss go?" Big John asked.

"That was strange too," Shorty said. "They went west. I guess they're heading for the Frenchwoman's Road. They're running from you, Marshal."

"From him," Dave said, pointing to Big John.

"Bad box, nothing is going right," Doc said angrily. "I'm going up to the house." He hurried out with Red right behind him.

Dave said to Shorty's brother, "What's your name?"

"I'm called Kid, and he's Ray." He pointed to the man sitting beside him.

"All right, boys, here's what I want you to do. Hitch up a wagon and take Luther into town and dig a hole on boot hill and throw him in. Then come back. Stop at the ranch house before you leave." Dave turned to Big John and Ted. "Doc and Red aren't going to want his sorry body buried on their land."

The men stayed at the table.

Dave laughed. "Ease up, Big John. You've plumb got them so nervous, they're afraid to move."

Big John lifted his Henry and rested the stock on his hip. "Sorry, boys. Go and do what the marshal said."

"Ah, sir," Shorty said hesitantly, "would you mind if I put my gun belt back on?"

"You any good with that?"

"No, sir. I just use it to shoot rattlers. I don't like snakes."

Big John's unsmiling black eyes bore into Shorty's face. "Me neither. Pick it up."

Shorty grabbed his gun belt, and the cowboys hurried out of the bunkhouse.

"You think they'll come back?" Ted asked.

"They'll be back," Big John said. "They're broke."

* * *

After the cowboys returned from burying Luther, Red invited them to the ranch house for dinner.

Red piled Shorty's plate high for the second time, and Shorty grinned his thanks. "Sure is the best meal me and the boys have had since we left home."

Kid and Ray nodded their agreement.

"Glad you boys like it," Red said with a chuckle.

"We didn't know this ranch was yours," Kid told Red.

"No way you would have known."

Kid looked up at him brightly. "I bet you could use three mighty fine cowboys."

Red laughed. "You're right, Kid. Doc and I talked about it while you took Luther into town for burial. We want you to stay on and take care of the stock. The problem is that you will be pretty much on your own until we can take care of some business."

"You've got to find your mom, huh?" Shorty said.

Big John leaned across the table and stared at Shorty. "Yup, that we aim to do first. Then we have to find and kill Butcher and his hired guns," he said in a hard voice.

Shorty gulped and said, "Yes, sir." Trying to change the subject, he turned to Doc. "I told Conrad like you told me—that you'd be back tomorrow morning. He said to tell you that the girls are doing fine."

"Good." Doc looked at Shorty sternly. "How'd you get along with Jesse?"

Shorty swallowed hard. "Sir, Ray and I were with Jesse when you beefed Tex."

"I remember," Doc said. "But you didn't answer my question."

"Jesse took good care of us. He tried to make sure we didn't get into trouble with the gunfighters."

"He protected us," Kid said. "We all appreciated that. Is he dead?"

Doc shook his head. "Rocky shot him, but he's mending. Are you three up to running this place until he's a bit better?"

"I'm no foreman, but I'm a good cowboy," Shorty said. "So's my little brother and Ray."

"If there's trouble," Doc said, "I don't want you to deal with it. You just drop whatever you're doing and ride hard to Conrad Spear's ranch. He'll help you. You know where it is, don't you?"

"Yes, sir. You mean like if Mr. Butcher, Cole, and Rocky return."

"Or Richie," Red added. "You just sneak out of here and hightail it to Spear's ranch."

"I've told Jesse the same thing," Doc said. "I 'spect he'll be coming back in a few weeks when he's healed more. He won't be able to do much because he took a nasty shot in his shoulder."

"We'll take good care of him, sir," Shorty said.

"All right, boys, we have a deal," Doc said. "Red's going to give you a double helping of apple dumplings. I'd like you to take them back to the bunkhouse. The rest of us have some private jabbering we need to do."

Shorty jumped to his feet. "I've been smelling them dumplings all through dinner. It just made my stomach do a jig in anticipation. For a double helping, I'd even sit in the middle of the corral."

"I reckon the table in the bunkhouse should be just fine," Red said with a laugh.

Red grinned as he watched the three cowboys spoon the dumplings into their mouths as they walked back to the bunkhouse.

Doc placed his hand on Red's shoulder and said, "You and your dumplings."

"It felt good to be back in our kitchen again."

"Come on," Doc said. "The others are in the study."

Ted had already started a fire in the stone fireplace. Big John sat in a solidly built rocking chair near the fire. "Finally, a chair I can sit in comfortably," he said as he took the cup of hot coffee that Red handed him. Big John pointed down. "And it even has a soft cushion for my tender behind."

Doc sat behind his dad's large oak desk and ran his hands over it tenderly. "I don't like the thought of Butcher using this desk or even being in this room. Red should be sitting at this desk. He told me he's a rich businessman."

Dave and Ted sat together on a hard pine couch covered with buffalo hides. Dave grinned at Red. "So how'd your little brother take the news of your business success?"

"I shocked him."

"Nothing has gone the way I figured it would go," Doc said. "Nothing. I figured after we got Mom, I'd be taking care of Red with the money I had left over from Mr. Bates's award. Instead, we don't have Mom, Red's complaining about having more money than I can even comprehend, and Butcher is still alive and dangerous." He put his hands behind his head, leaned back in his chair, and stared at the ceiling.

The only sound was the crackling from the fireplace. The sweet smell of burning pinewood filled the room.

"What are you planning to do?" Red asked Big John.

Big John held his cup of coffee and let its warmth soothe the arthritic ache in his fingers. "Got to help you find your mother. Told you that last night."

"Last night we thought we'd have a showdown with Butcher and he'd be dead," Red said.

"Yup, that's what I thought too. Sometimes, Red, plans don't work out. Plans are a lot like working cattle. Now and again they do what you expect, but most times they don't, so you just adjust.

"I don't have your brother's speed or your eyes, and my old body is a tad stiff, but I can still shoot, and with this Henry I'm a fighting force to be reckoned with. Since Butcher and his guns are still running loose, I figure having me along might make a difference."

"I'm obliged, Big John," Doc said softly. "After we find my mom and I know she's safe, then I promise we'll go after Butcher. But we'll have to toss to see who takes him down."

"Well, that seems fair." Big John paused and took a sip of coffee. "As long as I win." He asked Dave, "What about you two?"

"I've been pondering that myself." Dave turned and asked, "Ted?"

Ted frowned, then sighed. "We promised you a week, but this isn't how I figured it would turn out."

Red tapped the arm of his chair. Doc looked over at him as Red shook his head once.

"None of us figured this," Doc said thoughtfully. "Still, I believe we've broken the back of Butcher's gang. We've got our ranch back."

"What Doc is saying," Red continued, "is that you've got wives, children, and jobs. The search for our mom could take months."

Dave nodded and looked away. "Maybe we could let Ted go back, and I'll stick with you."

"No way," Ted growled.

Doc waved his hand. "You promised me a week. We promised your wives a week. When I asked for your help it was because I needed more firepower. We didn't know that Big John would be riding with us. He wants Butcher as badly as we do. He's a fine shot, and while not as young as you two, he's plenty trail wise."

Red stood and faced them. "It's time for you to go home to your families. The longer you are away from home, the harder it will be on you and your loved ones. Doc and I don't want that guilt."

"Just having you here with us these last few days has meant a great deal to Red and me," Doc added. "It's time for you to head home with our gratitude."

Dave sighed. "I don't like not seeing a job through, but you are correct, we did promise our womenfolk."

Ted nodded. "I'm like Dave. I hate to leave you with the job not done, but—"

"For you, it's done," Doc interrupted. "You leave tomorrow. I can't say I'll be happy to see you go, but it's the right thing for you to do."

"I just feel bad that we couldn't have been of more help," Dave said.

Red went behind the couch and placed his hands on their shoulders. "Right. Let's see, Ted saved me from a bushwhacker's bullet, and because I was alive, I was able to save my little brother's life. And then you two rode out to our ranch, not knowing what sort of gun battle we might be riding into. Yup, you're right. You certainly could have been of more help."

Ted grinned at Red. "Oh, shut up and give us another helping of your apple dumplings."

"Dave, I thought you told me Ted was the polite one," Red said in mock surprise. "I'm concerned that he's been riding with you too long."

Dave leaned back on the couch. "If you weren't such a good cook, I'd throw you out of the house, just like I did at that restaurant back at the stagecoach stop."

Red reached over the couch, grabbed Dave easily in his arms, and bounced him up in the air twice. Dave started laughing so hard he could hardly speak. "All right, my young buffalo, I apologize, but only if you feed me."

Red dropped Dave back on the couch.

Dave turned to Ted and said, "See, you just have to know how to handle him."

"I just saw." Ted smirked. "How much is it worth to you for me not to tell Mac?"

"A bunch!"

* * *

Doc came out of Esther's room with a big grin on his face. "Esther's walking great. She's healing fine. One more day, and if she's feeling as good as she is today, you can take her home."

Conrad smiled. "Esther or my baby, Ruth?"

"Why, Mrs. Bale, of course," Doc said seriously.

"The sad thing is that you're probably right," Conrad said.

"You know, Conrad, you're as much responsible for Esther doing as well as I am. All she and Mrs. Bale can talk about is going back home and fixing up the place for her, Martin, and the baby."

Conrad smiled. "What's remarkable is that Granville has told me how happy I look at least three times a day since Martin and I made up. I guess I must have been a bit grouchy over this last year."

"More than a little, boss," Granville said, coming up behind them. "More like a grizzly bear with a toothache."

"I think Doc plumb plucked that bad tooth out of me," Conrad said with a broad grin.

"Good thing too," Granville said. "You were making us all grouchy. Doc, I moved all your stuff into the back of Big John's wagon. I'll make sure your rig gets back to Helena soon."

Doc held out his hand. "Thanks, Granville. You take care of your boss and all like they're family."

"Son, they are my family. Been a real pleasure getting to know you, Doc. You come back soon and bring that wonderful mother of yours with you."

"That's the plan. Did Dave and Ted stop by?"

"About an hour before you. They didn't appear too excited about the stagecoach part of the trip, but you could tell they wanted to get back to their families as fast as they could."

Granville turned to go back outside, then stopped and reached into his coat pocket. "Dave said you might need these." He handed Dave's binoculars to Doc.

Doc smiled at the binoculars. "Damn," he said softly.

Martin hurried out of Esther's room. "There aren't words—"

"Then don't try," Doc interrupted with a wave of his hand. "I'm glad I could help. Keep an eye on my boys out at the ranch. I think they're a little overwhelmed and a little nervous about Butcher or his boys showing back up."

"I'll be checking on them. Joe's going to keep Jesse here until he's well enough to ride. Jesse's mighty grateful for all you did for him."

"Hmm. I still have mixed emotions about that."

"Shouldn't. You did the right thing, Doc. I'm proud of you for what you did for him. I'll ride with Jesse to your ranch to be sure he gets there all right."

"You take care," Doc said softly.

"You too, Doc. Come back to us soon."

Doc waved to Joe and Ann Simms and hurried outside, where Layton was holding Doc's horse. "What'll you be doing, Layton?" he asked. "Joe said you told him you were giving up your gambling ways."

"I love the game, but it's too hard on your life span. I've decided to open a billiard hall in Helena."

"Really? That's terrific. I learned to play in New York. It's a great game, relaxing and a bunch of fun."

"It's going to have a restaurant attached to it with a big variety of fresh-baked goods."

"You need some start-up money?"

"No, but thanks. I have a new partner who made a bunch of money in the California gold camps selling pies and apple dumplings."

Doc stared at him for a long moment. "A restaurant with fresh-baked goods. Hmm—and your partner sold pies and apple dumplings in the Sierras. He wouldn't be a moose of a man with a wild red beard and red hair, by chance?"

Layton smiled. "For you, everything will be on the house at our place. Thanks for saving my life, Doc. Safe journey."

Doc shook Layton's hand firmly, then mounted his horse and leaned toward Layton. "Just one piece of advice. Don't get him mad when he's holding a skillet in his hand."

"I'll remember that. Good luck finding your mom."

Doc turned his horse to where Big John and Red were waiting for him.

"Did he tell you?" Red asked, looking uncomfortable.

"He told me. I thought we didn't have secrets."

"I wasn't sure how you felt about Layton."

"Ah, yes, Layton. Here's what I know about Layton. After I delivered Esther's baby, he sat in a chair outside my room with a shotgun in his lap to protect me. I never asked him to do that. He knew I was exhausted and might not wake if Butcher tried to sneak in on me. Yup, I'd say you picked a good partner."

Red sighed in relief. "Thanks, little brother."

"He also said everything was on the house for me."

"Gosh, I don't know if I'd have gone that far." Red picked up the reins and spoke softly to the horses. "Let's go, girls."

Big John said to Red, "I believe I like having my own personal driver."

"That's all right, Big John," Red answered. "I like having a man who knows how to use that Henry you carry with you. I'm real glad you're with us."

"Me too," Doc said. "Let's go find Mom."

CHAPTER SEVENTEEN

Sinful hurried to Conrad. "Boss, I saw someone following Doc and the boys."

"You sure?"

"I know most folks around here, and he wasn't no cowboy. He was far off, but just from the way he was moving, I felt he was trailing them."

Conrad took a deep breath and frowned. "Sinful, you like Doc, don't you?"

"Sure do, boss. Almost as much as you."

Conrad smiled at Sinful. "Lad, I'm going to give you a new assignment. If you don't want to do it, you don't have to."

Sinful nodded seriously.

"You know that Doc saved my family and in a way saved me too. I want you to trail after them. If the man is just a lone rider, fine. If he's not, I want you to protect Doc, Red, and Big John."

"Yes, sir."

"Either way, I want you to stay with them and help them find Mrs. Whitfield."

"Really, boss? I'd consider that an honor. Thanks."

"Go, then."

"Yes, sir. I'm gone."

* * *

Doc rode alongside the buggy. "What's your plan?" Big John asked him.

"Mom's a Blackfoot. She'll try to get back to her people. I saw a small encampment of Blackfoot when I rode in. We'll start there."

"And if no luck with them?"

"Then we'll circle the area around Elk Forks and expand it until we get a lead. If that doesn't turn up anything, then we'll head up to Fort Benton. That's where she and my dad met."

"Can either of you speak Blackfoot?"

"We both can," Red explained. "How about you?"

"Yes, Golden Eagle taught me."

"We can also converse in sign language. Doc's better at speaking Blackfoot than I am, but I'm better at sign language. Doc has signed some strange things to other Indian tribes."

"Not intentionally," Doc said with a laugh. "Red softens their disposition with his cookies."

"Truly?" Big John asked in surprise.

"You can win an Indian friend faster with a cookie than a gun," Red said with a big grin.

Later that afternoon, Red pointed to a spot near a small stream. "That looks like a good place to stop for the night." He skillfully pulled the wagon under a small tree, then jumped out and tied up the horses.

Doc had already tied his horse to a nearby tree. He flipped his cape over the saddle and walked to the wagon to help Big John unload the supplies.

Doc reached up to take the cooking case from Big John.

"Freeze!" a loud voice behind them demanded. "Just keep those hands up, Doc. I've heard about you, so if you so much as flinch or move that right hand, I'll cut you in half with this shotgun." The man started to laugh. "In fact, that's just what I'm going to do..."

Big John was on top of the wagon facing the killer, and his face showed complete surprise.

Doc tilted his head slightly. He heard a soft thump, then a harsh groan, and suddenly the shotgun went off.

Doc flinched involuntarily, jumped to the side, turned, and drew his Colt in one smooth motion. The outlaw lay dead on the ground with the top of his foot blown off and Sinful's Arkansas toothpick sticking out of his back.

"Damn," Big John gasped.

Doc took a deep, nervous breath and let it out slowly. "Where are you, Sinful?"

Sinful stepped out from behind a tree. "I didn't want you to do one of those quick draws and mistake me for him. Figured I'd better stay out of sight till you called me."

Red rushed to Sinful and grabbed him in a big hug.

"Gently, Red. I'm just a tiny cowboy compared to you."

"Sinful, where did you come from? You just saved all our hides."

"I happened to see this one trailing after you, and when I told the boss, he told me to follow along after you three and keep you out of trouble. Look at that, the poor scorpion blew his foot off after I poked him."

"I'd say you were the scorpion and he was the nasty, owl-hoot killer." Doc tilted his head in thought. "How long have you been trailing him?"

"All day. A while after you left, I looked way down the road and saw this wood tick come out of nowhere. He was so intent on following you, he never did check behind himself." Sinful pulled his knife from the man's body.

"Are you saying Conrad sent you to join up with us?" Doc asked.

"He said I didn't have to, but I told him you were such greenhorns, I needed to."

Big John walked stiffly to Sinful and placed his hand on the cowboy's shoulder. "Boy, calling me a greenhorn under normal circumstances would call for me to teach you a strong lesson with my fist. However, since I can't much squeeze a fist any longer and you just saved my life, I might have to forgive you this time."

"Thanks, Big John. But I didn't mean you, just them two." He pointed at Red and Doc.

"Well, that's different, then."

"I hope you don't mind my staying on with you, but if you do, can you at least feed me?" Sinful asked Doc. "I had to leave in such a hurry, I didn't pack any food. I haven't eaten all day."

Doc put his hands on his hips and grinned. "Red, one more for dinner, and you'd better cook plenty. We've got one hungry tracker joining us. Come on, Sinful, we need to dig a shallow grave. I don't plan to waste much sweat on a back-shooter."

"You know, Doc, I'd like to see you draw someday, but it seems that everyone just wants to shoot you in the back."

"I guess that's why I'm glad you're along. Big John can protect Red's back, and you can protect mine."

"Does that mean I'm coming with you?"

"Yup, like you said, someone has to keep us out of trouble."

"Where do you suppose that killer came from?" Sinful asked as they were digging.

"I don't know, but that concerns me. Butcher's obviously put the word out to the bounty hunters that he'll pay gold for my body."

"I wonder if they know he doesn't have any gold."

Doc sighed. "Bounty hunters get real angry when they're promised money and none is delivered. Once they discover he's broke, that may take some heat off us."

* * *

The next day Doc and Red crawled slowly to the top of a high, grassy knoll. After looking down on three tepees for some time, Doc whispered, "What do you think, Red?"

Red glanced at Doc and frowned. "Something's wrong."

"I'm thinking the same thing."

"No women or children," Red whispered.

"It doesn't make sense," Doc scowled.

Doc and Red crawled back down the knoll, then stood and hurried down into a deep coulee where Big John and Sinful waited for them. "Red and I aren't sure if these are Blackfoot or not. The camp is wrong."

"Is it a trap for us?" Sinful asked.

"No, my guess is it's for some Blackfoot." Doc paced for a moment. "Big John, I hate to ask this, but do you think you can crawl thirty or so feet?"

"Not fast, but I can crawl. Just don't ask me to get up in a hurry."

"Red, you stay with the horses and keep your shotgun handy. If anyone comes over the edge of the ravine but us, sound off a round, then get under the wagon until we can get back."

When Doc, Sinful, and Big John got out of the coulee and close to the knoll overlooking the Indian camp, Doc took Big John's Henry and the three of them crawled forward. Big John groaned quietly as he padded along on his hands and knees. Finally they reached the top of the knoll and flattened out on their stomachs. The three tepees were directly below, and smoke drifted out of two of them.

Doc waited until Big John put on his glasses, then handed him his Henry and whispered, "You going to be able to shoot like that?"

"Not sure. The last time I tried to shoot while lying on my stomach was when I was a kid. I ain't a kid no more." Big John shifted around and finally got the Henry up in front of him. "I don't think I'll be any good this way. You might have to prop me up on my knees."

"Big John," Sinful said, "that means you wouldn't have cover."

"It's all right, Sinful. I know that Doc and Red want Butcher as badly as I do, so if anything happens to me, I know they'll get him for me."

Sinful looked askance at Doc but didn't say anything.

Doc pulled out Dave's binoculars and slowly scanned the area.

"It's set up as a trap," Big John whispered, confirming Doc's suspicion. "River on the left, steep cliff on the right. This knoll isn't high, but it's too steep for a horse to run up easily. Whoever they want to ambush will ride in from the prairie, and when they hit the tepees, they're caught."

"So that means whoever set this trap has to be out in the prairie somewhere."

"That would be my thinking," Big John whispered.

Doc lifted the binoculars and studied the area outside the camp. He pointed off to the left. "There's a bunch of cottonwood trees out on the prairie, beside the river."

"Who do you think set it up?" Sinful asked.

"Difficult to tell. Could be the Crees or Crows. They're both enemies of the Blackfoot. Might also be the Assiniboins, although they sometimes are and sometimes aren't friendly with the Black-foot."

"What do we do?" Sinful asked.

"We wait. If we see some Blackfoot coming this way, then Big John's going to fire a bullet toward those cottonwood trees."

"I'm glad you said those cottonwood trees. For a moment, I was afraid you really wanted me to hit something. I'm a good shot, but not at that distance. But I understand what you're up to. My shot will take the surprise away from the Indians who set it up. Give whoever they want to attack time to retreat."

"Since most of my plans haven't worked out yet, I'm almost fearful of what will happen with this one."

"Yeah, you haven't been too great with your predictions so far, that's for sure," Sinful said as he scratched his nose.

"Thanks. Dad used to tell us if we can't say something nice, it's best not to speak at all." Doc grinned at Sinful, then lifted his binoculars and studied the horizon. "Wait, I see something. Too far away to tell who they are, but..." Doc paused as he waited for the riders to get closer. "It's a Blackfoot raiding party heading home, and they have a large herd of horses with them."

Big John cocked the Henry. "Tell me when."

"Just a bit longer. I want them to be even with the cottonwood trees when you fire. That should confuse the tribe hiding behind them."

"That's if there is anyone hiding there," Sinful said.

"You aren't great at building a person's confidence, are you?" Doc said. "They're about there. Let one go, Big John. Let's see what happens."

John fired, and immediately there was shooting in all directions. A large group of Crows rode out of the cottonwoods, but by then the Blackfoot had turned and dashed back to the open prairie. Some Crows started trying to round up the horses that the Blackfoot had left.

One of the Crows pointed to the knoll.

"Dang, I think they figured out where that shot came from," Sinful said.

Doc bit on his lip in thought. "That wouldn't be good. Perhaps they're just guessing."

Big John sighed. "I think not, Doc. Here they come."

Sure enough, eight braves were riding hard, straight for them. Big John slowly pushed himself up onto his knees.

"Big John," Doc said, "get down."

"Can't shoot flat on my belly. You and Sinful ain't no help with your toy guns at that distance. It's up to me." He brought the Henry up and, taking his time, started firing shot after shot in a smooth, steady pattern. One out of every three shots found a target. Horses and Indians fell. As the braves got closer, the ones still on their horses realized they'd left four behind. Then another horse went down, throwing the brave over its head. The brave jumped to his feet and pointed. The Blackfoot raiding party had regrouped and was charging across the grassland, firing at the Crows.

Big John sat back on his legs and asked, "Will you two help get me back up? I've got cramps in both my legs and my knees are killing me."

Sinful and Doc pulled Big John to his feet. He hobbled around the top of the knoll, moaning and cussing. He stopped and said to Sinful, "I'm not much of a cursing man, but these cramps truly hurt."

"It's all right, Big John. I've heard all those words. Just never heard them arranged so colorfully before."

The Crows were riding in all directions. Some were trying to rescue the wounded that Big John had hit. Others were scooping up the Indians who had lost their horses.

A small group of Crows tried to face the regrouped Blackfoot charging at them but realized they were outnumbered and turned and rode away hard. Soon all the Crows that were alive were galloping across the river as the Blackfoot raiding party rode after them, firing rifles and taunting them. The Blackfoot stopped at the river's edge and whooped after the rapidly disappearing Crows.

"Uh-oh!" Doc frowned. "It looks like the Blackfoot want to chat with us."

Four Blackfoot warriors rode straight toward them.

Doc raised his hand in greeting as the braves rode through the fake camp. "Don't shoot. I'd like to think they're smart enough to know we were the ones who warned them."

The lead brave rode to the bottom of the knoll, stopped and pointed at Doc. "Who are you?" he asked in Blackfoot.

"Little Medicine Boy."

"Who am I?" the brave asked as his horse danced around.

Doc studied the brave for a moment, then remembered. "You are Wild Coyote, and you and I don't like each other much."

Wild Coyote laughed. "Yes, Little Medicine Boy, it is you. You've grown up. Why are you here?"

"We are looking for my mother, Yellow Bird. Have you seen her?"

"No," Wild Coyote said. "But Chief Black Cloud's camp is south of here. They may know."

"Thank you, Wild Coyote. I hope your hunt was successful."

"It almost wasn't. Do I have to like you now?"

"No, but we must respect each other as Blackfoot warriors," Doc said.

"Wise words, Little Medicine Boy." He turned his horse. As he rode away, he held his rifle out to the side and lowered it quickly.

Big John asked, "What was that he just did?"

"I believe he just said thank you. Usually you just put your hands out, palms down, and lower them to say thank you in sign language, but he did it with his rifle."

Doc turned to Big John. "When we met as children, he didn't like that I was only half Blackfoot." Doc grinned. "Then I scared him a few times playing hide-and-seek and that was it. He never liked me after that."

Just then he heard Sinful yell at him to come to the top of the coulee, where Red stood with blood running down the side of his face. He was holding his red bandanna on his head.

Doc ran to him. "You all right?"

Red pursed his lips disgustedly. "Stupid. I was under the wagon, and when the firing started I jerked up my head, and this is what happened."

Doc checked the damage. "Just a scratch, but head wounds bleed easily. Let me get my bag, and we'll get the bleeding stopped. Next time, you stay with me and not under the wagon." He turned and ran down to the wagon for his medical bag.

Sinful stared at Red's face. "Your blood isn't nearly as pretty as your hair. Your hair is a much brighter red. Still, with the red bandanna soaking up all your blood, they're all starting to look the same."

"Thanks for that information, Sinful."

"Just trying to cheer you up," Sinful said with just a hint of laughter in his voice.

"Sinful, if you're not nice to my big brother," Doc said as he ran up with his medicine bag, "I'll make you get down on your hands and knees so Red can sit on something while I patch him up."

"Then you'd have to patch me up too."

Red started laughing. "There's an image that does cheer me up, Sinful."

"See, I knew I could do it."

Big John walked up. "I'll go get the wagon. Looks as if I'm back driving. Are we going to head south for a while before making camp?"

Doc shook his head. "Nope. We're going to spend the night in the tepees. Then tomorrow we'll break them down and take them to Chief Black Cloud as a gift."

CHAPTER EIGHTEEN

Doc threw the tarp off, pulled on his moccasin boots, then stood and slipped his Colt into his holster. Spending the night in the tepee two nights ago had spoiled him. His breath puffed white in the cold, bracing morning air, and the buffalo grass sparkled with the early morning frost.

Sinful was starting a fire. Red was down at the creek cleaning out a cast-iron skillet, and Big John sat mournfully in the wagon seat, trying to wake up and wishing for a cup of hot, black coffee.

Doc glanced to the west at the Rockies, their peaks stretching to the sky, then turned his gaze east over the endless plains and smiled. He turned to Sinful, then felt the whiz of the Arkansas toothpick pass within inches of his body. Doc drew his gun and fired. He heard Big John firing two quick shots from his Henry. Sinful and Doc glanced toward Big John and saw two Indians squirming on the ground in pain.

At the stream, Red turned just as an Indian started to plunge a knife into his back. He parried the thrust with his skillet, did a quick sidestep, brought the skillet back up, and smashed it hard against the side of the Indian's head. The Indian fell backward, unconscious.

A second Indian, a youth of perhaps thirteen or fourteen, drew back his spear. Just then a shot from Doc's Colt shattered the spear point. Red lifted his skillet threateningly, and the Indian dropped his pole and spread his hands in defeat and fear.

Sinful grinned at Doc. "I wasn't sure if you'd think I was throwing at you or not. Then you drew and fired." He shrugged. "I figured I was a dead man."

"Well, for just a moment I wondered, but the Indian behind you convinced me that you'd missed me on purpose." He glanced up at Big John, standing in the wagon. "What'd you get?"

"Two more down up ahead."

"Dead?"

"I don't think so, but I 'spect they're hurting."

"That sure woke you up." Doc grinned up at Big John.

"I needed coffee before they stopped in for a visit. Now I truly need a cup."

Red came from the streambed, directing the Indian lad to the wagon. "I'll just tie him up on the wagon wheel while we gather the wounded. Doc, you're on call. Get your bag."

"You mean I've got to patch up these savages who just tried to kill us?"

"Doc!" Red exclaimed. "That's not even a bit funny. I don't need to remind you that you're half savage yourself."

"Yes, the good half," Doc said with a smile. "Go get the two that Big John shot and take your skillet with you for protection."

"I'll go with Red," Sinful said, "but you'd better look at this one, Doc. My knife did some real damage, and I don't want to just pull it out. The other one has your bullet in his side, but I don't think he's hurt that badly. I'll wrap a cloth around his wound and tie him to the other wagon wheel till you can look at him."

Doc hurried to the Indian lying on the ground with Sinful's knife buried in his thigh. The brave's face was twisted in pain.

Big John climbed out of the wagon. "I'll drag up the Indian that Red banged by the stream."

Doc felt around the Indian's thigh. He asked him in Blackfoot, "Do you understand Blackfoot?"

The Indian looked at him blankly.

Doc looked down at the Indian's moccasins. "Cree," he said aloud. He sighed and frowned as he tried to dredge up in his mind his hand signal skills. It had been more than three years since he'd used them, and, as Red said, it wasn't his greatest talent.

"How do you know they're Crees?" John asked as he dragged the Indian from the stream up to the camp.

"He's wearing soft-bottom moccasins. All the Blackfoot Indians wear hard parfleche soles. Get my medical bag, Big John. This one is going to be difficult. If Sinful's knife hit an artery, I may not be able to save him."

Doc used sign language to the wounded Indian. "I, Blackfoot medicine man. You, hurt bad. I fix."

The Indian quickly flicked his head to indicate that he understood.

Red and Sinful hurried into camp carrying the other two Indians.

"How are they?" Doc asked.

"Both alive." Red pulled his hat off and roughly scratched his wild red hair. "I hope you realize, gents, that six Cree Indians attacked us and with all your fancy rifles, guns, and knives, you didn't kill a single one."

"I thought you were part of this group too," Sinful said.

"Sure, but my weapon's a skillet, and it did exactly what it was supposed to do," Red said with a wide grin. "Put him to sleep." He pointed with his skillet to the still unconscious Indian Big John had dragged from the creek.

Big John scanned the four wounded Indians and asked, "Who said we wanted to kill them, Red? Doc's half Indian, your adopted mom is Blackfoot, and I was married to a Blackfoot. Maybe that's the way we planned it."

Red bent over the fire, blew on a hot spark, and finally got it going. He settled back on his heels. "You know, Big John, while I was in the Sierra goldfields, the miners were killing the defenseless Sierra Nevada Indians—men, women, and even children. It made me sick. You're right. I'm glad we didn't kill any of them. I'm ashamed of what I just said."

Sinful walked to where Doc was working on the Indian with the knife in him. "Can I help, Doc?"

"You all right around blood?"

"As long as it's not mine. How come he's letting you work on him without fussing?"

"He knows I'm a Blackfoot. I told him I was a powerful medicine man and that I was going to help him."

"And he believed you?"

"Wouldn't you if you had a huge knife sticking out of your thigh?"

"Yup, that I understand. What do you need?"

"I've got to put him to sleep. Since I don't speak the language of the Crees, I've tried to explain in sign language what I'm going to do. I hope I've told him correctly. He believes I'm going to give him a cloth with a sweet smell, and he is to breathe it and he will see Notawinan."

"What's that?"

"The Cree's supreme god. I'm pretty sure it means 'our father.'"

"And he's just going to let you do it?"

"Nope, he's going to do it. At first he was afraid that I was going to try to suffocate him, but I explained that he had to do it to see his god. I guess he figured that was all right."

Doc carefully poured chloroform onto the cloth and handed it to the Indian brave. The brave cautiously sniffed the sweet smell, and when Doc gestured for him to lay it over his face, he did so.

"Now what happens?" Sinful asked.

"When his hand drops away, he'll be asleep."

"That stuff can really put you to sleep?"

"Yup." Doc said as the brave's hand fell away from his face. "I'll leave it on for a few moments more just to be sure he's totally out."

Doc dug into his medical bag, pulled out his instruments, and laid them on a cloth on the ground.

"What's that nasty-looking knife?"

"That's a bistoury knife. I can use it to enlarge bullet holes." Doc glanced up at Sinful. "It's no good for tossing."

Sinful grinned. "I was just checking."

"When I tell you, I want you to pull your knife straight out. Then you may have to place a finger where I tell you to stop the blood until I can take care of it."

Sinful got down on his knees on the other side of the injured Cree. Doc had a handful of muslin ready. "All right. Pull it straight out and make it a smooth pull."

Sinful closed his hand around the handle of his knife and with one quick jerk pulled it out.

Doc examined the wound carefully, and a hint of a smile crossed his face as he pressed the muslin over the wound. "Press down on this."

Sinful did and felt the warm, red blood slowly cover his hand. "Is it bad?"

"Better than I expected. I've got to go in, clamp some problem areas and then tie off some blood vessels, but your knife didn't hit an artery."

"Is that good?" Sinful questioned.

"For him, it is."

* * *

Red handed Doc a plate of food. "I don't know what you should call this. It's too late for breakfast and too early for dinner."

Doc sat tiredly against a cottonwood tree and started eating quickly.

"Hey," Red said. "Slowly. That's quality food you're eating there. You look like you've got your face in a nose bag."

Doc didn't slow down but just gestured for Red to add more to the plate, as he continued to shovel the stew into his mouth.

"You'd think," Red said to the others, "that someone who has spent three years in New York City would have learned some eating manners." He took a large ladle and spooned another big helping of stew onto Doc's plate.

Big John stared at the six Indians watching them, all on the ground with their hands tied. "We've got four wounded, another with a serious headache thanks to Red's skillet, and a young one who's trying to be brave but is really terrified. What're we going to do with them?"

Sinful was stretched out in the shade of another cottonwood. "And don't forget, we also have forty-two new horses."

"How'd you and Red ever find those, anyway?" Big John asked.

"Don't ask me," Sinful said as he pointed at Red. "The big red-head went out there, bent over like an old hound dog, and started sniffing the ground. Before you knew it, he'd found their stash of horses."

Red reached over and playfully slapped Sinful with his hat. "I was not sniffing the ground. I was looking for signs."

"Nah, I positively heard you sniffing."

Red looked at Doc. "Should I just throw him into the creek?"

Doc laughed at them. "Sinful, Red is about the best tracker I've ever seen. He and I spent many moons with the Blackfoot when we were growing up, and he could even out-track some of their best. Dad always got such a laugh out of it when Chief Red Hawk told him about it."

Doc stood and went to the brave with the wound in his thigh. He knelt and carefully lifted the bandage, then studied it for a few moments. "It looks good."

The Indian brave watched warily.

He stood. "They all do. They're as patched-up as I can do. We should just go. We'll leave them their horses but no weapons, except for one bow and a quiver of arrows so they can find game to live on. We'll take the stolen horses with us.

"Only the young one is healthy. The others will have to ride slowly and won't be able to go far each day. They'll head for home. Red, what can we use to leave some of your stew for them to eat?"

"There's some large pieces of bark I believe I can use."

Big John rubbed his hands slowly. "Good plan. We can get in four or five hours today. The shape they're in, they may not even move until tomorrow."

The Crees watched them anxiously as they started packing to leave.

"You take off," Doc said. "I'll speak with the young one after you're down the trail a piece."

"What about the horses?" Red asked.

"Right. Sinful, you stay too. We can herd the horses when we leave. Besides, I want them to see you toss your toothpick."

Doc squatted under the cottonwood tree and slowly twirled the cylinder of his Colt. Its distinct clicking noise made the Indians even more uneasy. "Lift that old log and lean it against that tree over there," Doc said.

"What now?" Sinful asked.

"Walk off about ten paces and then give that toothpick of yours a toss."

Sinful walked away, then turned swiftly and threw his knife. It struck the log with a loud thump.

Doc stood, reholstered his Colt, then drew and fired two shots so fast, none of the Indians even saw him draw. One shot struck the log above Sinful's knife and the other below it.

"Dang, Doc. You've got them so spooked that if they were cattle, we'd have a stampede on our hands."

"Good. I don't want them to think they can just come after us again and have easy pickings."

"I don't reckon that's what they're thinking," Sinful said with a short laugh.

Doc went to the young Indian brave. "Cut him loose, Sinful."

Sinful flipped the knife back and forth between his hands. The brave's eyes grew huge.

Doc signed to him, "No, we are not going to scalp you. Once we leave, you can untie your brothers. Eat and rest tonight here. Tomorrow go home. Do not return. Only death awaits you if you return. Do you understand my signs?"

The young brave slowly got to his feet and signed that he understood. He tenderly rubbed his sore wrists.

Doc and Sinful mounted their horses and began herding the forty-two others down the trail.

The young brave watched them go but did not move to untie his brothers until Doc and Sinful were out of sight.

"Do you think they'll do as you said?" Sinful asked.

"Only three of them are in shape to ride. The other two wounded ones might need a travois to get them back to their tribe."

Sinful looked at Doc, puzzled.

"A travois is like a sled made of poles. They use it to carry their gear, and a horse or dog pulls it. They can also use it to carry a person."

"Doesn't sound too comfortable."

Doc grinned. "Isn't, but it's better than being dead."

* * *

Three days later, Doc rode quickly back to the wagon late in the day. "Indian camp coming up."

"Bad ones?" Red asked.

"I don't think so. It looks like a Blackfoot camp, but after that last camp we found, I'm leery."

Red halted the wagon. Big John said to Doc, "Why don't we let Sinful keep the horses back here while we meander in, peaceful and slow-like?"

"Probably a good idea." Doc circled his hand at Sinful. Sinful gestured that he understood.

As the wagon approached the camp, a semicircle of Indians formed in front of the chief's tepee.

"They're Blackfoot," Red said softly, "but they've got war paint on and don't look happy. I'm not feeling comfortable about this."

"Which one's the chief?" Big John asked quietly.

"The fierce-looking Indian on the white pinto," Doc whispered. "The horse he's on is called a medicine hat. See the red-brown warbonnet markings on its head and ears and the brown shield that covers its chest? Only a chosen warrior or chief is allowed to ride these sacred pintos. The Blackfoot believe that these horses have magical powers and make the rider invincible in battle."

The chief raised his hand and asked in Blackfoot, "What do you want here?"

"We seek the camp of Chief Black Cloud. I am Little Medicine Boy and he's Fire Hair." Doc pointed at Red. "We seek our mother, Yellow Bird."

The chief frowned at Doc.

"This doesn't look good," Big John said under his breath.

"I do not know of your mother, Yellow Bird. Four nights ago, Crees attacked our camp," the chief said. "They stole our horses, wounded two of our young braves."

"Why have you waited so long to go after them?" Doc asked.

Red groaned and mumbled, "That's pushing it, Doc."

"We were away," the chief said. "We just returned and heard the news."

"Were there six Crees, and did they take forty-two of your horses?" Doc asked.

The chief leaned back on his horse, looking puzzled. "How do you know of this?"

"The Crees are no more. We are returning your horses. We also have tepees we took from a Crow hunting party. These we will give you."

"Doc," Red whispered. "I surely do hope you know what you're doing. They find those Crees, and they might decide to come after us."

"It's been three days. The Crees are back in the mountains by now," Doc said softly to Red.

"Where are their scalps?" the chief demanded.

"I travel with white men. They don't believe in taking scalps."

"Some do."

Doc shrugged.

"Where are our horses?"

"I will get them for you. Wait." Doc spun his horse, rode quickly over the ridge, and whistled for Sinful to bring the horses in. Then he returned to the wagon.

A few moments later Sinful drove the horses into the Blackfoot camp.

Doc pointed to the poles and tepee coverings in the back of the wagon. "These are a gift from us."

The chief told his people to take the items out of the wagon. "Chief Black Cloud is two days south of here," he said, pointing quickly.

Doc extended his hands, palms down, and lowered them.

Red watched the chief closely. When the chief said, "Leave," Red quickly turned the wagon and they headed off.

After they were back on the trail, Sinful grinned and said, "That wasn't very neighborly. That chief didn't even ask us to have a smoke with him."

"I believe," Red said, "that we were lucky to get away with our scalps still attached. One brave kept eyeing my head, and I could tell he was looking forward to seeing my red locks flopping on a pole in front of his tepee."

Doc smiled at Red. "I believe Sinful was being sarcastic."

"This wagon doesn't do sarcasm," Red said.

Big John growled up at Sinful. "Red's correct. And I don't need to remind you that irritating our cook and my driver is bad business. And irritating me is even worse."

"Goodness," Sinful said, chuckling. "You two are sure crabby. We got away with our hair still in place. We did a good deed and brought their horses back to them, which means we don't have to herd them anymore. We dumped that load of poles and tepees, which was extra weight we didn't need, even though it was supposed to be a gift for Chief Black Cloud. And we know we are heading in the right direction." Sinful threw up his hands. "What more do you want?"

Big John lifted a warning eyebrow. "Peace and quiet."

Sinful thought for a moment, then said, "Ain't going to happen." He rode away quickly, laughing as he went.

CHAPTER NINETEEN

Sinful rode rapidly back to where Doc and the wagon slowly climbed the grade. "Doc, can I borrow your spyglass? There's something moving toward us that I'm not sure I believe."

"Trouble?"

"No, a wagon so huge, I can't believe it's real."

Doc reached into his saddlebag and handed the binoculars to Sinful. Doc grinned at Red. "Keep coming. I'm going to ride ahead with Sinful and see if he's losing his sight or his mind."

"Doc, you won't believe it." Sinful waved the binoculars in the air. "Wait until you see it." He turned his horse and galloped back up the grade. Doc followed at a slower pace. When he got to the top of the crest, Doc stopped his horse beside Sinful's and stood in his stirrups to get a better view.

Sinful held the binoculars to his eyes. "That's the biggest rig I've ever seen." He handed the binoculars to Doc. "Look. You won't believe it. There must be eight horses pulling that thing. And look at the size of the wagon. It must be twice as tall as a normal one."

Doc studied the wagon intently. "Sinful, that's not eight horses, that's twelve."

"Dang! Twelve horses."

"And they aren't pulling one wagon, they're pulling three."

"Let me see again, Doc, please."

Doc handed the binoculars back.

"Isn't that the most incredible thing you've ever seen?" Sinful grinned at Doc. "Can you imagine driving twelve horses? I've driven four a few times, and once I got to sit beside a driver running six, but never twelve. How far do you think they can go in a day?"

"Oh, I'd guess about six to ten miles a day with a full load and good weather."

"That would take a long time to get from Virginia City to Helena."

"A bunch of long, boring days, I'm afraid." Doc reached out his hand for his binoculars. He studied the wagon for a long time. "Ride back and tell Red to pull off the road when he gets to the top. I need to see if that's who I think it is."

Doc spurred his horse toward the huge wagons before Sinful could ask him who he thought it was. "Dang," he said as he watched Doc moving rapidly down the road.

When Doc neared the huge freight wagons, he pulled his horse off to the side of the road and waited. Four roughly dressed, grimy men were riding on either side of the team that pulled the wagons. They looked at him guardedly, but he smiled and said brightly, "Morning."

They stared back. One man tipped his hat hesitantly. The driver rode the left-hand horse at the rear of the team and controlled all twelve horses with a single jerk line.

An older man with long, white, bushy sideburns sat on top of the first wagon. He studied Doc suspiciously. When the wagon got even with him, Doc had his horse fall in step with it.

"Howdy. You wouldn't be Tom Frost from Elk Forks, the world's greatest lumberman, would you?" Doc asked.

The man leaned over the seat and squinted at Doc. He shook his head as if to clear his vision. "Doc, is that you hidden behind that unshaven face and black cape?"

"Hi, Tom," Doc said with a huge grin. "Red and I have sure missed your terrible coffee."

"Doc, grab my horse from the back of this rig and bring it around for me." Tom climbed gracefully down the side of the two-story wagon. When Doc brought his horse even, he slid easily onto it.

"Still as agile as ever, I see."

Tom shook Doc's hand strongly. "How long have you been here?"

"A spell. Red's at the top of the ridge. We need to talk to you."

"Let's go." Tom immediately urged his horse into a lope. At the top of the ridge, Tom started yelling, "Red! Red!" He jumped off his horse, ran up to Red, and gripped his hand. "How wonderful to see you," he exclaimed as he slapped his friend firmly on the shoulder.

Doc tied his horse to Red's wagon and joined them. "Tom, have you seen Mom?"

Tom frowned in concern. "What's happened to Yellow Bird?"

Red filled him in on all that had occurred since they'd come to Elk Forks, including what had happened to Big John and his wife. Tom paced in anger. "I can't tell you how many times I've thought I just needed to get a force together and go out to your ranch and shoot them all. But look at me. I don't carry a gun. I can barely fire a rifle. I'm a great lumberman, but I'm no gunfighter. I can't even hunt for food."

Red started a small fire and heated some coffee. Soon he handed a cup to Tom. "We don't fault you for that, Tom. We were just glad you were there for Mom."

"I heard that Rocky was in Bannack. We'd just delivered a load of wood to a big mine, and someone told me Rocky had moved into town. I thought that was strange but just figured he and Butcher had broken up."

"Didn't hear anything about Cole, Richie, or Butcher, did you?" Big John asked.

"Only Cole. Odd that you should mention his name. I talked to a man who saw him killed just a few days ago."

"How?" Doc questioned.

"Cole came into a digging next to his, drew his gun, and demanded their gold. One man smacked him in the back of the head with his shovel. Apparently, the rest of the men were so distressed with how bad the digging had been going, they just became outraged at him for trying to steal what little they had. They pounded him to death with their shovels and picks. Must have been horrible to witness."

"Dang!" Sinful said. "Butcher's men are dropping like cow dung."

Tom said to Big John, "I'm so sorry about what Butcher did to you and your wife. I just hope he hasn't killed Yellow Bird too." His face creased in pain.

"We don't think he has," Red said. "Butcher has tried too hard to find her alive. She took off with Butcher's money and gold and just disappeared."

"Your mother was always such a curious mixture of the Blackfoot and the white culture. She was the best of both, and that's what made her so wonderful." He said firmly, "I'm riding with you boys. I'm just worn out worrying and praying for her and not doing anything. I'm no good with a gun, but I'll give you whatever support I can."

The freight wagon had just reached the top of the ridge road and stopped to let the horses blow. Tom hurried to them and yelled to the driver, "Percy, climb up in the jockey box and hand me down my rifle and my bag. I've got some work to do with these men, so you take the wagons on to Helena."

Percy handed down a rifle in a deerskin case and a traveling bag. "You know what to do. I'll be back as soon as I can," Tom said.

Sinful asked Tom, "What's in all your wagons?"

"All the necessities of life, my boy. They started out from Elk Forks full of lumber for all the gold mines down south. Once the wagons are empty, we fill them back up with supplies for all the shops and stores in Helena."

Tom pulled the rifle out and checked it.

"Has that Minié been modified?" Big John asked.

"It's a breech-loading, single-shot action now." He handed the Minié to Big John.

Big John handled it knowingly. "This is a fine rifle. Extremely accurate," he added.

"In the right hands," Tom said.

"And in your hands?" Big John asked.

"I've been practicing hard, but…" He let the sentence fade.

Big John nodded in understanding. "You have anyone to help you?"

"My workers are all lumber people."

"I'll teach you."

"I'd be willing to pay—" Tom stopped when he saw he look on Big John's face. "Sorry, I didn't mean to insult you. I'd be much obliged."

Red put his arm around Big John. "Don't let his mean old face fool you, Tom. When you're Big John's friend, you know your back is covered."

Big John's eyebrows shot up. "I'm okay with the 'mean' part, but you give me any more mouth about 'old' and I might have to take you on." There was a hint of a smile on his face. "If I can tie you up hand and foot before we start," he added.

Sinful laughed. "I'd still put my wages on Red."

Big John wagged a warning finger at Sinful.

"It's all right, Big John," Tom said. "Those of us with a little white in our hair may not be as fast as these young bucks, but we sure are a lot smarter."

Big John agreed with a rapid tip of his head.

"Your rig going to be all right?" Doc asked.

"Don't worry, Doc. Those men have been with me for years. Don't let the dirt and grime fool you. They are loyal, hardworking men. What's the plan?"

"Chief Black Cloud's camp is down this way, off the trail and toward the Belt Mountains."

"Do you think Yellow Bird is there?"

"Don't know. If Chief Black Cloud doesn't know where she is, my plan is to ask the nearby Blackfoot camps. If that doesn't bring us success, then we'll head for Fort Benton and try to find Chief Red Hawk.

"It's getting late into the season. The tribes will be heading for the Marias River encampment for the winter."

"We're not sure if Mom was on foot when she left the house, but she knows how to survive," Red added. "So many Blackfoot travel through this area, she could have found help with many different tribes."

"Let's hope so," Tom said, the concern heavy in his voice.

CHAPTER TWENTY

Chief Black Cloud stood before them and made it clear that they were not to step down. "You brought sickness to our people. You killed our buffalo and left them to rot in the tall grass. You killed our people…"

A young Indian child wobbled toward Sinful's horse in the unsteady way of a toddler who has just learned to walk. She could not have been more than a year old. Sinful glanced at the girl, then saw the large rattlesnake about to strike her.

Sinful yanked his Arkansas toothpick and flung it at the snake in an action so fast that unless you were watching him closely, you wouldn't have seen it.

Chief Black Cloud shouted out when he realized what had just happened. He rushed to the young child and swept her up in his arms. His yell stopped everyone in the camp.

Doc had just glimpsed Sinful's movement out of the corner of his eye. He leaned forward and saw the snake pinned to the ground. It was dead, with the dagger stuck through the middle of its triangle-shaped head. The snake's body wiggled wildly, then slowly stilled. Doc let out a breath of air and said, "Sinful, I thought I was fast, but you just put me to shame."

Many of the Indians had rushed to the snake and were now gesturing at Sinful and talking loudly. Sinful looked nervously at Doc. "Are we in big trouble? They don't look happy."

"I think you stunned them with your throw," Big John said as he glanced around.

"You don't suppose they think I was trying to kill the little girl, do you?"

Doc shook his head. "If they had, I 'spect we'd all be dead. I agree with Big John. I don't think they've ever seen someone throw a knife the way you did."

"You need to remember, Sinful," Red added, "that these are people who have used knives all their lives. To see someone throw one like you just did makes you appear almost magical."

"Do you think they'd mind if I got my toothpick back?"

Doc tried to get a sense of the mood of the braves. "Do it slowly."

Sinful eased out of his saddle. The braves moved away from him as he went to the snake. He placed his boot on its neck and withdrew the knife. Then with a swift downward motion he sliced off the snake's large head.

"I really don't like snakes," Sinful said to Doc. "If we were out by ourselves, I'd keep it and have it for dinner and save the skin for my hat. They taste real good."

He made another slash at the tail of the snake, smoothly cutting off the large rattle. He reached down, picked it up, and gave it a little shake. It made a distinct rattling sound. He held it out uncertainly to the chief, who still held his daughter in his arms. The Indian girl reached for it excitedly.

The chief leaned forward so she could grab it. He smiled as his daughter eagerly wiggled it back and forth while jabbering at her father.

"What's she saying?" Sinful asked Doc.

The chief answered Sinful in English. "My daughter is thanking you for saving her life in child talk. I don't know how that snake was able to get so close to our camp with all the dogs about." He handed the child to his wife and then whispered to another daughter, a teenager who stood beside him. She rushed away. The chief said to Sinful, "Show us how you throw your knife."

Sinful glanced up at Doc, uncertain what to do.

"Do it," Doc said.

The chief looked at Doc and said in Blackfoot, "Get down. Come, all."

Doc and Tom got off their horses. Red and Big John climbed down from the wagon. They followed the chief across a shallow stream to a spot near the edge of camp.

Sinful quickly splashed his knife in the stream as they crossed, cleaning it of blood, and dried it on his pants. He slipped the knife into its sheath on his belt. All the men and women of the tribe had followed them.

Chief Black Cloud pointed to a dead tree trunk, cut in two by lightning and about twelve feet from them. The bottom of the burned-out trunk stood more than eight feet high. The bark was gone; all that remained was the shiny white trunk.

Sinful was turned sideways to the trunk, facing the chief. Faster than anyone could believe, he grabbed his knife from its sheath and flung it toward the trunk in a sideways motion.

The knife struck the center of the trunk with a resounding thunk.

A teenage brave came to Sinful and gestured that he wanted to retrieve the weapon. Sinful grinned and nodded for him to go ahead. The brave raced to the trunk and tried to pull the knife out. He grunted and tugged, but it would not budge. Finally Sinful walked over, grabbed the knife, pumped it up and down twice, and pulled it out.

The chief's older daughter rushed up to her father and whispered into his ear. He nodded.

Sinful handed the knife to the brave, who held it as if he held the tribe's sacred peace pipe. He ran back and handed it to the chief.

Chief Black Cloud said to Sinful, "What can we give you in trade for this?"

Sinful glanced at Doc. Doc made a barely perceptible shake of his head. Sinful remembered Doc's admonition never to insult an Indian and asked, "Chief Black Cloud, you have a sacred pipe, do you not?"

The chief nodded.

"And if I asked to buy your sacred pipe, what would you say?"

"We would never part with our sacred pipe."

"Why?"

"It has been handed down from my father and my father's father before him. Our pipe is part of our tribe."

Sinful touched the knife that the chief held in his palms. "The knife that you hold was handed down from my father. Like your pipe, my knife is a sacred tool to me, which I hope to hand down to my children."

"I understand." He handed the knife back to Sinful. "You saved the life of my daughter. I wish to give you many horses in thanks."

Sinful pulled off his black slouch hat and said slowly, "That's mighty kind of you, chief, but I have plenty of horses."

Doc gasped, rolled his eyes, and slapped his hand over his mouth.

The chief frowned. He stared at Sinful angrily. "What don't you have plenty of?"

Sinful scratched his head. He looked down at the chief's feet, then over at Doc. "That." He pointed at Doc's moccasins. "See the moccasin boots he wears? That's what I don't have. I have boots that are always tight and hurt my feet something fierce. I'd really love to have some boots just like that."

"Moccasins?" the chief repeated in surprise. "Not horses but moccasins?"

"If that's all right," Sinful replied innocently.

The chief's head went back and he laughed loudly. He yelled to six of his bucks, and before Sinful knew what was happening, they grabbed him by his arms and legs. They turned him on his back and were trying to tug his boots off.

Sinful's blue eyes were huge. "Help, Doc, they're getting ready to scalp me."

Doc, Red, Tom, and John were laughing along with the chief. "Don't worry, Sinful. They're just going to make you a pair of new moccasin boots."

Sinful frowned anxiously at his legs held up in the air as one Indian pulled his left boot off. One brave stuck his head down in the boot; he immediately made a terrible face and started coughing. He passed Sinful's boot to the brave beside him, and soon everyone had to take a smell. They all coughed and made horrible faces.

"Is there something dead inside this?" one brave asked Doc in Blackfoot.

"Just Sinful's foot," Doc replied. "I think he needs a bath."

Just then the second boot popped off. "I don't believe it would be right to give him new boots unless he's all clean," Doc said to the chief.

The chief spoke to his braves.

"What did you just tell them?" Sinful yelled at Doc.

The braves picked Sinful up, pulled off his pants, vest, and shirt, and rushed him to the creek.

"Doc, what have you done?" Sinful cried out wildly.

"Sinful, they're just going to give you a bath so you won't have to put your dirty feet into their new moccasins."

"Doc, it's not even Saturday and this water's cold."

"Be brave, Sinful. You don't want these Indians to think you're a milksop."

"I just want my shirt and pants back on," Sinful wailed.

"Do you think I should help him?" Red asked.

"Absolutely not," Doc said with a laugh. "He'll talk about this experience until he's as old as Big John."

"Hey, watch it there, boy," Big John said. "You're just between grass and hay yourself."

Doc looked puzzled.

"That means you're halfway between being a boy and a man," Red explained.

The chief turned to Doc and asked, "You are known to me?"

"Yes, I'm Little Medicine Boy and my brother is Fire Hair, but it has been many years since you have seen us. We were just children then."

Chief Black Cloud studied them seriously.

* * *

Later that evening, Sinful sat outside the chief's tepee wearing his moccasin boots. His legs were stretched out in front of him. "Aren't they the most beautiful boots you've ever seen?" he asked no one in particular.

"Did you know that some believe the dark color of your boots is how the Blackfoot got their name?" Doc asked.

Sinful held up his left leg, reached down, and patted it. "Does that make me a Blackfoot, since I wear their boots?" He grinned at Doc. "Sort of an honorary member of the tribe because of my moccasin boots. What do you think?"

"I think that would be up to the chief."

Chief Black Cloud smiled across the fire at Doc and spoke to him in Blackfoot. "Never have I seen someone enjoy a gift as much as your man Sinful. My concern was great that he would not take my horses in return for saving the life of my youngest daughter. But watching him enjoying his new moccasin boots, I realize that this was the proper gift."

"You are correct," Doc said. "I thank you for not becoming angry at his refusal to take your gift of horses."

"Yes, for a moment I was, but when he asked for moccasin boots, I realized his innocence. He has brought much laughter to our camp."

"Well," Doc said, "seeing him get a bath was almost as much fun for us."

Chief Black Cloud smiled. "Yes, I tried to be serious, but he was hollering and screaming like a young child, and how could you not laugh at such behavior? Then to watch him step about the camp, once he had the boots, with all the young children matching his steps, was wonderful."

Doc smiled as he remembered. All the children had stretched out in a line behind Sinful as he lifted one foot and laughed at his new boot, took two steps and lifted the other foot and laughed again. Then he'd clap his hands over his head. The children matched his steps, clapping and laughing while everyone enjoyed their performance as they danced around the camp.

The chief went on, "Yet, after that he spent time with our young warriors and showed them how to better throw their knives. He is a good white man."

"Yes, he is." Doc studied the fire for a moment, then said, "We came to you because we search for our mother, Yellow Bird."

"Yes, I know."

That surprised Doc. "How is it that you know?"

"While we were waiting for Sinful's gift to be made, a rider came to camp with a message for me."

Doc waited.

"This message was from Wild Coyote, and he spoke of your bravery in warning them about the Crows. His message ended by saying we must respect Little Medicine Boy. I found that a strange thing for him to say."

"Wild Coyote and I respect each other as warriors, but we don't enjoy each other's company."

Chief Black Cloud smiled knowingly.

"I have heard that Yellow Bird has great fear of a white man named Butcher. What of him?"

"Butcher chased Fire Hair and me off our land and hunted us. Recently our mother escaped with all his wealth. The yellow rocks that the white man uses to buy things. His men found out that I had returned to Elk Forks and came to kill me, but my friend"— Doc pointed to Big John, —"heard them come. Because of his bravery and that of other friends in town, we were able to kill many of Butcher's gunmen.

"Then men with government badges came to help us, and we went to our ranch, but Butcher had fled. First we will find our mother, Yellow Bird, and then we will hunt down this bad white man. The hunted have returned."

The Indians from the camp were seated around the campfire listening to their chief and Doc and his friends. A female voice behind them spoke in Blackfoot.

"Is Yellow Bird finally free?"

Red and Doc leaped to their feet in unison. They searched the crowd of seated Indians. Near the back, a tall, beautiful, older Indian woman stood. She wore her long black hair in two thick braids. Her white smile shone in the dark night.

"Mom!" Doc and Red said together as they stepped cautiously but quickly through the crowd of seated Indians to her. The camp was silent as the Indians watched the two sons embrace their mother.

After the embrace, Yellow Bird gently touched each son's cheek with her fingertips and spoke so quietly that only her sons could hear. When they turned and escorted her to the fire, their broad smiles told all who watched that this was total happiness.

Yellow Bird rushed up to Tom Frost, and they came together for a quick embrace. He spoke softly to her, and she gently laughed and touched Tom's face with her fingertips. Doc told her to sit with Tom.

"Mom, why didn't you speak up when we came in?" Red asked in Blackfoot.

"I was afraid Butcher was still after you, and I didn't want to cause any harm to come to you. Just to see you all grown up and handsome made me so happy." She turned to Tom. "And to see Tom with you brought me much happiness. I know for him to ride with you required great courage on his part."

"Well, we are going to make sure your nightmare is over," Doc said. "How did you get here?"

"I'd planned my escape since April, after Butcher wouldn't let me go to church anymore. It was the only place where I could see and talk with Tom," Yellow Bird said in Blackfoot. "I was all set to go a month earlier, but they didn't all go to Helena as planned. I had to wait until they got careless and everyone was gone."

Doc quietly translated for Sinful and Tom.

Yellow Bird continued. "I had already decided that I would take away all the wealth of Butcher, but I had to plan with great care. I had to wait until Tom was taking a load of lumber south to the mines. If Tom were around when I escaped, Butcher would think Tom helped me. That would have put Tom's life in great danger. Butcher never liked Tom, but Tom always had so many of his workers around him, they were afraid to try to kill him.

"Then I found out that Tom had left for Bannack with three freight loads of lumber two weeks earlier. The day before the Sabbath everyone went to Helena except for Tex and four ranch hands. I waited patiently, and soon I saw Tex riding away with three of the hands toward town. I knew the young one was sick and in the bunkhouse, so I felt certain I could get away. The time had come for me to escape."

"What happened to everything in the safe?" Red asked. "Jesse said you took it all when you escaped from the house."

Yellow Bird laughed. "There was no way I could have carried it all. Don't you remember how your father was always afraid that he'd be trapped in the safe and would suffocate?"

Red grinned in understanding. "Dad's hidden escape tunnel out the back of the safe."

"I just moved everything from the safe to the hidden escape tunnel behind it," Yellow Bird explained. "The gold and silver chests were heavy. I pushed everything in with my legs. I took all the paper deeds with me in case he found the tunnel."

Tom jerked in surprise. "As far as Butcher knew, you'd hauled his wealth away with you."

Yellow Bird's shiny black eyes sparkled. She reached over and took Tom's hand. "Yes, that was my plan."

Doc thought for a moment. "But something went wrong."

"The freezing wet snow fell heavily from the sky, and the roads were slick with mud and ice. This was good, because soon my tracks would be covered, but my horse slipped and I was thrown off. The horse raced back to the ranch."

"That's why they thought you'd left on foot," Red said.

"Yes. I walked the rest of the way to the old tribe camp that I'd taken you to so many years ago. The camp was empty, so I crawled into a dark cave.

"I was cold and soaked with mud and icy rain. I covered myself with my buffalo robe and waited to meet the Sun."

Sinful asked quickly, "The morning sun?"

"The Blackfoot god," Doc whispered.

"Yes," Yellow Bird said. "I was ready to die. I was sad that I would never see my sons or Tom again, but I was free. And I had the stolen deeds with me. I believed that whoever found my body would at least know that I tried my best."

"Then what happened?" Big John asked anxiously.

"I heard sounds in the cave. I expected it to be some wild beast. I pulled out my knife. I would fight to my death if I must."

Sinful's eyes had grown huge. "Dang!" he exclaimed, followed by deep gulp of air. He hadn't realized he'd been holding his breath.

Doc fought back a smile.

The camp was silent as everyone leaned forward to hear what happened next.

"I froze, trying to see in the darkened cave. Unexpectedly, a young voice asked, 'Yellow Bird, are you all right?' I could not tell who spoke, but I answered that I was in trouble. Then a light was made, and I saw Sinopa-Fox, Chief Black Cloud's oldest daughter. She had seen me crawl into the cave and followed me."

Yellow Bird held up her hand, and a beautiful young Indian maiden came shyly to her. Yellow Bird pulled her down in front of her and wrapped her arms around her.

"She had returned to the camp to search for a beaded necklace that her mother made for her. She was afraid to tell her mother that she'd lost it, so she returned alone, without telling anyone from the tribe where she was going."

"And she will never do such a thing again," the chief said firmly. "Great was the worry of our tribe when we found that she was missing."

Yellow Bird smiled at the chief. "She has promised, but even you have to admit that she has the great courage of a chief's daughter."

Chief Black Cloud looked tenderly at his daughter but refused to smile, even though the pride for his daughter showed in his eyes.

Yellow Bird continued. "She had just found the necklace when she saw me crawl into the cave. Sinopa-Fox saved my life and brought me back to her camp. Her father, Chief Black Cloud, was exceedingly brave to hide me, because I told him that many bad white men would be searching for me."

"That is the reason I wanted you to leave," Chief Black Cloud explained. "I had great fear for the safety of your mother. I had only seen you when you were small." Chief Black Cloud shrugged. "Then Lightning Knife saved the life of my daughter."

"Who's Lightning Knife?" Sinful asked in a whisper to Doc. "You."

"Dang!" Sinful glanced up and saw that Chief Black Cloud had stopped speaking and was watching him. Sinful lowered his head and mumbled, "Sorry, Chief."

The chief continued after a smile. "This was not the action of a bad man. I sent Sinopa-Fox to Yellow Bird to come quietly and observe you."

Yellow Bird placed her hand on Tom's. "This has been a long winter for me. At last I feel safe and free."

Doc stood and said to Chief Black Cloud, "Great is the debt that Fire Hair and I owe Chief Black Cloud and his people and especially Sinopa-Fox. I'm happy that my friend, Lightning Knife, saved your daughter, for that in some small way starts the repayment of my debt to you, but it will take many moons before I can fully repay you for what you have done. My brother, Fire Hair, and I thank you."

CHAPTER TWENTY-ONE

Tom Frost leaned against the willow-rod backrest inside the tepee and smiled. "I've dreamed of this day for so long, I'm having trouble finding the words to describe how happy I am."

"It's the same with us," Doc said. "To have our mother safe after all these years is almost inconceivable."

Sinful stretched his legs and beamed at his moccasin boots.

"Sinful," Big John said. "You're going to break your face if you don't stop grinning at your new boots like that."

"But, Big John, I not only got this great pair of moccasin boots, I even got a great Indian name, Lightning Knife. Isn't that wonderful?"

"I believe, Sinful," Yellow Bird said, "that the tribe has had as much pleasure from your gift as you have. Seeing you step around the camp with your new moccasin boots and all the children following you made everyone laugh."

"He was crazy, Mom," Red said. "Even Chief Black Cloud kept laughing when he was with the children. And he's not a chief who laughs much."

Sinful shrugged. "I loved the children. They are just like ours."

"Yes, they are," Doc said. "It's too bad that a whole bunch of white folks don't understand that. I didn't realize you loved kids so much."

"They're my weakness. Kids just seem to take to me. I had so much fun dancing around the camp with them all behind me."

* * *

Later that evening, Yellow Bird reached over and took Doc's hand. She said sadly, "It just doesn't seem fair."

"I know, Mom," Doc said. "But I have to agree with Tom's plan. It's the best one to assure your safety. There's a stagecoach swing station not that far from us. Tom and Red will go with you. Once you get to Helena, let as few people see you as possible until we get back with word about Rocky, Richie, and Butcher. Do not, under any circumstance, go to Elk Forks."

"I understand. But why can't you just come home?" Yellow Bird said, her voice sad. "I've missed you so much."

"You know why, Mom," Doc said. "This business with Butcher has to be taken care of."

Red rubbed his wild red hair roughly. "Doc, I don't like your going off without me."

"I know, but it's not fair to place that responsibility on Tom. He's not good with a gun, and if there's trouble, he's more likely to be killed than anyone."

Tom sighed heavily. "I'm sorry, but I'll stand in front of Yellow Bird no matter what. Even if I can't shoot." Tom frowned when he realized what he had just said. "That's not what you needed to hear, was it?"

"Don't worry about it, Tom," Doc said. "You're skilled at so many things that not being able to use a gun isn't really that important. Perhaps there will come a time when none of us has to carry one."

"With men like Butcher around, that's unlikely to happen anytime soon," Big John said with a black glare at the fire.

"Tom, when you get to Helena, talk to your lawyer friend you were telling us about and see what he advises as the best way to handle the stolen deeds."

"I'll take care of it."

* * *

Outside in the warmth of the sunlight, Yellow Bird, Red, and Doc talked quietly while they waited for the stagecoach to arrive. Although the nights were cold, the days were filled with fall: yellows and reds, smells of the changing season, and gentle breezes.

The station agent said that the stage had been running on time; he didn't expect a delay. He and the stock tenders were busy harnessing up the fresh horses. This would be a quick stop for the stage, with only enough time for the passengers to use the outside facility, walk about a bit to relieve their cramped muscles, and grab a cup of coffee or a drink of fresh water from the well.

Big John pointed up the road, and they could make out the stage heading toward them. The stagecoach rushed into the swing station trailing a huge cloud of dust that spilled over everyone once the stage stopped. Only two passengers stepped out. One was a drummer, thin of face and tired looking. The other was a tough-looking man with a wide hat and an unruly, bushy mustache and goatee. He glanced over at Red, did a double take, and came to him. "Are you Red Whitfield?"

Then he saw Doc standing behind Red in his black cape. "And you must be Doc Whitfield. Well, Marshal Kramer said I'd have no problem spotting you, and he was right. I'm John Beidler, deputy US marshal."

"When did you see Dave…uh, Marshal Kramer?" Red asked.

"The stage had a stopover in Virginia City, and when I saw them step off, I had a chat with them. Good men. They were heading home, back to Colorado. He and Marshal Jones told me about your situation. They asked me to help you out if I ran into you. They filled me in on your problem. How's it going?"

Red pointed at his mom. "We found our mother, and we're taking her home."

"Well done, boys. What about this criminal named Butcher and his gang of cutthroats?"

"We're still looking for them," Doc said.

"I, of course, can't condone this vigilante stuff, but this territory has too many outlaws for me to get them all."

"Marshal," Red said, "I was planning to go back to Helena with my mom because our friend Tom, here, isn't the best with a gun. You wouldn't be heading to Helena, would you?"

"Stopping there." His head dipped slightly in thought. "You wouldn't need someone to ride shotgun and keep an eye on them?"

"We'd be mighty obliged, if you wouldn't mind," Red said. "I'd like to stay with my brother and finish this business."

"I understand." He turned to Yellow Bird. "I'd be honored to offer my protection to you, ma'am, and your friend, if that would be all right with you."

Yellow Bird smiled graciously and said, "That would be most kind of you, sir. I'd feel better if my boys were with each other during this difficult time."

Tom, the last to get on the stage, yelled back at Doc and Red, "Come home soon, boys. Your mom won't marry me unless her sons are with her."

"As soon as we can, Tom, and that's a promise," Red said with a final wave.

* * *

Doc watched the stagecoach rumble out of sight in a moving cloud of dust, then slowly turned and went back to his horse. "That was hard. To have finally found her, then send her away from us again." His face muscles tightened.

Red sighed deeply. He sat in the wagon with Big John and asked, "Should I have gone anyway?"

"I don't mean you any offense, big brother, but Marshal Beidler is the best man for getting her home safely. Tom can't shoot, and you need to be within three feet to bang anyone on the head with your skillet."

"I have my shotgun."

"Right. And how long has it been since you fired it?"

"A while."

"How long?"

Red slowly grinned. "All right, a long time."

"Besides," Big John said, "I've gotten used to having a coachman. Not sure I could even drive this rig by myself anymore."

"Is it Rocky time?" Sinful asked with a big grin.

"You're having a fine time, aren't you?" Doc asked.

Sinful lifted his left leg and showed off his new moccasin boot. "Look at that. I'd never be wearing them if I were out minding cattle. I've had more excitement since I joined up with you than I've had in my whole life." He slipped his foot back into his stirrup and added, "Today is the first time since I was a kid that my feet haven't hurt. I just love your Blackfoot people."

"Well, dang, Sinful," Red said. "Let's go find Rocky."

Big John took off his hat and slapped Red on the shoulder with it. "Don't you even think of picking up Sinful's bad words."

Red picked up the reins and called out to the horses, "Git up, girls. Big John's getting crabby."

Big John growled under his breath, but he had a slight grin on his face.

CHAPTER TWENTY-TWO

Red parked the wagon down the street from the Bannack Saloon. Doc waited for him and Big John on the wooden sidewalk. His nervous breath puffed like Indian smoke signals in the cold air. He took off his cape and laid it in the back of the wagon. Instantly he felt the cold penetrate his black vest and long-sleeved black wool shirt. He rubbed his arms to keep himself warm.

"You sure you want to leave your cape here?" Red asked.

"Can't afford to have it snag my gun, even as good as the cape is. Rocky's too fast for even the slightest mistake. Sinful told me that Rocky is inside drinking and playing cards. Looks like three gunfighters have joined up with him."

Doc took a deep breath and flexed his shoulders to relax. "I sent Sinful back inside. He's sure that Rocky's never seen him in Elk Forks. He'll cover my back. Red, I want you to make sure no one walks in the front door while I'm having my little chat with Rocky. Big John, if you'd keep an eye on the back door, I'd be obliged."

Big John reached into the wagon and lifted out his Henry. "Ask him where Butcher is, won't you?"

"I'll do that. I'll give you a few minutes to get around back."

Big John walked quickly between two buildings and soon was out of sight.

Red held his shotgun pointed downward as they walked to the saloon door. "You want me to watch you from here?"

"No, stay away from the door. I don't want a stray bullet hitting you or some innocent folk. Just stand to the side. Once the shooting stops, you'll know it's safe to come in." Doc paused, "Or you will need to finish what I started."

"Understand." Red sighed. "Let me come in with you."

Doc shook his head. "No. We've talked about this. It has to be this way."

Red stared at Doc for a long, silent moment. Finally, he said, "I sure don't like this. I don't like the odds." He reached up and nervously readjusted his hat. "You," he paused, "be smooth with your draw."

Doc reached out and grabbed Red's arm. "Thanks, big brother." Then he turned and walked in the door.

Two cowboys came down the walk and started toward the saloon door, but Red blocked their way, bringing up his shotgun. He shook his head. "Sorry, boys, there's going to be some shooting going on in a few minutes. I don't want you to meet your maker any sooner than needed."

The younger cowboy started to sit on the bench to the right of the door. The saloon window was behind it. "Mind if we wait?"

"I'd sit on the other one." Red pointed to the bench on the left side; there was a solid wall behind it. "That glass window won't be of much use in stopping a bullet."

"Friend of yours inside?" the older cowboy asked as they moved to the left bench.

"My brother."

The older cowboy pulled out a tobacco plug and bit off a chew. "A personal matter?"

"A man inside shot our uncle in the back."

"Damn!" the younger cowboy exclaimed. "Don't suppose I could peek through the door?"

Red shook his head somberly. "Not if you value your life."

* * *

Doc stood for a moment inside the door and let his eyes adjust to the dim light. The long, narrow saloon had a twelve-foot fancy oak bar that ran along the left wall with a long mirror behind it. Two men were at opposite ends of the bar, each drinking a beer.

Unlit oil lamps hung from the crossbeams, and the exposed slate roof showed where it had leaked. The rough-hewn log walls and wide plank floor were dark with age and smoke from the lamps. A long shelf under the mirror held various bottles of whiskey and glasses.

To his right, next to the front window, a man was getting a shave in a barber chair. Neither the barber nor his customer noticed Doc; the barber was busy soaping up the man's face.

Without a coat or heavy vest on, he stood out, and a few men eyed him uneasily, with his Colt hung low and ominous.

Five tables were in a line along the right wall, with men drinking or playing cards at three of them. Sinful leaned casually against the wall, pretending to watch a poker game at the middle table.

Doc took a quick, nervous breath, lifted his Colt slightly from his holster, and let it slide back smoothly. The movement didn't go unnoticed by two men at the front table. One leaned over and whispered to the other. They gulped the last of their drinks, then quickly got up and left the saloon. Doc watched them silently as they hurried past him.

Rocky and three other gunmen were playing faro at the table at the rear of the saloon. Rocky had his back against the wall so he could face the bar and the front door. Doc walked to the middle of the bar and with a quick glance at the bartender, said softly, "I'd be obliged if you kept your hands on top of the bar."

The bartender started to argue, then took a good look at Doc's determined face and placed his hands on the bar.

"Hello, Rocky," Doc said in a loud voice. "Shot anyone in the back lately?"

Instantly there was silence in the saloon. Rocky laid his cards down and took a swig from a half-empty glass of whiskey. "Time for you to die, Doc. Hoping you'd show up so I wouldn't have to waste time looking for you." He stood and his two hired guns got up with him.

The man at Rocky's table with his back to Doc stood slowly. The faro board was on the table in front of him. He turned and showed his empty hands to Doc. "I'm only the gambler here. Not my fight." He moved quickly behind the bar and stood with the bartender.

The two gunmen with Rocky were young. One had four scars that ran down his left cheek. The other wore his gun at an angle for a cross draw.

"I'm sorry Tex isn't here to see me kill you, Doc. He'd enjoy the show."

Doc remained silent and waited, realizing that the third gunman accompanying Rocky was one of the men at the bar, and he was between the two.

Before Doc could decide what to do, he heard a whoosh behind him followed by a sharp, raspy wheeze.

The hired gun behind him fell against the bar, then to the floor. His gun skidded across the plank floor toward the barber's chair.

"Dang it, Doc," Sinful said softly. "Someone's always trying to shoot you in the back."

Doc glanced quickly in the mirror behind the bar. He saw the dead gunman on the floor as Sinful hurried to retrieve his knife. Doc's eyes snapped back to Rocky.

Rocky frowned at his dead man.

"Shouldn't have been drinking, Rocky," Doc said softly. "Slows a man down."

"I'll show you," Rocky said as he went for his gun. He fumbled the draw slightly as he started his move. Doc's first shot lifted Rocky off his feet and slammed him against the wall—dead.

The cross-draw gunman had just pulled his weapon from its holster when Doc's second shot struck him in the left shoulder. He yelled and crashed to the floor. The third hired gun got off one wild shot before Doc's next bullet hit him in the stomach and slammed him back against the wall. Before the man could get off a second shot, Doc's fourth bullet struck him in the chest. He slid silently to the floor.

The cross-draw gunfighter was struggling to bring his gun up to fire at Doc when there was a flash of metal and Sinful's knife struck the gunman in the chest. The man's arms flung backward. Sinful's knife had finished him instantly.

Red came through the door with his shotgun raised and hurried to where Doc stood. The men in the saloon immediately dove under the tables.

Doc quickly checked the bartender. The man wasn't even looking at Doc; with shaking hands he was trying to pour himself and the gambler a drink. The whiskey mostly missed the glasses and splashed over the countertop.

The back door swung open with a crash and Big John came through with his Henry pointing forward. The bartender and gambler immediately ducked behind the bar. Big John took in the destruction and said, "I bet you forgot to ask him where Butcher was, didn't you?"

Doc took a long breath and said in a tight voice, "Sorry, Big John."

Big John studied Doc intently, then said seriously, "You did good. Put your Colt away."

Doc reholstered his Colt smoothly. He glared at the dead men in front of him and mumbled angrily, "That was for you, Uncle Herb."

"Come on," Red said. He hurried Doc out of the saloon.

Sinful went to the cross-draw gun slick and pulled his knife from the body. Big John grunted for Sinful to go before him as he covered their exit by walking out backward, keeping his Henry pointed at the men left in the saloon.

The bartender and the gambler slowly rose from behind the bar. "Ain't never seen anything like that before in my whole life," the gambler said.

All the bartender could do was clear his throat in agreement as the rest of the men in the saloon slowly moved closer to look at the four bodies.

* * *

Later that evening, Red paced outside the Blackfoot sweat lodge. Sinful joined Red and said, "He's been in there a long time."

"The shaman is flushing the angry spirits out of Doc. No telling how long it will take."

"How do they do it?

"Mostly they use hot stones and pour water on them to make steam seven times, then they repeat the cycle four more times. The songs they sing are sacred songs."

"What's that I smell?"

Red sniffed. "Sage or sweetgrass, I think."

Sinful fell in step with Red. "Red, I don't understand why he's angry. I would have thought he'd be really happy to kill those men who killed your uncle."

Red stopped and put his hand on Sinful's shoulder. "It's about not being able to bring our Uncle Herb back after he killed Rocky. That got Doc angry and sad at the same time. I know it sounds strange, but that's how he is."

"I guess I can understand that." They walked together a few more steps and Sinful said, "Red, I've never seen a man draw a gun and fire as fast as Doc did today. I didn't even see it happen."

"Doc told me if you hadn't gotten the man behind him, he'd be dead," Red said.

"I'm glad I was there for him. I've never had a friend as special as Doc."

Red placed his hand on Sinful's shoulder and gave it a squeeze. "You've saved all our lives a number of times on this trip. Thanks."

Sinful grinned up at Red. "This has been the most incredible trip I've ever been on. Where to now?"

"We'll hit a couple of mining camps close by here and then decide where to go next."

"I heard Doc say that Big John won the draw. What was that about?"

"Doc promised that after we found Mom, they would draw to see who would get to kill Butcher. Big John won. That pleased him."

"Really?" Sinful asked with a knowing grin.

Red smiled down at Sinful. "Well, Doc may have rigged the draw. That was another thing that made Doc mad. That Butcher had Big John's wife killed. Doc told me it wouldn't be fair unless Big John got to take Butcher down."

* * *

Late that evening, Doc and Red sat by the fire; Sinful and Big John were asleep. Doc spoke softly, his voice relaxed as he stared into the flames, slowly drinking cold water from a tin cup. "You know, after I killed those men today, I just got angry. I kept thinking not a single one of them was worth Uncle Herb. I know that was stupid of me, but it just sort of bubbled up out of nowhere."

"I understand that, Doc."

Doc let out a long frustrated sigh. "We've met our share of evil men, huh? Remember the two men who Butcher sent to kill us?"

Red nodded.

"They tried to kill us just for money. To take a life for money doesn't make any sense to me at all. Life is so precious, and to kill someone is such a waste. It just makes me so angry. I'm trying to keep people alive, and these evil men are going around taking innocent lives. You'd think anyone would have more sense— would want to cherish life." Doc scowled at the fire.

"I told you about what happened on the train coming back here," he continued. "Two robbers stopped the train, and one shot a pregnant woman. Can you believe that? He shot an unarmed, pregnant woman! I couldn't believe it. I drew and killed him while he held his gun on me. That was really stupid of me, but I was so angry, I knew I couldn't be stopped." Doc sighed.

"Then a bad thing happened in town where the train stopped to drop off the body of the robber. A drunken cowboy almost forced me into a gunfight. For the first time I was worried I might have to kill someone who I didn't want to hurt. The Wells Fargo special agent I told you about, Robert Mock, convinced him to try a practice shooting. When the cowboy saw me draw, that sobered him up quick." Doc smiled slightly.

"Robert told me he wasn't too quick with a gun, but let me tell you, he was plenty quick with his brain. I learned a valuable lesson from him on that one. I've got to be smarter about using this weapon."

"Did the shaman help?" Red asked.

Doc slowly sipped the water from his cup. "Yes. Yes, he did. He told me not to get angry at evil men because it was a waste of my energy. I must concentrate on healing. If I become angry it might cloud my judgment, my skills. He told me to just try to be the best medicine man I can be."

"That sounds like good advice," Red said.

"It is, of course, but it's easy to say and much harder to do. Sometimes I wonder if I'm a doctor or really a gunman." Doc turned to Red, and his black eyes glittered orange and red from the reflection of the fire. "What do you think?"

Red poked the fire with a stick. "Doc, you aren't a gunman. You're a doctor, even if you do carry a gun. That Colt is just another instrument in your medical tool kit. You've always been a doctor, a healer, and the fact that you're good with your Colt doesn't change a thing."

Doc stared at Red and nodded slowly as he thought about what Red had said. "I've never thought about it like that, but you're correct. My gun is just like a scalpel. Just another tool for me to use to cut out diseases. I like that."

"Just know," Red said, "that Big John, Sinful, and I aren't standing beside a gunman when we travel with you but beside our friend, the doctor, and my little brother." Red paused, roughly scratched his beard, and added, "However, if it helps, the next time I see you getting angry or losing your concentration, I'll just swat you with my hat."

"Well, I'm all right with that. Just make certain it's your hat and not one of your skillets." Doc reached over and gripped Red's arm. "Thanks. Just having you to talk to helps. It helps a great deal. I've really missed my big brother."

CHAPTER
TWENTY-THREE

"You be Doc Whitfield?"

Doc stopped in front of the man who'd addressed him and nodded suspiciously. He pulled his right hand inside his cape and rested it on the handle of his Colt.

The man had tobacco juice stains on his shabby beard and down the front of his dirty shirt and vest. His smile was forced, and what few teeth he had left were darkly stained. The odor of the man's unwashed body mingled with his stale whiskey breath.

"What do you want?"

"I have information I'd be willing to sell you. Twenty dollars gold. No paper money."

Doc shook his head and said, "Twenty dollars is too much money for information. How about a ten-dollar gold piece if I believe it's worth it?"

"Oh, it's worth it, you'll see." The man spit a stream of tobacco juice into the street and thought a moment. "Buy me a drink, just in case you don't." He started for the saloon behind him.

"Wait," Doc said, thinking the man might be trying to set him up for an ambush. "That one." Doc pointed to a saloon two doors down.

"No matter to me." The man turned and stumbled down to the saloon Doc had indicated. Doc turned around when the man had his back to him and waved at Sinful. Sinful tipped his hat to show that he understood and hurried into the mercantile store to get the others.

The man went directly to the bar. "Whiskey, Tony."

"Show me your money, Scrub," the bartender said gruffly.

Scrub tilted his head at Doc, and Doc laid two coins on the rough wood bar. "Give him a whiskey, and I'll have a beer." Doc waited until they were served, then said, "All right, what do you have that's worth a ten-dollar gold piece?"

"Butcher," Scrub said softly.

"Go on."

"I know you want him. I know where he is."

Doc's eyes narrowed as he studied Scrub. "How do you know Butcher?"

"He tried to hire me and my brother. Sometimes we do a little bounty hunting. Offered us a hundred dollars apiece for all four of you."

In his peripheral vision, Doc saw Sinful come in, followed shortly by Red and finally Big John. They spread out through the saloon.

The bartender saw them, and his lips tightened. He reached under the bar for his shotgun, then stopped when he realized that Big John had placed his Henry on the counter, pointed directly at him. "A beer, my man," Big John said. "And I suggest you keep your hands up where I can see them."

Tony glanced up at Big John's hard face and his dark, threatening eyes and swallowed. He handed Big John the beer and said, "On the house."

"Thanks."

Doc asked Scrub, "So why didn't you take Butcher's offer? Or maybe you did, and you're trying to set me up."

"Nah, no chance of that. I ain't dumb. My brother and me were in the saloon at Bannack when you wiped out Rocky and his boys. Ain't never even saw you draw—you was so damn fast." He let out a breath. "I never saw it." Scrub shuddered as he remembered the scene. Then he grinned at Doc. "Besides, you've got that big redhead over there who just came in." He nodded toward Red, who was standing back in the corner and cradling his shotgun in his arms. "Then there's that blue-eyed, golden-haired kid with the blade that's almost as fast as you and the tall, frightening old man with the Henry standing down the bar right behind me. He's the one I heard ask you if Rocky told you where Butcher was."

"You've got good eyes, Scrub."

"And good ears." Scrub took another sip of his whiskey. "Yup, in my line of work I can't take chances. I may look bad, but I'm not stupid. There's no way I want to go against the Doc Whitfield gang."

Doc tried not to let Scrub's reference to the Doc Whitfield gang bother him. He looked skeptically at Scrub and took a sip of beer as the man continued.

"My brother asked Butcher for half the money. Butcher said he'd only pay us when we brought him your bodies. Four hundred dollars was more than we've seen in a long time. Just then the bartender came up to Butcher and told him to pay for the bottle we was drinking from. That's when we found out he didn't have a tail feather left." Scrub drained his glass and signaled the bartender to fill it again.

The bartender glanced at Doc. Doc laid another coin on the bar.

"Obliged," Scrub said with a quick wipe of his mouth on the back of his hand. "The bartender threw us all out, and we threatened to kill Butcher for trying to set us up. He gave us his pocket watch to let him go." Scrub fumbled in his vest pocket and pulled out a large watch with a slender gold chain attached to it. He displayed it proudly to Doc.

"So where is he?"

"Up near the top of the pass, there's a series of mines that look like old caves. They was dug by some old miners. They never found color, but sometimes people who are down on their luck live up there. You know where I'm talking about?"

"I know."

"He's holed up there. That worth a coin?" Scrub asked.

"Scrub, I'm going to give you a ten-dollar gold coin, and then I'm going up there to see if you're telling the truth." Doc paused. "You remember how good that man was with his knife?"

Scrub's eyes opened wide. "Yes, sir. I remember."

"If Butcher's not there, I'm going to give my man a hundred dollars, the same amount Butcher offered you for my hide, to make sure you don't ever lie to me again."

"He's there, honest." Scrub took the second whiskey and drank it in one gulp. "I don't want your gang after me. It's the truth." He started pulling nervously on his left ear.

"For your sake, I hope so." Doc laid the ten-dollar gold piece on the bar and added two more small coins for a tip to Tony. "You just stay where you are, Scrub, until I'm out of here."

"Yes, sir, I'm not moving." He grabbed the bar as though he needed help standing.

Doc signaled to the others with a quick flip of his head toward the door. Sinful followed him out, then Red. Big John took another swig from his glass and said to Tony, "Thanks for the beer." He walked past Scrub and just let the end of his barrel brush against the back of Scrub's vest. Scrub's back muscles tightened.

Big John turned and quickly scanned the saloon. Satisfied, he slipped sideways through the door and was gone.

Tony went up to Scrub and asked, "Who was that?"

"That was the Doc Whitfield gang. You don't never want to mess with them."

"They outlaws?" Tony asked.

"Nope. Like vigilantes, but they don't hang their men. They shoot them dead, right on the spot when they find them. The man in the black cape was the one who killed Rocky and his three boys in Bannack. He has the fastest draw of any man I've ever seen. Rocky and some others shot his uncle in the back. Bad pox for Rocky."

"That tall, older one looked plenty mean to me."

"They're after Butcher. You know him?"

"The fancy dresser with the big red nose and no money?"

"That's him." He slid the gold piece to Tony. "How about a bottle?"

A man in a suit came up to Scrub. "Sorry, I couldn't help overhearing your story. I'm a writer and new in town. If I bought you dinner and a few drinks, would you mind telling me about that man in the black cape? What'd you call them, the Doc Whitfield gang?"

"That's their name." Scrub's eyes opened wide, and he scooped the ten-dollar gold piece back off the bar. His lips spread into a tobacco-stained smile. "Happy to oblige you, sir."

* * *

"You think he was lying?" Red asked as the wagon moved up the road to the abandoned mines near the pass.

"He could have been," Doc said, "but somehow I've a feeling he's still sore at Butcher for getting them all excited about earning four hundred dollars and then discovering he didn't have any money."

"Sure was a pretty watch Butcher gave them," Big John said with a small chuckle.

Red turned to him in surprise. "Big John, I think that's the first time I've ever heard you laugh."

"I don't know, Red, but I have a good feeling about this." He leaned toward Doc. "Remember, Butcher's mine."

"I know, Big John," Doc said grimly. "I'll only be there to back you up."

"Something else is bothering you," Big John said.

"Scrub called us the Doc Whitfield gang."

"Dang!" Sinful exclaimed. "I'm part of a gang."

"That's not something to be proud of, Sinful," Doc said. "That's a label that will bring gunmen looking for you, looking to make a name by killing you. Folks will shoot you before finding out that you're an honest, hardworking cowboy. People in gangs... well, they die."

"Dang, I surely don't want that. How about we just call ourselves Doc Whitfield's friends?"

Doc managed a grin. "That you are, Sinful. A mighty good friend."

After a long ride up the grade, they came to the road that led off to the abandoned mines. They rested there, giving the horses a chance to blow.

"Do you think I can get this wagon up that road?" Red asked.

Doc and Sinful rode a little way up the road. "It's going to be bumpy, but you shouldn't have any trouble," Sinful yelled back. "Wagons have used it before."

Doc leaned over and spoke softly to Sinful. "You ride back down and tell Red and Big John I see people up ahead with rifles. I don't want to ride into an ambush. Once you tell them, you drift behind the wagon and protect our rear."

"You be careful, Doc," Sinful said seriously.

Doc rode slowly up the road, his eyes scanning ahead for danger. Occasionally, he stopped to study the pine forest on the right. The road was skirting the edge of the mountain and there was a steep drop-off on the left.

Red caught up with him soon after they came out of the trees. "We're above the tree line, but I don't like all these rocks on our right."

Doc ran his hand nervously through his long, black, shiny hair. "What do you think, Big John?"

"I agree with Red. We're easy targets. They start shooting, where will we go? Cliff on our left. Barely enough room for the wagon on the road."

Doc rode his horse around to the rear, dismounted, and tied his horse to the back of the wagon. He placed his cape and vest in the wagon.

"Give me five minutes, then start forward slow and easy."

"Doc, what're you up to?" Big John asked.

"Letting the Indian in me out. Tell them, Red." Doc turned and quickly trotted up the rocky slope and behind some large boulders. Suddenly he was gone.

Sinful sat back in his saddle in surprise. "Dang, did you see that? One minute he's up there by that big boulder, and next minute he's gone."

Red glanced at his pocket watch. Big John waited and finally asked, "All right, Red. Tell us what?"

"Doc used to love to play hide-and-seek with me. I could never find him. When he got older, he'd do the same with our Indian friends. Hardly anyone ever found him. He was like a ghost. And what's even scarier, he used to wait, and then jump out at me. He'd frightened me so much I'd jump around like I had yellow jackets in my pants. Some of our Indian friends quit playing with us because Doc would scare them so badly."

Red picked up the reins, and the horses moved slowly up the rocky road toward the abandoned mines. When they got closer, Big John pointed to three men with rifles watching them approach. Red stopped and yelled up at them. "Permission to come on in?"

"Who are you and what do you want?"

"We just need to talk to you for a minute."

"Turn your wagon around and—"

The men on the hill abruptly dropped their rifles and lifted their hands in the air. Red turned to Big John. "See what I mean?" He touched the reins, and the horses moved forward into the makeshift camp.

The three men walked forward with their hands in the air and Doc directly behind them. When they got to the wagon, Doc said, "Big John, keep an eye on them for me. I need to get my vest and cape back on. It's cold in these mountains."

Sinful frowned at one man. "Elias, is that you?"

The man glanced up at Sinful and his eyes opened wide in surprise. "Sinful, good to see you. Tell your friends that we have no money and damn little food."

Sinful gestured to Big John, who pointed with his Henry for the men to put their hands down.

"Elias, what happened to your plans to find the big gold stream and strike it rich?" Sinful asked.

Elias pushed out his lips in an ugly pout. "Worst years of my life. Worked from sunup to dark in freezing water, shoveling and digging until I thought my back was going to break, and all I ever got was enough flakes to keep me from starving. Couldn't dig during the winter, so even badder then."

"Sorry," Sinful said. He looked at the squalor the men were living in. "What now? Find another gold field?"

"My gold fever's gone. I just want to get home and get a real job with real pay. We—my buddies here and me—finally dug enough to get us back when this fancy dresser came up here and asked if he could stay a few nights. Said he was down on his luck."

Doc came around the wagon with his black cape back on.

Elias pointed at Doc. "Where'd you come from? One moment there was no one behind us and the next we hear you cocking your Colt. Plumb near scared us to death."

"See what I told you?" Red grinned at Big John. "Just like old times."

"You two friends?" Doc asked Sinful.

"Elias and I grew up together. We traveled out West together to become cowboys after my folks died, but he got gold fever."

"You were talking about a fancy dresser. He give you a name?" Doc asked.

"Yeah, Butcher. Then this morning he came riding back into camp like he'd just seen the devil himself. He was all pale and sweaty and having a hard time breathing. Kept mumbling that they'd joined forces and were going to hang him.

"When I asked who was after him, he just shook his head and kept looking down the trail like whoever it was be right behind him."

"Dang," Sinful said. "So what happened?"

"He drew a gun on us and took the little gold we had and our horses. Then the thieving bastard rode off north. Made me tie up my friends, then he tied me."

"But Elias didn't tie me tight," the man standing beside Elias added. "So once Butcher was gone, I got us all untied. We'd have gone after him, but he got our horses, so wasn't nothing we could do."

Elias shrugged. "Don't have bullets for the rifles either, so it probably wouldn't have mattered even if he had left them, except now we don't have any way to get home. Too late in the season to try to pan more flakes."

"You sure he was heading north when he left?" Doc asked.

"Oh, I'm sure. Said he was going back to his ranch and get his gold."

"But he was hurting," the other man said.

"What do you mean, hurting?"

"Breathing bad, and he must have been in some pain because he was sufferin' and his face showed it."

"You don't think he's going back to our ranch?" Doc asked Red.

"That doesn't make sense. Maybe he saw us in town."

"I agree," Big John said. "It sure sounds like he was talking about us."

Doc mounted his horse and said, "I thank you for the information. Sorry about your circumstances."

Red started to lift his reins when Big John reached over and stopped him. "Sinful, are you and Elias good friends or just acquaintances?"

"We're good friends, Big John. We grew up in the same town. Our folks were friends. Makes me feel bad to see him hurting like this."

Big John waved his hand. "Elias, come here a minute."

Elias walked to the wagon. Big John reached into his vest pocket and pulled out one of the bags of gold he'd taken from the killers in Kansas. He handed the bag to Elias. "Maybe this will help you and your friends get back home."

Elias judged the weight with his hands. "Mister, this bag is almost double the weight of what Butcher took from us." Elias shook his head in wonder. "I don't know how to thank you."

"You already did when you told us about Butcher." Big John paused and added, "But, boys, I don't want you taking that gold and going into town and drinking or gambling or talking to the pretty ladies. You buy some horses and go home straightaway. You hear me?" Big John looked at them sternly.

"Yes, sir, we won't go astray. We all just want to get home."

Big John's black eyes bored into each man. "Do that, boys. Do that." Then he told Red to get going.

"Wait, sir," Elias yelled. "Might I ask your name?"

The wagon was already moving. "Warner. John Warner."

Elias held up the bag and yelled, "Thank you, Mr. Warner. We won't ever forget your kindness."

After they'd gone back down to the main road, Red pulled the horses to a stop. "That was a mighty fine thing you did back there, Big John."

Sinful rode up to the wagon. "Red's right, Big John. You just made me feel real warm inside when you did that."

Big John shook his head, embarrassed.

Doc leaned forward and crossed his hands on the saddle horn. "Yup, that surely hurts your tough cowboy image."

Big John's eyes lifted quickly to Doc from under his hat, and for a moment a slight grin crossed his face. He jabbed Red in the side with his elbow and said, "Let's get this freight train rolling, Red. We've got Butcher to catch."

Red gently flicked the reins.

CHAPTER TWENTY-FOUR

Red and Doc squatted on the road and studied the marks. The hour was late, and in the dim light it was hard to see.

Sinful leaned from his saddle and asked, "How can you make sense out of all the horse tracks on this road?"

"Well," Doc said as he stood, "the rain last night washed a bunch of the old tracks away."

Red pointed down. "But the most important thing is that Butcher is keeping the three horses he stole from your friends, and one has a cracked horseshoe." He pointed to a single track in the road.

"That's a mighty distinct mark," Sinful said.

"He's pushing those horses too hard." Doc pointed off to the left. "There's a small Blackfoot camp up ahead. I'm going to ride over and see if they saw him."

"You want us to come along?" Red asked.

"Sure. Sinful, maybe you can knife another rattler and get a second pair of moccasin boots."

Sinful watched Red search around in the back of the wagon. "What're you digging for?"

"Cookies."

"For us?" Sinful asked with a grin on his face.

"Nope, for them." Red pointed to the Indian camp.

* * *

Later that night, Doc squatted in front of the fire. "Kind of Chief Heavy Runner to invite us to stay with him in his camp."

Red grinned. "It was my cookies that did it."

"I hate to admit it," Doc said, "but you do have a way with your baked goods that always makes us welcome."

"So Butcher had to trade three of his horses for food," Big John said. "That will slow him down."

"Chief Heavy Runner told me he thought Butcher would have tried to rob them if his braves didn't all have rifles. The chief didn't like him, so Butcher just ended up trading for food. The chief said they would have given him food if he'd been a good man."

"That chief was a good judge of character," Big John said. "So what did they give him for three horses?"

"A parfleche bag of pemmican and dried apples," Sinful said. "I tried the pemmican and it didn't taste too good."

"I remember eating that," Big John said, his face suddenly sad.

"Doc told me they pound meat and mix it with melted fat. I tried some that had berries in it." Sinful made a face. "I'd have to be mighty hungry to enjoy it."

Doc laughed. "It was good. You notice that Red didn't have a problem gulping his down."

"Felt like old times to be eating it again," Red said.

"Golden Eagle and I would eat it while we sat at our favorite place overlooking the valley by our home." Big John quickly glanced away from them and blinked rapidly.

"Why don't you finish up what's left in my bag, Big John," Red said gently.

"What was interesting was the medicine woman, Pana," Doc said. "I'd met her many years ago up at the Marias River encampment near Fort Benton. When I told her that Yellow Bird was my mom, she remembered me. She told me that Butcher is sick. She could tell."

"Good. He'll feel even worse when I shoot him in the stomach and watch him die," Big John said as he munched a mouthful of pemmican from Red's bag.

* * *

The next morning, Big John pointed to a large meadow off to the right of the road. "See that loose strawberry roan up there?" he asked Doc. "That's not a wild horse. It looks like it's limping bad."

"You and Red stay here. Sinful and I will ride up and see what's wrong."

As they neared the horse, Sinful looked down and pointed to the mark in the wet grass and mud. "Got a broken right horseshoe. It's Butcher's horse. That was dumb of him. The horse he kept was a real broom-tail."

"Never try to outsmart a Blackfoot when it comes to trading horses."

"He obviously doesn't know much about horses," Sinful said. "This one has gone lame."

Doc stood in his stirrups and called for Red to bring the wagon up. "If it's Butcher's horse, then we need to be extremely careful." He pointed ahead to a cabin at the edge of the meadow. "No smoke coming out of the chimney, but he might be holed up there."

Big John stepped down from the wagon after Doc told him about the horse and the cabin. He grabbed his Henry.

"I don't think Butcher had a rifle with him," Sinful said.

"Just a handgun, according to the chief."

"Boys, here's where my Henry is better than your fancy toy guns. I'll just meander up to that cabin and see what we have."

Doc dismounted, slipped out of his cape, and threw it over his saddle. "If you don't mind, I'll go along too." He held up his hand. "I know, Butcher's yours, but I'd feel better if I were covering your back."

"That makes sense," Big John said without taking his eyes off the cabin. "Someone's up there. I just saw some movement by the far front window."

Doc grabbed his binoculars from his saddlebag and the men set off. When they got closer, they stopped, and Doc studied the cabin with the binoculars. "No glass in the windows. Just shutters they can pull closed. Looks to be one room, and tiny. A mighty poor family. No animals."

Big John scratched his week-old beard. "I figure I can walk to that water well, and if he's inside, he still couldn't hit me at that range with his handgun."

Doc scanned the area around the cabin. "All grassland, as far as I can see. No place for someone to hide. I'll just hang back about ten feet in case he's got a surprise for your back."

"Appreciate that."

Big John cocked the Henry and started walking slowly forward. After he'd gone ten steps, Doc matched steps with him. When Big John got to the well, he stopped. A rifle barrel came out the window, and a young boy yelled, "Stop right there or you're a dead man."

Doc hurried to Big John. "Well, that's certainly not Butcher's voice."

Big John yelled out. "We mean you no harm. We're chasing a very bad man who was on that lame strawberry roan back there. Did you see him?"

"He tried to get in but I chased him off."

"What'd he want?" Doc asked.

"Wanted to use our water, but it's gone."

"How are you getting by without water?" Big John asked.

"We make do."

Big John turned and pointed to some markers off to the left. "See what that is."

Doc studied the spot with his binoculars. "A cemetery. Two graves, and they look fairly recent."

Sinful hurried to them on foot. "It's not Butcher, is it?"

Big John shook his head and turned to Sinful. "Run back to the wagon and bring a canteen of water. Make those new boots of yours move fast."

Sinful took off at a dead run.

"What are you thinking?" Doc asked.

"I've a feeling we've got a really scared little boy in that cabin, all alone."

The depth of sadness in Big John's face surprised Doc. "Well then, we need to help him."

Big John said softly, "A frightened little boy with a loaded rifle is a dangerous animal. We have to be extremely careful." He thought for a moment. "Doc, I need an Indian ghost that can sneak around back of that cabin and see if there's another way in, nice and quiet-like. We don't want to frighten him more than he already is."

"I understand."

Sinful ran back with the canteen. He handed it to Big John.

"Boy," Big John called, "we have water we'd be happy to share with you. I 'spect you're hungry too. So we'd be happy to share some food with you." Big John opened the canteen and took a long draw and let the water dribble out the corner of his mouth.

The rifle barrel disappeared from the window, replaced by a thin little boy's face. "I'd like some water but you can't come in."

"That's fine," Big John said. "You have a cup?"

"Yes, sir."

"Go get it," Big John said. When the boy's face disappeared from the window, Doc ran toward the back of the cabin.

Big John slowly walked to the cabin. In a moment the boy returned to the window. He was so eager for the water that he didn't appear to even notice that Doc was missing.

Big John told the boy to hold out the cup, and he filled it. The boy gulped the water down quickly and held out the cup for more. This time, much to Big John's surprise, the boy rushed away from the window. Big John leaned in and saw that the boy was trying to pour some water down a frail little girl's throat. She coughed and refused the water. "Please, Jenna, try to drink a little."

The back of the cabin didn't have a door, but a cloth hung over an opening. Doc silently came inside the cabin and knelt beside the children. He placed his hand on the little girl's forehead. "How long has she been sick?" Doc asked, his voice gentle and soft.

"Three days. Two days after we ran out of water." If the little boy was surprised or frightened by Doc's sudden appearance, he didn't show it.

Big John and Sinful entered the cabin through the unlocked front door.

"Dad died first. Then a week later, Mom died. Powerful hard burying my mom."

Sinful knelt beside the little boy, gently placed his arm around him, and said, "That's Doc Whitfield. He's a mighty fine doctor, and he's going to make your sister well."

The little boy put his arms around Sinful and said tearfully, "I'm so hungry and tired."

Sinful picked him up and said, "We're going to get you something to eat right now."

Red hurried into the cabin. Doc looked up and said, "Red, you've got a baker's nose. Do you smell anything strange or different in here?"

Red sniffed. "There's a bad smell in here, not quite as bad as the inside of Sinful's old boots, but bad."

"Dang, Red. That's not a kindly thing to say. I'm going to take the boy out to the wagon and get him something to eat." Sinful hurried off to the wagon.

Red grinned after Sinful, then said to Doc. "We need to get this little girl out of this place. I'm not sure what that smell is, but it has the smell of death to me."

Doc reached down and picked up the child. "She's burning up with fever. Big John, check the cabin and see if there's anything that has information about the children."

Big John glanced around the barren cabin doubtfully.

"Anything that tells who these kids are. Any papers. Pictures. Maybe a Bible with the family history in it." Doc hurried to the door, cradling the little girl in his arms. He stopped in the doorway and added, "Then burn this place down."

* * *

Both children were asleep in the bed of the wagon. It was early afternoon. Doc paced, frowning and mumbling to himself. Finally he stopped and told Sinful, "You keep putting cold cloths on Jenna. I need herbs. I'm sure she's got mountain fever."

Red stood beside the kettle where he was making a stew. "You're going to ride into Chief Heavy Runner's camp and get herbs from Pana, the medicine woman, aren't you?"

Doc shook his head. "I'm going to get Pana. I remember Mom telling me Pana was the wisest medicine woman she'd ever known."

"Smart doctor. Not too proud to ask for help," Big John said. "Go. I'll keep a watch on things here."

"Big John, I know this means Butcher is getting away from us."

"Never mind. Butcher's not worth the lives of these little ones. Besides, he's on foot." He turned and looked north. "Somehow I just feel we're still going to catch him. You go, Doc. I'll make sure our family is safe."

Doc leaped onto his horse. "I like that. Keep our family safe."

* * *

Sinful pointed at the tepees around them and said to Big John, "Dang, when Doc said he was going after the medicine woman and her herbs, I didn't expect him to bring the whole tribe back with him."

Big John grinned. "Where Doc's concerned, I'm beginning to learn not to be surprised."

Sinful thought about Big John's words. "You know, you're right." He looked down at his boots, then at the boy he held in his arms. "This trip has been so remarkable. Here I am wearing Indian moccasin boots that are so comfortable, I don't know that I have them on. And I'm sitting here holding Dane as though he were my own son."

"I surely wish we had found some records about the children," Big John said. "I guess it's not surprising not to find anything. Dane told us his folks couldn't read. But not to have any record of them just..." Big John sighed, leaving his thought unfinished. "They sure have latched onto you, Sinful. That's a serious responsibility."

"I know. I've been thinking about that a bunch. They don't even know when they were born. Dane thinks he's ten and was born in May. He says Jenna is six and that she was born in March." Sinful slowly rocked Dane back and forth. "He's too old for me to be rocking him like this, but he's so dang little."

"And so frightened and hurting," Big John added.

"They both are," Red said as he came out of a tepee and sat beside them. "Doc figures it's been a long time since they've had enough to eat, and then to have to bury your parents..." Red slowly rubbed his eyes. "They're too young to have to go through that," he said in a husky voice.

Big John leaned over, poked the fire with a stick and asked, "How's Jenna doing?"

"That's why I came out. Doc wants Sinful to go into the tent and sit with her. She's drifting in and out, and every time she wakes she cries,"— Red looked at Sinful, —"for you."

"Well, dang, Red, I'd better get right in there. If I wrap Dane in this buffalo robe, will you keep an eye on him for me?"

"Of course."

Sometime after Sinful went into the tepee, Doc came out and smiled tiredly at Red and Big John. "That Sinful. After watching him playing with the children at the Indian camp, I should have figured he'd be the daddy sort."

"How's she doing?" Big John asked.

"Better, much better. Pana thinks she's out of danger. Jenna woke up and looked up at Sinful's blue eyes and smiled. She whispered that she thought his eyes were as pretty as the sky and immediately fell back asleep holding his hand."

Pana stepped out of the tepee and came to Doc and sat beside him. "Your Sinful is a most gentle man."

"Yes, more than I realized." Doc reached in a bag and pulled out his ceramic mortar and pestle.

Pana's eyes opened wide.

"I've been trying to decide what I could give you to thank you for your kindness." He handed the white mortar and pestle to her. "Then I remembered your excitement when I used this to grind your herbs and flowers. Will this gift please you?"

"This gift will please me much." She took it gently with both hands and smiled at it with pleasure.

"Thank you for the supply of herbs and dried flowers you've given me, Pana," Doc said. "Your skill is miraculous. I have learned much by watching and speaking with you."

She smiled her thanks. "Your Golden Hair child is better. Tomorrow you can travel with her back to your land, but move slowly."

She rose and quickly disappeared among the many tepees.

Red handed Doc a cup of coffee.

Doc took a sip. "Big John, you were terrific today, the way you handled the situation with the children."

Big John grunted.

"I also felt there was something personal about it."

Big John stared down at the fire. "Dane reminded me of me at his age, when I had to bury my mother and was left all alone. His pain was mine."

"I'm sorry," Doc muttered. "I had no right."

"It's all right. Dane's life will turn out better than mine. Sinful will see to that—and so will I."

Red bent, handed Big John three warm cookies and whispered, "And so will we, old friend." He patted the man gently on the shoulder. "And so will we."

"Big John," Doc said, "what say we drop Sinful and the kids off at Conrad's ranch, then head to our ranch to see if Butcher really is going back there?"

"Yes." Big John stood and looked at the stars filling the dark clear sky like tiny beacons. "Butcher's not that far away. I sense his ugly presence and smell his nasty odor. He won't get away this time. This time I'll get him. This time I'll pay him back for what he did to me—to us." He glanced down at Doc. "I'm glad he's running scared from us. I want him to know fear. That gives me almost as much pleasure as I'll get when I kill him."

CHAPTER TWENTY-FIVE

As the wagon approached the gate leading into Conrad's ranch, Martin Graham rode across a meadow with a small herd of cattle. He saw them, told Charlie to handle the herd, and rode to greet them.

They filled him in on all that had happened. "I'd better ride ahead and warn Dad what Sinful is bringing with him," Martin said. "I've learned that Dad doesn't like surprises." He turned and rode off quickly.

Sinful sighed. He was perched in the back of the wagon on a makeshift seat with Jenna in his lap and his arm around Dane, who snuggled beside him.

"It's all right, Sinful," Red said. "Like Doc and I told you last night, if Conrad doesn't want the children, you will come home with us."

"I'm obliged, but I hope he doesn't say no. He's the one who took me in and taught me to be a cowboy. I'll feel real bad if he sends me off."

As the wagon pulled up in front of the ranch house, Conrad, Martin, Granville, and Esther stood on the porch waiting for them.

Esther held her baby and had a big smile on her face.

Red pulled the wagon to a stop, and Conrad quickly came over to them. He asked Doc, "How'd Sinful do?"

"Saved my life—four times. I wouldn't be here if it weren't for him."

"Hmm, Sinful, are these your new children?" Conrad asked.

"Yes, sir, boss. Their parents died, and this little one came down with the mountain fever, but Doc and a Blackfoot medicine woman saved her life. They are fine little people."

Before Conrad could respond, Mrs. Bale hurried to the wagon, pushed him aside, and smiled at Jenna. "Do you like gingerbread cake?" she asked.

"I don't know," the little girl said softly as she tucked her head shyly into Sinful's shoulder. She looked up at Sinful. "I don't think I've ever had it."

"Well, Jenna, Mrs. Bale makes the best gingerbread cake I've ever eaten, anywhere," Sinful said.

Mrs. Bale had a piece in a cloth, and she broke off a small piece. She held it under Jenna's nose.

Jenna took a tentative sniff and smiled. "It smells good."

"Open up, darling." Mrs. Bale popped the piece into Jenna's mouth. She looked at Dane. "You too."

"That sure was good," Jenna said.

"Then come on, darling, and I'll give you a big piece and a big glass of milk." She held out her arms.

Jenna looked at Sinful and cried, "You aren't leaving me, are you, Sinful?"

Mrs. Bale smiled knowingly. "You have captured their hearts, haven't you, Sinful?" She touched Jenna gently on the arm and said, "He won't leave you. As he told you, he loves my gingerbread cake too."

Jenna held her arms up, and Mrs. Bale took the child into her arms. Jenna wrapped her arms tightly around Mrs. Bale's neck and whispered, "You smell just like my mommy used to smell."

Mrs. Bale's eyes misted for a moment, then she composed herself. "Come on, Sinful. Bring your son."

Sinful looked worriedly at Conrad.

Conrad glanced at Mrs. Bale, who was already going into the house. "Well, go on. The last thing I need in this house is to make Mrs. Bale angry with me."

Sinful and Dane hurried into the house behind Mrs. Bale.

Conrad looked down at his daughter and tried to speak.

"Dad," Esther said, "as far back as I can remember, you've told me you wanted sons and grandchildren. Today you gained a son and two more grandkids."

"But Esther—Sinful?"

"Yes, Dad, Sinful."

"Why not, Dad?" Martin added. "He's a much better cowboy than I'll ever be."

Granville smiled. "As long as he doesn't have to shoot a gun, he's one fine cowboy. Great with cattle. A hard worker. The best cowpoke on this ranch except for me."

"Who taught him all he knows about being a cowboy?" Esther added. "Except for Martin, he's been more like a son to you than anyone. You know, Dad, you can't pick the sons you get. You can only love them."

Conrad turned to Red, Doc, and Big John. "Boys, let me give you some serious advice. Don't have a daughter and a strong-willed housekeeper. No matter what you want, these women will always get their way."

Esther reached up and kissed him on his cheek.

He sighed and flipped up his hands in surrender. "Tarnation, and I was just getting used to having a granddaughter and a new son." He shrugged. "Well, what's three more in the family. You all come on in. If I know Sinful, if we don't get in there quick, he'll have eaten all the gingerbread cake by himself."

* * *

The road between Conrad's ranch and Doc and Red's ranch was filled with ruts, so Red took it slow and easy. Big John complained at every bump they hit. Doc, Red, and Big John talked about the stop at Conrad's all the way back.

"Poor old Conrad didn't have a chance," Red said with a laugh and a shake of his head. "When Mrs. Bale came out and grabbed up Jenna, that was it."

"Yeah," Doc agreed, "but did you notice the smile on Conrad's face as he watched his family eating and laughing around the kitchen table? I'd call that pure bliss."

"Or how about when you told them how Sinful got his moccasin boots and did his dance around the camp?" Red added.

"And his bath," Big John said. "Old Granville was holding his suspenders so far out in delight that if he'd let go, they would have snapped him into the next room."

"Poor Conrad was laughing and pounding the table so hard, it's a wonder everyone didn't fall off their chairs," Doc said with a long laugh.

"And that Granville is like an uncle to Sinful—half the time sticking up for him and the other half teasing him," Red added with a chuckle.

"What I noticed," Big John said, "was the pride on Conrad's face when you told them how Sinful had saved your life and ours.

That was the look of pride of a father for a son. I don't think we have to worry about Sinful and the kids having a home."

Red and Doc agreed.

"We even got a few smiles out of you," Doc said to Big John.

"Yup, for just a few moments, that black pain I carry inside my soul was gone." He shrugged. "With Sinful, how can you not smile? He's a good lad, even if he can be exasperating at times."

"You know," Red said as he scratched his beard, "now that Sinful's got two children, we need to think about helping him get a wife."

"What do you mean, 'we'?" Doc exclaimed. "Help Sinful get a wife! Goodness, that's really a stretch for my imagination. How about one for you?"

"Nah, not me." Red said. His face flushed briefly.

The wagon banged over two large ruts in the road. Red grinned at Big John and said, "I'm not sure what I'm looking forward to more. The kitchen or a real bed."

"The way you've been hitting every pit in the road, you may need to carry me to a bed."

"I'm only hitting those ruts to keep you alert," Red said.

As they came around a large grove of trees, Big John pointed to the ranch in the distance and the two riders galloping toward them, trailing a storm of dust. "That looks like trouble blowing our way."

Jesse and Kid rode to them with terror on their faces. They pulled to a panicked stop beside the wagon. "Butcher just showed up," Jesse said between breaths. "Not sure how he got here."

"We didn't see a horse," Kid said. "I happened to look toward the house and saw him splashing water from the well on his face."

"Kid came and got me," Jesse said. "I'd just ridden in, so we circled the house and took off for Mr. Spear's ranch like you told us."

"Where's Shorty and Ray?" Doc asked.

"Up in the hills, rounding up strays. They aren't due back until tomorrow," Kid said.

"Get behind the wagon," Doc said. "When we get to the gate, stay there until we call you."

"Yes, sir," they said in unison.

"He came back to the ranch," Red said as he shook his head in disbelief. "That doesn't make any sense at all. I never thought he'd be that stupid."

"I agree, but he's here," Big John said. "That's all I care about."

"We go in together," Doc said to Big John.

Big John licked his lips, cocked the Henry, and levered a shell into the firing chamber. "I'm ready."

Red drove quickly to the front of the ranch house. Big John leaped out with more agility than he'd shown since they'd been together. The front door stood open. Big John walked in first, with Doc behind him.

Butcher leaned with his hands on top of the large desk in the study. He looked up as Big John and Doc silently entered the room. A revolver lay on the desk between his hands, but he made no move to reach for it.

"It's over, Butcher," Doc said.

Sweat dripped from Butcher's face onto the desktop. For a moment Doc thought it might have been fear. Then he realized how white Butcher's face was and heard the wheezing coming from his throat.

"The weekend you came, she robbed my deeds, all my gold." He coughed, and his right hand came up and rubbed his left shoulder. Pain fleetingly crossed his face. "I never wanted her, just the gold mine. You made me an offer to trade your mom for this place, and everything I wanted was right at my fingertips and I couldn't deliver." He snarled at Big John. "Then you show up too." He glared at Doc. "Damn you—" Suddenly Butcher collapsed to the floor.

Doc hurried over and felt for his pulse. "Dead."

Big John rushed to Butcher's body. "No! No! No!" Big John shook his head violently. "That's not fair. I wanted him to look into my eyes and see who was killing him. For him to know he killed my Golden Eagle. For him to know I was about to kill him. Is he dead? Is he really dead or just faking it?"

"He's really dead," Doc said.

Red hurried into the study. "I didn't hear a shot. Who shot him?"

"He just toppled over dead," Doc said. "I guess all his badness finally caught up with him."

"He just keeled over dead?" Red exclaimed.

Doc stood. "Heart attack, I'd say, or perhaps a stroke. He said something that confused me, though. He talked about a gold mine."

Red looked puzzled. "Could he have been talking about the gold that Mom hid in the passage?"

Doc frowned in thought. "It doesn't make sense. The gold in the safe was his gold. No, he specifically said 'gold mine.'"

Big John pointed his Henry at Butcher's body.

"No!" Doc exclaimed. "Don't pull that trigger. I understand what you want to do and why, but we don't want blood on your floor."

Big John's hands quivered angrily. "I don't care if he is dead. Just let me shoot him four or five times." His face contorted in pain. "I want my Golden Eagle back," he whispered. Finally he took a long, painful gulp of air and slowly regained control over his emotions.

"Doc is correct—*your* floor," Red said.

Big John glanced from Doc to Red. "What are you two talking about?"

Doc shrugged. "Red and I were talking. Mom's going to marry Tom and live with him. Red wants to go to Helena and open a restaurant and bakery with Layton in his billiard hall. He figures once the railroad gets finished between here and California, he can run all his businesses from there and just travel to California a few times a year. I may go to Europe to further my medical studies on my big brother's money. That leaves only you to run the ranch. We're going to give you a third of the place."

Big John stared at them, his face showing amazement. There was a long silence in the room. "Me?" he finally sputtered.

"Yup," Red said. "We can't think of anyone else who could do as good a job. Doc promised Jesse he could stay here, but Doc doesn't want to reward him for lying the way he did. We'll split the profits three ways."

"You do all the hard work, and we get all the easy money," Doc added.

"Our ranch?" Big John said slowly as he looked from one to the other.

"So, your first job is to drag this worthless piece of cow dung out and throw him in the pigpen," Doc said.

"Then what?" Big John asked.

"After he has a good smell, tell Kid and Jesse to take his filthy body into town, dig a hole on boot hill, and throw him in. I don't want his rotten body stinking up our land."

"Somehow I like that. I'd still rather shoot him a few times, but I do like the idea of the pigpen." Big John grabbed Butcher's arms and dragged him out of the house.

Doc turned to Red. "Shall we see about the safe?"

Red went to the bookcase. Butcher had already released the hidden latch behind the book *The Woman in White*. The first four shelves of the bookcase had swung out, exposing the safe opening behind the bookcase. The safe was four feet high, three feet wide and three feet deep.

Red pointed to the empty shelves at the back of the safe. "Mom did clean him out," he said with a grin. He got down on his knees and stretched an arm toward a small, unobtrusive hole at the top right corner of the top shelf. He grinned up at Doc. "Okay, you do it."

Doc patted Red on the back as Red crawled out. "What's the matter, that thick arm of yours still too big to reach the release?"

"You never complained when my thick arm had to lift something heavy for you."

Doc crawled into the safe, grunted, and finally grabbed the release handle hidden inside the hole. Then Doc slowly pushed open the secret passageway door behind the shelves.

Red whistled softly. Inside were five chests of gold and loose bags of gold, silver, and paper money. They stared at it in silence. Finally Red said, "Doc, I wasn't expecting this much. Were you?"

Big John came into the room and overheard Red. "Wasn't expecting what?"

"Come look at this," Red said to him.

Big John leaned around Red and drew a quick breath. He removed his hat and shook his head. "Did you boys just strike the mother lode? I've been in banks that don't have that much gold and silver in them."

Doc frowned at a circular parfleche pouch tied with a buck-skin thong. He reached out, grabbed it, and handed it behind him to Red. After he crawled back out, he said, "We need to talk."

Doc leaned against the back of the desk. Big John eased himself into the rocking chair by the unlit fireplace. Red sat in the big chair that had always been his when they lived there.

Doc paused in thought for a moment before he spoke. "We know much of this gold and silver is stolen money, maybe all of it. Big John, I suspect a big bunch is the gold that Butcher used to frame you."

"I reckon you're right about that."

"So we've got to figure out some way to get it back to the people that Butcher stole it from."

"Not going to be easy," Red said.

Doc glanced at Big John.

"Red's right," Big John agreed. "If people learn about it, every scoundrel in the territory will be here saying it's his."

Red untied the pouch Doc had handed him and removed the map inside. He looked at it incredulously, then started laughing. "Doc, you're not going to believe this. Big John, you wanted justice. This might be it."

Big John shrugged. "What?"

"Just before Butcher died, Doc said Butcher told him something about not wanting to give up the gold mine," Red said. "Doc didn't understand what that was about. Neither did I when Doc mentioned it to me. I thought Butcher was confused and talking about his own gold."

Red handed the map to Doc. Doc quickly scanned it. "I haven't seen this in years. You don't think he thought this map was real, do you?"

"It makes sense, if he did," Red said.

"What are you two talking about?" Big John asked again.

Doc grinned. "Inconceivable. Red and I could never figure out why Butcher wanted our ranch. I mean, we think it's a great ranch, but Butcher was never a rancher."

"He was too busy being a thief, rustler, and killer," Red added.

"So why our mom, and why this ranch? It just never made sense to us, but this may explain it." Doc handed the map to Big John.

Big John took off his distance glasses and put on his reading glasses. He studied the map. "This looks like your ranch." He pointed to the X on the map. "And if I'm reading it correctly, this mark is the location of a huge, rich gold mine."

Red and Doc grinned at each other. "One great-looking map, huh?" Red said to Big John.

Big John lifted the map questioningly in the air.

"Red drew that map when he was—what?—twelve or thirteen years old," Doc explained.

"Maybe younger," Red added.

"Are you telling me this map is a fake?" Big John asked.

"Hey," Red said. "I resent your saying it's a fake. I did a great job drawing it. Remember I was just a little kid."

"You were never a little kid," Doc said.

Red chuckled. "Well, I admit that the gold mine X was a wishful dream, but the map turned out swell. Dad thought it was great, and he loved all the details. I still remember the time we spent going over all the fine points. He told me to put it in the safe because he wanted to keep it forever. He made me feel real proud of it."

"But Butcher didn't know it was a fake," Big John said.

"Somehow, he must have found it in the safe and thought it was real," Doc said.

"I made the X vague against the eastern edge of our ranch," Red explained. "There was no way he could just ride out and find it easily."

"Why didn't he just marry your mother, or kill her and start digging?"

Doc grimaced. "He knew if he hurt our mom and we were alive, we'd never stop looking for him, or the community would get the vigilantes after him. Just keeping her here against her wishes must have worried him a bunch."

"That's pretty strange thinking on Butcher's part," Big John said. "Maybe he thought that was going to be his retirement when he quit robbing folks for a living." Big John studied the map further. "It's a fine map, Red, and you're correct, I like the idea that Butcher never knew it wasn't real. That's real twisted justice."

They sat silently.

"What about Tom Frost?" Big John suggested. "Perhaps he could go through all this gold and stuff and match it up with the deeds and such your mother took. Maybe he can find who some of it belongs to. He knows people in Virginia City, Bannack, and other gold fields. We can put this into a bank in Helena, and that way we don't have to worry about robbers coming to us."

"Good idea," Red said.

"I agree," Doc said. "I'll talk to Tom about it."

"What about what's left over?" Red asked.

"The four of us will share it, you, me, Mom, and Big John."

"Me?" Big John said in surprise.

"Why not?" Doc said. "Hey, let's include Sinful. He deserves a share too. And since he's a family man, he'll need money for his kids."

A hint of a smile crossed Big John's face. "Boys, your sense of justice is sure a treat for me." He slowly rubbed his arthritic hands together, lowered his head, and said softly, "I have a favor I'd be obliged if you'd do for me." He gave a long, pained sigh. "I'd like to visit my old homestead and see if my wife's bones are there. I don't think I can do it alone, and..." John's voice broke and he coughed and looked away.

Red and Doc looked at each other. "Of course, Big John. How far is it from here?"

"Maybe three hours," he answered, his voice just a whisper. "I'd like to give her a proper burial."

"We'll leave after breakfast tomorrow," Red said.

CHAPTER TWENTY-SIX

Red brought the wagon to a halt at the end of the narrow road. The horses were winded and glad to rest. Tall pines had blocked their view of the burned-out cabin until they were right beside it.

Big John slumped in the wagon. "I don't think I can handle seeing her in there," he said as he stared at the shell of the cabin.

"It's all right, Big John," Red said. "We'll check it out. You just stay here."

The cabin was a burned pile of charcoal logs on three sides, but it hadn't burned completely. One side and one corner still stood. Only the bottom of the rock fireplace was still intact, the burning logs having knocked down the upper stones.

As Doc and Red stepped inside the tiny cabin, their feet kicked up small clouds of charcoal dust. The faint smell of burnt logs was still present. Doc picked up a long stick and meticulously picked through the remains on the floor of the cabin. Finally, he stopped and shook his head at Red. "She's not here."

"Any chance an animal could have carried her body off after they killed her?" Big John asked.

They had been so intent on their search that they hadn't heard Big John come up to the cabin.

Doc's face tightened in thought. "Possibly, but if she was here when it burned, there should be some signs. I don't see any graves around either."

Big John looked at a narrow path that led to a lookout over the valley. "We loved to go up there—just sit, talk, and look over the valley. She called it our peaceful place."

He looked away and started back to the wagon, then stopped, turned, and with a hesitant shrug, started up the trail to the top. Red and Doc followed him.

Big John pointed to a rustic log bench that looked out over the valley. "This was the first thing I built. Even before the cabin. Golden Eagle loved this view so much." He slowly lowered himself onto the bench. The sorrow in his face was in stark contrast with the beauty of the view.

Doc walked to the edge and looked out. Herds of buffalo grazed in the lush valley below, and dark green pines stood out against the pale green grass that rolled over the hillsides like a carpet. The sight captivated him. He felt Big John's pain.

Red had gone off to the side, and now he returned and asked Big John, "You did say your wife was Blackfoot, right?"

Big John nodded as he rubbed his knees.

Red pulled off his wide-brimmed hat and briskly rubbed his bright red hair. He was deep in thought. He kicked the dirt with his boot and slowly bit his lower lip. "Doc, come and look at this." Red turned, went to a spot on the side of the overlook, and pointed. "What do you make of it?"

Doc studied the rocks Red had found. They were meticulously arranged in patterns on the ground, with sticks placed at various angles. Close by, grasses were tied in bunches. "Red, you were the best at figuring this out when we were kids. What does it say?"

Again Red removed his hat and ruffled his hair. "Some of the rocks have moved. It's hard to read after all this time. The grass is even harder." He rubbed his hand over his mouth. "Sticks have fallen." He gave a quick shake of his head. He leaned in closer to Doc and whispered.

"What're you two whispering about?" Big John asked as he glanced over at them.

Doc frowned, uncertain whether to proceed. "Come over here and look at this. Have you ever seen anything like this before?"

Big John looked at the rock, stick, and grass patterns. He shook his head. "They weren't here while Golden Eagle and I were together."

Red squatted and studied the objects. "They were placed so there would be less chance of an animal disturbing them." Red frowned and said softly to Big John, "I can only guess what some of this means, but if I'm correct, this message is for you."

"Who left a message for me?"

Red stood and stepped away. "Not sure. The message says travel north. This person has gone north to be with her people. You must come and find her."

"Her? Who's 'her'?" Big John's face twisted in pain. He reached over and grabbed Red's shoulder. "Are you telling me that Golden Eagle may still be alive?"

Red shook his head. "I'm just telling you that the message says a woman. We don't know who wrote it."

"Don't get your hopes up, Big John," Doc said. "We don't know if the signs were from her or not."

Big John looked around wildly. "Who else would have left a message up here?" he asked excitedly, his voice choked with emotion. "She's alive. But where, Red?"

"Well, that's the problem. Whoever left this message probably left a location, but so much time has passed, it's been erased. I'm pretty sure it says north, but even that is really a guess."

"There's a bunch of ground—north," Big John said. "Well, I'm going north, boys. You may be right, and it might have nothing to do with Golden Eagle, but I'm going north. I have to know. Even a little hope is better than the despair I've been living with."

Doc turned and stared over the valley below them. "I'm going with you, Big John," Doc said.

"Me too," Red said with a grin.

"Boys, we have no idea how long it's going to take to find her or even, as you say, if this message is from her. No idea how far we might have to travel. I can't ask you."

Red flopped on his hat and said, "Gee, Big John, I don't recall your asking us."

"Who was by our side when we went looking for our mom? I don't recall we asked you to come along, yet there you were," Doc added.

Big John sighed and frowned slightly. "Boys, we could be mistaken."

"I agree. Still, no bones, no grave. A message saying to look north." Doc pointed north. "How can we not go and find out for sure?"

"I have to go, you know," Big John said.

"And you won't ever rest easy until you discover what happened to her, will you?" Red asked.

"I 'spect not."

"Right. And Doc and I won't either." Red walked to the edge of the overlook and stood beside Doc. "You thinking of the Belt Mountains or the Forks at Warm Spring Creek and the Judith?" Red asked.

"Yup, sort of. They might have already decided to move up to the Marias River near the trading post at Fort Benton."

"What are you two talking about?" Big John asked.

"We need to go to a big Blackfoot encampment if we hope to find your Golden Eagle," Doc explained. "The problem is the Blackfoot tribes might have already started moving toward the big winter area north of Fort Benton by the Marias River. This time of year the Indian tribes do serious trading. The buffalo doesn't get its best winter coat until November, but the Indians will trade deer, beaver, and elk hides till then."

Red shrugged. "Doesn't much matter. We have to head that way anyway. We'll check them all."

"Agreed." Doc turned to Big John and asked, "You all right with that as a plan?"

"Boys, I didn't have a clue what to do. I figured I'd just ride north and stop every Indian I saw until I found her. I can find a lost heifer easy, but looking for a lost wife..." He shrugged. "I'm obliged."

"Big John, I don't want you to get too hopeful about all this," Red said. "But I know you won't rest easy until we give it a try."

"Red, just not finding her bones or a grave up here has given me new hope." He turned to the wagon. "You think we can get where you want to go with me in that? I can try a horse."

"Big John, I'm a big boy, but lifting you onto a horse every day and then pulling you down every time you need to make a stop would just wear me out. We should be fine. Just make sure you bring a soft pillow for that hard butt of yours," Red added with a grin.

Big John climbed slowly into the wagon. "I thought when a man got older, he was supposed to get some respect from young whelps like you."

"I never heard anything like that. Did you, Doc?" Red asked.

"Nope, surely never did." Doc grinned at Big John. "You two head back for the ranch and tell the boys that we are on the move again. I'm going to cut over to Conrad's ranch and see how Sinful's kids and Esther's baby are doing."

"Sure appreciate Joe letting us keep our stuff in his storeroom," Red said. "The advantage of having the wagon is we can take winter clothes with us. What we don't have, we can pick up at Todd's store. We'll meet you in town tomorrow around dinnertime at Joe's."

"That sounds good."

"You take care. We still don't know where Richie is."

"I'll be wary, big brother. See you tomorrow."

CHAPTER
TWENTY-SEVEN

Doc, Red, and Big John had ridden through intermittent cold rains for five days since leaving Elk Forks. The first day, they rigged a cover over the wagon, and that helped a little. By the second day, Red and Big John were soaked after two hours on the trail.

Doc's cape had worked well the first few days, but by the fifth it looked like the wagon cover—soggy and soaked with rain. His hood drooped limply around his face.

Red caught Doc's attention and nodded toward Big John. Doc rode around to the other side of the wagon where Big John sat.

Big John was slouched forward, rubbing his knuckles gently, trying to soothe his wet, cold, aching hands. Occasionally he looked up and scowled.

"You knew it wouldn't be easy," Doc said as he rode beside the wagon.

"It's not just that. It's your mom and Tom." Big John sighed. "I'm feeling real low that we didn't stick around long enough to get them married. Time is so precious when you love someone."

"You know we couldn't wait. We've been lucky with the weather so far, but it could close in on us momentarily."

"It's raining like someone pulled the cork out of a rain barrel, and you're calling this lucky?" Red harrumphed.

Doc grinned at Red. "It could be four feet of snow we're traveling through."

"And this muddy road is better?"

"It's better and you know it. Remember the time the wagon got stuck in a snowdrift coming back from Helena when I was thirteen or so?"

Red harrumphed again.

Doc said to Big John, "Mom understood why we couldn't wait. She knows what it's like to miss someone you love. She told me she would pray that we would find your Golden Eagle alive and waiting for you."

"That was kind of her, but I don't think Tom was nearly as understanding," Big John said. "I wouldn't have been."

"I talked to him. He wasn't happy about it, but he told me that being with Mom made a difference. Besides, he and Mom are busy working with the stolen deeds and figuring out what to do with all that gold and silver."

Doc flicked raindrops from his forehead. "Tom told me he'd already found some claims of miners he knows Butcher robbed, but he didn't think he'd find many more. He said we'd all get a big share of what was left over of the gold and silver. There's no way he can find everyone who was robbed. No way to prove that Butcher and his boys were the ones responsible."

Red grinned and said, "Can't you hear Sinful when we tell him he's going to get a potful of money? 'Dang!' he'll say."

Big John smiled slightly; then his face turned serious. "It's so frustrating, not knowing if she's even alive. And then not finding anyone who can help us."

"That's why we're heading for Fort Benton," Doc said. "Our trader friend, Jeff Pickrell, can help us. If anyone knows where Chief Red Hawk is, it will be Jeff. He started his trading post up there at the same time our dad opened his. We should be there by midafternoon if this rain doesn't get worse."

Doc glanced at Red. "And what are you grinning about?"

"Nothing."

"Right, you're thinking that Jeff's wife, Lisa, is going to send you into her nice warm kitchen and force you to make your world-famous apple dumplings for her."

"I don't know which I'm looking forward to more, her warm kitchen or just getting dry." He reached in his pocket and pulled out three gingersnap cookies for each of them. "Here. These will hold you till we get there."

* * *

Doc, Red, and Big John trudged into the trading post, dripping water and looking like a mop just pulled from the bucket. Five Blackfoot Indians were examining the products in the store.

Jeff Pickrell looked up from the counter and yelled, "Fire Hair, is that you dripping water on my clean floor?"

"You've never had a clean floor since I've known you."

Jeff limped around and rushed to him. "I'd give you a big hug, but it would be like getting my spring bath early." He stopped and stared at Doc. "Little Medicine Boy? No, it can't be. He's just a little tyke."

"I'm not a little tyke anymore, you simpleton," Doc told Jeff. "You still hobbling around like you still have that arrow in your knee?"

"Only hurts when it's cold and rainy," Jeff said with a laugh. "Like today."

One Blackfoot Indian stared at Doc and Red, then immediately hurried out of the trading post.

"Still trying to give me a bad time, huh?" Jeff said. "As full of trouble as your dad used to be. Get those wet things off." He turned and yelled toward the back room. "Lisa, get out here. Our baker has arrived, just in time for tonight's meal."

Lisa hurried out. "Oh, Red," she exclaimed. She paused, then continued, "And is that you, Doc? You've grown a foot. How wonderful to see you both."

"Meet our good friend Big John. He's as wet as we are," Doc said.

"Tell her something she can't see," Jeff said. "Lisa, take them home and see if you can't dry them off." He turned and stopped. "Wait a minute." He yelled into the next room, where four men were playing cards, "Barry, quit taking all their money for a moment and come out here and meet two great friends of mine."

A tall, good-looking man came out. "This calculating machine be Barry Metzler," Jeff said. "He's my banker, a good friend, and dangerous with a deck of cards."

"You having any luck teaching Jeff how to take care of his money?" Red asked.

Barry looked solemnly over at Jeff and said, "I'm good, but he's a tough case."

"What'd you mean a tough case? I've done everything you've told me to do."

Barry looked at Red and sadly shook his head. "Nah, not even close."

"Don't listen to him, Red," Jeff said with a sad look on his face. "How can you trust a man who doesn't enjoy a good glass of wine? All he wants to do is sit around and drink my cheap beer and complain about what I drink. Except for that one serious flaw in his character, Barry's a good man."

"Well, that is mighty serious," Red said. "Except I'm a beer man too. And so is Big John."

"Oh no, not you both. Doc, what about you?"

"A good glass of wine is liquid gold."

"See, Barry? Doc's a man of worldly experience, not like you and those two big water bugs beside you dripping all over my floor."

Barry reached out and solemnly shook Red's hand, then Big John's. "You are obviously men of great taste and culture, not like those beastly wine drinkers over there."

"Thank you, my good man," Red said seriously. "I agree. Beer over that rotgut they drink any day."

"No class," Jeff said sadly to Doc. "Hey, Barry. Get Dina and come over for dinner with us tonight. Red makes the best apple dumplings in the land."

"For apple dumplings, I won't even complain about your wine." Barry turned back to the card game but mumbled softly, "Any more than I usually do." He winked at Red and Big John.

"I heard that," Jeff yelled after him.

* * *

After dinner, Dina turned to Lisa and said, "These menfolk sure know how to eat."

"I'm not sure whether they're enjoying my food or just glad to be warm and dry."

Big John delicately wiped his mouth with the cloth napkin. "Ma'am, it's because we're warm and dry that we can truly enjoy the most wonderful meal I've had in more years than I can remember."

Lisa shook her head, embarrassed.

"Good one, Big John," Jeff said.

Doc turned to Barry. "Jeff said you left the military in the spring of 1866. You were stationed in Colorado?"

"Yes, my last assignment was at Fort Livermore. We lost our commander and more than half our men in an ambush the year before I got out. "

Doc and Red glanced at each other quizzically. Red asked, "You ever meet anyone from Quiet Valley named Dave Kramer?"

"You mean Major Kramer? He was the best officer I ever met in my whole career in the military."

Doc and Red immediately stopped eating. Red dropped his fork noisily on his plate. "Dang!" they exclaimed in unison.

"Boys, that's got to stop right now!" Big John said sternly.

"What's that all about?" Dina asked.

"That's an expression a good friend of ours is always using. I guess it must have rubbed off on us," Red explained with a brief chuckle.

"Well, unrub it," Big John said. "Sinful doesn't know better, but you two do."

"How do you know Major Kramer?" Barry asked.

"Dave Kramer is a good friend. He was just here helping us find our mom." Red pointed at Doc. "They've taken turns at saving each other's life more times than we can keep count."

Barry sat back and took a swig of beer. "He was the most courageous man I've ever met. If he hadn't shown up when he did, our whole garrison might have been wiped out. Brave, tough, and smart. Totally fearless."

"Yup, that about sums Dave up," Doc agreed.

"So is business good?" Red asked Jeff.

Jeff shook his head. "Last year we had seventy steamboats dock here, this year half that."

"Thirty-seven," Barry corrected.

"See?" Jeff said. "Always the banker. Always the numbers."

Barry shrugged. "But Jeff's right about business falling off. We're not sure if it's because the gold rush is starting to end or because of all the Indian trouble or because of the railroads taking the business away from the steamboats."

"And getting the steamboats here is always a gamble. They hit snags or sandbars and sink, or they catch on fire," Jeff added.

"That happen often?" Red asked.

"More than we'd like," Barry said. "We lost the *Emilie* in June."

Jeff explained, "It was the first side-wheeler to come to Fort Benton. It got hit by a tornado near St. Joseph. I believe that's the only steamboat we've lost that way."

"Red and I know St. Joseph, don't we?" Doc smiled at Red.

"Oh, yeah. I thought that was one huge city until we stepped off the train in New York. Then we were overwhelmed. If it weren't for Bob Bates's friend, Larry Swartz, meeting us there and befriending us, I don't think we would have made it."

Jeff accepted an apple dumpling from Dina. "Ah, smell this." He held the dumpling near his nose. "Magnificent. This might be worth having to mop up my floor after you left."

Lisa smirked. "You've never mopped that floor—ever."

Doc asked Jeff, "Have you seen Chief Red Hawk this season?"

"His tribe came through just a few days ago. Strange things are going on with Red Hawk. He's always been friendly with me, but not this year. He was most evasive. He came through so fast this year, I hardly had a chance to say hello. Not like him at all."

Doc sat back in surprise. "That's strange."

Lisa asked if anyone would like some coffee. As she poured a cup for Big John, she said, "I know how desperately you want to find your wife, but you need to be extremely careful, all of you." She turned to Red and asked, "How many years since you've spoken with Chief Red Hawk?"

Red thought for a moment. "Probably three or four years."

"That's a long time." Lisa poured Doc a cup of coffee. "These are not good times for Indians. Smallpox and measles killed so many of them. White hunters are killing the buffalo and just taking the hide. They leave the rest to rot on the plain. The Indians don't understand such waste. Jeff figures he shipped more than fifteen thousand pelts down the river this year."

"What's even worse," Dina added, "is that here in Fort Benton, a drunken white man will kill an Indian for no reason at all, and it's suppressed." She shook her head. "You can't do that without repercussions."

"We'll be vigilant," Doc said. "But if we're ever going to find Big John's wife, I still think Chief Red Hawk is the best place to start. We grew up in his tribe."

Jeff stood and raised his glass. "Therefore, we beer and wine drinkers need to stand, united, and wish Big John success on his quest." They stood and tapped their glasses together.

CHAPTER
TWENTY-EIGHT

In the middle of the third day after leaving Fort Benton, Red paused the wagon. The rain had stopped a day after they'd left, and the sun felt warm on their clothes. Ahead of them were hundreds of tepees stretching out in a huge Blackfoot camp. Big John stared in astonishment. "I wasn't expecting anything this large!" he said.

"Yes," Doc said. "The size of the Marias encampment always stuns me."

They spent a few minutes looking at the enormous camp, then started down toward it.

"How will we find Chief Red Hawk?" Big John asked.

"The design on the tepee will tell us."

Suddenly an Indian brave rode out from behind a tree and stopped in front of them with his bow already strung with an arrow. He wore a buckskin tunic and leggings. Two of his three braids fell forward in front of his ears, and his topknot was stiffened with grease.

Doc stopped his horse and raised his hand in greeting. "Running Wolf, it's good to see you again."

"My brothers saw you at the post three days ago. They told me you were coming here. Leave at once. I do not want to kill you."

"Kill me? Why would you want to kill a brother?"

"You have come to take me to the white man's jail. I will not let this happen."

"Why would I want to take you to jail?"

For the first time, Running Wolf looked away from them. He sighed and shook his head. "You have come because I killed a white man."

"We need to talk." Doc pointed his finger at Running Wolf and then at a tall tree to their left. He told Red to join him and asked Big John to stay in the wagon.

Doc stepped off his horse. He undid his gun belt and laid it across his saddle. Running Wolf watched his every movement. Doc went to a rotten log, sat, and told Red to do the same.

Finally Doc looked up at Running Wolf, spread out his hands, and said, "Well?"

Running Wolf sat motionless on his horse; then he finally placed the arrow in his quiver, slid off his horse, and hurried to Doc and Red. He sat cross-legged on the ground across from them.

Doc stared at Running Wolf. "Speak to me, Running Wolf. All. What is this thing that has happened that makes you believe I would turn against my sacred brother and take you to jail? After all these years, my disappointment in you is very great at this moment. What has happened?"

Running Wolf placed his hands on his knees and spoke quietly. "The white man you know as Richie came into our camp near your ranch. I saw him coming, so I placed my arrow in my bow and when he got closer I told him to leave, that he was not welcome. He had his gun in his hand. He told me he looked for Yellow Bird. When I said I had not seen her, he fired at me. He missed. I heard the bullet pass close to my body. I shot my arrow at him. I saw his eyes watch the flight of the arrow as well. I remember watching the arrow go straight into the chest of this man Richie. The force of my arrow lifted him out of his saddle, and he landed on the trail behind his horse."

"Your arrow killed him?" Red asked.

"No, he was alive when I rode to him."

"So what did you do then?" Red asked.

"I looked down at this man who had killed two of our people. My arrow quivered in his chest, and I felt no pity for him. He'd even scalped an old man from our village after he killed him. This old man was not able to defend himself and had harmed no one."

"When did Richie kill the old man?" Doc asked.

"Two winters ago. After you had been gone one winter."

"Go on," Doc said.

"This man Richie was making bad sounds and trying to lift his gun to shoot me, so I kicked the gun out of his hand. After he died, I scalped him."

"Funny thing about justice, huh, Doc?" Red said. "If you had found him first, you would have killed him. One shot and he's dead. Running Wolf did it his way, and somehow I can't help but believe that justice was served better this way."

"Yes." Doc paused in thought. "Maybe it was." He turned to Running Wolf. "So you thought that's why we came here?"

"Yes, to take me to the white man's jail. To hang me. Do I understand you wanted to kill this man too?"

"Yup. You just got the first crack at him. Chief Red Hawk must be worried and upset."

"Chief Red Hawk is afraid that the whites will come to destroy our village. Kill all our people."

"What happened to Richie's body?"

"We took him deep into the hills where no white man goes, removed all his clothes and let the wild things eat on him."

"And his clothes?" Red asked.

"Everything was burned, including his gun. Then we took all the ashes and buried them far from here."

"And his horse."

"We ate it."

For the first time, all three of them smiled. "I'm sure glad I missed that feast," Red said.

"The horse is sacred to us, so the chief made the shaman bless the horse many times. No one got sick, so his magic worked." Running Wolf looked down at the ground. "Running Wolf is sorry he mistrusted Little Medicine Boy."

"Know well, Running Wolf, that I would have stood in front of you before I'd have let anyone take you," Doc said.

"Running Wolf understands."

Doc stood. "I need to talk to Chief Red Hawk. I want no one from the tribe to tell anyone about this incident with Richie. Who has the scalp?"

"I do. Do you want to see it?"

"I believe I'll pass on that. It must be burned."

Running Wolf made a face.

"This scalp is not a victory of war, Running Wolf. Your courage is known in the tribe and a scalp is not needed, but if the scalp is found, it could bring harm to the tribe. Someday you will be chief, so now is the time for you to show wisdom over pride."

"You think I will someday be chief?" Running Wolf asked. He thought about what Doc had said. "Your words are wise."

"Good. I'll talk to the chief and explain that no white man will come looking for you because of Richie. Richie had no friends.

But I will also tell the chief that they are never to speak of this to anyone."

"The chief will be happy to hear your words."

"Running Wolf, we traveled here for another matter that is of much more concern to us than Richie. My friend Big John, over there in the wagon, has lost his wife, Golden Eagle. She was Blackfoot. The bad man that Richie worked for did bad things to Big John, and we believe Golden Eagle ran away because they wanted to kill her also. I need your people to help us look for her."

"Did you find your mother?"

"Our mother is safe. She found safety with Chief Black Cloud's tribe."

"Good. Your mother always liked Running Wolf. Come, follow me." Running Wolf ran to his horse and leaped onto its back.

Doc quickly mounted and followed him. "If you had shot me, my mother would have been most unhappy with you," Doc yelled.

Running Wolf turned his head back toward them. "Yes. So there was no way I could shoot you."

"You were playing a joke on me."

"Not about Richie but about shooting you, yes."

"That wasn't wise of you," Doc said.

"Yes, but worth it to see the look on your face. Race you."

Red called after Doc from the wagon. "You've never beaten him in a race."

"Thanks for reminding me," Doc said as he raced after Running Wolf.

Red clicked to the horses, turned to Big John, and said, "We'll just let the children run and play. It's too pleasant a day to get all hot and sweaty."

"Do you think they will help me find Golden Eagle?"

"Well, this village is like a second home for us, so if anyone can help us, they will."

Big John sighed softly.

Running Wolf rode quickly up to the tepee of Chief Red Hawk. He leaped off his horse and gloated. "Again, Running Wolf show puny white man how to ride horse fast. Little Medicine Boy is even slower than last time."

The camp had heard the yelling and laughing as they rode up, and everyone came out of the tepees to see what the noise was about.

Doc dismounted and said, "Running Wolf, if I'd known you were going to be this bad, I wouldn't have brought you a present."

"You brought Running Wolf a present?"

"Maybe. Is Chief Red Hawk here in camp?"

"Where is Running Wolf's present?"

"After I speak with Chief Red Hawk, we will discuss if Running Wolf is worthy of my present."

"So you try to do Indian trick on me."

Doc shrugged. "Chief Red Hawk."

"Patience, Little Medicine Boy. First is the Indian way, and then there's the crazy white man way."

Running Wolf asked Doc, "Does he really love her?" He pointed at Big John.

Big John replied in Blackfoot, "More than life itself."

"You speak our language. Very wise. I will speak to our chief about you and slow, puny paleface you ride with."

Red grinned at Doc. "Oh, is he ever having fun with you. I'm sure glad I was never mean to him."

"I don't believe that," Doc said. "Running Wolf, was Fire Hair ever mean to you?"

"Fire Hair understands the gentle, kind nature of Running Wolf."

"Ha!" Red said with a laugh.

"Right," Doc snorted. "That means he bribed you with his cookies."

"Best Blackfoot bribe I know," Running Wolf said, as he flashed Red a triumphant smile. He hurried into the tepee.

Big John paced nervously. After some time, Running Wolf came out and told all three to go inside.

They stepped into the warm tepee, filled with the scent of pinewood burning. Red and Doc turned and smiled at each other as memories of winter nights spent listening to ancient stories of the tribe returned to them. The chief sat with two elders on either side of him. Many other Indians sat inside the large tepee. Doc and Red greeted the chief, told Big John to come forward, and introduced him.

The chief told them to sit.

Big John stared at the buffalo hides on the ground and frowned. He spoke in Blackfoot, "Oh mighty chief, I would not want to show you or any of your tribe disrespect, but my old bones will not allow me to sit on the ground. And if I were to get down, I'm not sure I could get back up again without much help. May I please just stand?"

The chief looked at Big John thoughtfully. "You speak Blackfoot well."

"My wife, Golden Eagle, taught me. I speak it as a sign of my respect for the Blackfoot."

The chief pulled his buffalo hide around his shoulders. He told Running Wolf to come to him. Running Wolf bent down as the chief whispered in his ear. Running Wolf grinned and hurried out of the tent. A moment later he returned with a rocking chair, placed it in the circle, and gestured for Big John to sit in it.

Big John was totally taken aback. "I thank Chief Red Hawk for this honor." He slowly sat in the rocking chair, and, once seated, an Indian placed a buffalo hide over his legs and lap and another one over his shoulders. Big John bowed his head in thanks to the chief.

The chief slowly pulled away some of his buffalo hide to show them that he also sat in a rocking chair. The ground under the chair had been dug away so that it looked as though the chief were sitting on the ground. "Chief Red Hawk understands about old bones. These two chairs were given to me by Yellow Bird, the mother of Little Medicine Boy and Fire Hair. Chief Red Hawk does not want to sit in white man's chair, but old bones do better when I do."

The chief turned to Doc. "Welcome, Little Medicine Boy. Your wisdom of the white man is needed. Running Wolf tells me we do not have to fear about the death of this man Richie."

"That is true, but things must be done to ensure the safety of the tribe. No one will search for Richie. He was a bad white man. Still, Running Wolf must destroy the scalp of Richie."

"Yes, Running Wolf spoke of this. The medicine man will guide Running Wolf in doing this."

"And most important of all," Doc continued, "the story of the death of Richie must never be spoken of again. If white men should ever hear of it, they would not care that Richie was a bad man, only that he was a white man killed and scalped by an Indian."

The chief turned to the elder on his right and they whispered back and forth. Then he turned to the elder on his left and did the same thing. "Your words are wise. It will be done," the chief said.

"I give you many thanks, Chief Red Hawk, but our visit here was not made about the bad white man. My friend Big John married a wonderful Blackfoot woman named Golden Eagle. This man Richie, he worked for a very bad white man who had Big John placed in the white man's jail for crimes he did not commit. The bad man told Big John that he'd had Golden Eagle killed. Big John felt great sorrow at the lost of his Golden Eagle. He did not smile because of his loss. Sometimes he has tears in his eyes when he thinks of her.

"Some days ago, we returned to the home he'd built for her high in the mountains. There we found what we believe was a message left by her, but time had destroyed much of the message. We are not even sure if it was left by Golden Eagle, but we hope it was.

"Big John will never stop until he has found his beloved wife. The task is like finding one special buffalo in a large prairie filled with many buffalo. We are here to ask your help in finding her."

Chief Red Hawk rocked slowly in his chair. "Such a search might need many moons. The earth is large." He waved his hand. "To find one Blackfoot woman among all the Blackfoot nations will be a most difficult task."

Big John leaned forward. "It does not matter how difficult it will be. I must find her."

"What if you get tired of the search?"

"I will never get tired," Big John said. "I will never stop until I find her. There can be no happiness for me without Golden Eagle."

"Hmm. Such words are easy to say."

"If the winter snows come and I have not found her, then I ask Chief Red Hawk to allow me to stay with the tribe and continue my search. Little Medicine Boy has told me that many tribes will spend the winter here by the Marias."

Doc stood and placed his hand on Big John's shoulder. "Chief Red Hawk, Big John is a good man. His heart is heavy with the loss of his beloved Golden Eagle. If he must stay through the winter to search for her, I will make arrangements at the trading post for many points to be credited to you for extending him your help." Doc sat back down.

"You travel with caring friends, Big John. You were wise to come here for help," Chief Red Hawk said as he rocked back and forth slowly in thought. "Such a search will not be easy. It would almost be easier to find a white buffalo. Still, Chief Red Hawk is old and has gained much wisdom with age." He paused. "Sometimes when you start a difficult search and expect it to be long and hard, the unexpected happens. The search turns out to be different from what was expected. Perhaps it will not be necessary to look as far or as long as you thought." Chief Red Hawk signaled with his hand.

Big John looked confused. "I do not understand." He glanced anxiously at Doc and back to Chief Red Hawk. "Do you know where she is?" he asked. "Is she still alive?"

An older Indian woman came silently up behind Big John. She wore a long deerskin dress, fringed and decorated with porcupine quills. She gently placed her hands on his shoulders, leaned over, and said softly, "Did your eyes really fill with tears when you thought I was dead? Is that true?"

Big John twisted around in his rocking chair and gasped, "Oh, Golden Eagle, oh my dearest Golden Eagle, is that really you?"

"My husband, I never gave up believing that we would once again be together."

Tears flowed from Big John's eyes. He tried to speak but no words came out. He pulled her around to the front and into his lap as he stroked her hair and gently rocked back and forth. She wrapped her arms around him. He placed his cheek on top of her head and cried.

Chief Red Hawk signaled to all in the tepee to leave silently. Two braves helped the chief get out of the rocking chair and up the earth steps to the tepee floor.

Once outside, Chief Red Hawk said to Doc and Red, "I fear much for my people, but to see a white man love Golden Eagle the way he does gives me hope for our future."

* * *

Doc glanced up at the huge, puffy white clouds casting moving shadows over the land. The blue of the sky reminded him of Sinful's eyes. The sound of rolling thunder echoed out of the high mountains to the west. He took a deep breath of the pine-scented air and smiled at the glorious day.

Running Wolf rode up. He held up his new knife. "Well, paleface, it is good I spared you."

"Listen, you wild Indian, I should have just tossed that knife away or given it to a chief."

"Perhaps you did," Running Wolf said with a broad smile. "Fire Hair, thanks for the cookies. Your little brother has much to learn. Teach him well."

Red tipped his hat at Running Wolf.

Running Wolf grinned at Doc. "Thank you for the knife. No one has a knife as fine." He made fists and crossed his arms against his chest. "Ride like the wind, Little Medicine Boy."

"You as well," Doc said as he mirrored Running Wolf's sign of affection. "You as well, my brother," he repeated softly.

Running Wolf turned his horse and rode off with a loud, happy whoop.

After the wagon had been loaded and good-byes had been exchanged all around, Big John climbed into the back of the wagon and sat in the rocking chair that Chief Red Hawk had insisted he take with him. Golden Eagle sat on two planks covered with buffalo hides beside his rocking chair, holding his hand. Her radiant smile was all for Big John.

Red twisted around, grinned, and shook his head.

Doc rode up beside the wagon and smiled at them. "That's got to be the strangest sight I've ever seen, Big John."

"Not to me, Doc. I feel as if I'm in a golden chariot. Fire Hair is driving, you are my guardian angel, and I have my precious Golden Eagle sitting beside me, holding my hand. I'm so happy, I feel I'm in heaven." He smiled at Doc.

"Big John," Doc said in surprise, "that's the first time I've ever seen you really smile since we met."

"Golden Eagle gives me a reason to smile again."

"Well, hold that smile," Doc said. "We've got to get home to a wedding. I thought Tom was going to either cry or tie us all down when we told him we had to go searching for your wife. He's a man who wants that same smile."

Doc winked at Red.

"Git up, you old girls," Red said, as he picked up the reins. "Let's go home."

ACKNOWLEDGMENTS

Special thanks to editors Joy Ann Fischer for the first edit and Perry Crowe and Elise Marton for the last edits. Joy Ann Fischer and Elise Marton were particularly astute in their editorial suggestions, and their advice has helped make this a better book. And thanks to Su Wu, publishing consultant, for helping me get this book published.

Thanks to the following: Sara Delano and Ken Boyer for the Colorado/Montana mountain adventures. Lisa, Todd, and Hossegor Harmon, my French connection. Barry and Dina Metzler for giving me the time to write part of this novel on their front porch, eat apple dumplings, and drink wine in the beer garden, and Jeff and Lisa Pickrell for the wine and laughter. Sandy Aldinger for the magic of the dance. My buddy Sinful, who demonstrated how to throw an Arkansas toothpick and allowed me to ride with a real cowboy. Special Agent Bob Mock for the music, paintings, straight shooting, and friendship. Dane and Jenna Anderson for showing me once again what the joy of childhood is all about.

As I researched my book, these folks offered Old West history with Midwest hospitality: In Fort Madison, Iowa, Sam Fiorella at Pendemonium has a store filled with unique old pens and writing instruments. Andy Andrews, at the North Lee County Historical Society, shared his knowledge of the Mississippi and old steamboats. In Leavenworth, Kansas, Joanie Kocab, Vivian Ross, and Lisa Weakly of the Carroll Mansion and home of the Leavenworth County Historical Society shared wonderful information about their community. In Helena, Montana, at the Montana Historical Society Library, staff members were friendly, helpful and very knowledgeable. Their collection has 95 percent of all the newspapers ever published in Montana—an amazing resource for a writer. In Fort Benton, Montana, tour guide Bob Doerk took the extra time to share insight into the mystique of early Fort Benton. And three Blackfoot Indians who asked me not to use their names, but I want them to know they made a difference in my book.

And a special thanks to the magnificent buffalo in a snow-covered Yellowstone National Park that allowed this author to walk beside him for half a mile in a gusting snowstorm. When something as magical as this happens, Native Americans say we have walked together in the shadow of a rainbow.

ABOUT THE AUTHOR

 To research *The Hunted Return*, the author set out from Fort Madison, Iowa, to Leavenworth, Kansas, then joined the Oregon Trail up to Colorado and over to Utah. From Utah, he veered north through Idaho up to Helena, Montana, before taking to the waters of the Missouri and Marias rivers and riding through a rainstorm into Fort Benton. This epic trek was made to ensure the historical and geographical accuracy of the travels of his characters in the novel. Many of the novel's scenes describe actual ghost towns and historical sites visited by the author. Spalsbury has published western novels, Christmas short stories, science fiction, and contemporary fiction. He currently lives in Visalia, California.

Visit his website at: www.JeffRSpalsbury.com.

Made in the USA
Monee, IL
21 October 2023

44902801R00156